FAKE BOYFRIEND
BREAKAWAYS

A SHORT STORY COLLECTION

EDEN FINLEY

REBOUND

FAKE BOYFRIEND 2.5

PREMISE

Aron:

I've always known Wyatt was hot, but scotch and half a bottle of tequila makes him so Goddamn beautiful.

After my last disastrous relationship with a close friend, you'd think I'd learn my lesson and choose someone else for a rebound. Someone I don't have a solid friendship with.

I should definitely stay away from Wyatt. But when have I ever listened to logic?

Wyatt:

I'd long forgotten my college crush on Aron. He was never a possibility, having friend-zoned me from the beginning. But now he's drunk and looking for a rebound.

It'd totally ruin our almost decade-long friendship. I have to say no and be the bigger person ... right?

**_Rebound_ can be read as a standalone but would be better understood if read in conjunction with _Trick Play (Fake_

Boyfriend book 2). **While this story belongs to the Fake Boyfriend universe, it does not contain a fake boyfriend trope.****

1

ARON

There were rules, damn it. Important ones. Then I went and broke them. *All* of them, including the most important one.

"Don't fall for me."

I agreed, thinking I was bored, horny, and lazy, and therefore, I could have a reoccurring casual thing with a friend, and it wouldn't be a big deal. I didn't expect that casual whatever to last twelve months, and I never expected to start getting feelings for the guy.

He's Noah Huntington the Third, and his attitude matches his name. He could be elitist, arrogant, and definitely cocky, so when we started fooling around, there was no real danger of me falling for him.

I don't know when that changed exactly, only that it did.

Of course, when Noah found out I had "real feelings," he did what he does best. He shut me out and ran away. I hated it, but I understood it, because he told me it would happen.

When you confess your feelings for a commitment-phobe,

they run away faster than Road Runner being chased by Wile E. Coyote.

I expected it to happen. Yet, here we are, a month later, and the words on my laptop screen don't change no matter how much scotch I drink to make them blurrier ... more blurry ... a blur? Whatever.

I'm sorry. I met Matt and it just happened. I didn't expect to fall so fast, but I have.

I've been staring at the same Messenger conversation all fucking day, because I don't understand it.

He's fallen head over heels apparently.

It's been *one month*—thirty days since he told me we couldn't keep doing what we were doing because he can't handle a relationship. With *anyone*. Those were his words. Now he's all over the internet and in the tabloids on the arm of a famous football player and calling him his boyfriend. He never once gave me that label in the twelve months we were screwing around.

I don't know whether to be angry or just really fucking depressed. A few hours ago, I decided to let the alcohol choose for me, but all it's done is make me tired and numb.

The knock on my door doesn't bring any form of hope. It won't be *him*. He's in the middle of the Atlantic on a romantic cruise with the new guy.

I shove my laptop aside and get my ass off the couch to stumble to the door. It's either going to be Skylar, Rebecca, or Wyatt, and I hope for the latter. I love the girls to death, but I can't handle their good-cop-bad-cop routine right now. Plus, if they turn up, it means Noah's and my secret is out. Wyatt's the only person who knows about Noah and me, and he told me to walk away as soon as he found out it was happening. Even he knew it would end badly.

On second thought, I hope it's not him.

There's a chance it could be our other friend Damon, but I doubt it. He's been in the honeymoon bubble with his new boyfriend, Maddox, and I'm pretty sure he wouldn't know if a meteor was headed for Earth let alone if one of his friends was upset. He's also not supposed to know about Noah and me, but the way he eyes me sometimes, I think he at least suspects.

There's a group of about six of us from college who still catch up at least once a month, and considering how close we are, it's surprising it's taken this long for two of us to fuck up the dynamic by fucking each other.

Through the peephole, all I see is the top of Wyatt's long blond hair. As if he knows I'm staring at him, he looks up, and his sympathetic expression asks me silently to open the door. And when I open up, his blue eyes cut into me and roam over me as if assessing the damage. At five-foot-six, he doesn't come across as an intimidating guy most days, but today, I can't even look him in the eye.

"You saw the news," he says, his voice soft.

"I don't need an *I told you so* speech."

Wyatt's pouty lips turn up into a tiny smirk, and a strand of his long blond hair comes out of his bun and falls by his face. He's always been the prettiest guy I know and has the looks of a model, but the guy is smart too. He's a data manager for a multi-million-dollar start-up and owns stock in the company. I slave away as an office assistant for a giant corporation where I have to wear a suit and there's a line of people waiting and qualified to fill my job if I fuck up. He's going to work in sneakers and jeans and making bank.

He pulls out a bottle of tequila from behind his back. "I'm not here for *I told you so*."

"Fuck, I love you."

Warm laughter bubbles out of him. "I'm guessing by the smell of your breath, I have some catching up to do."

I sidestep so he can enter my cramped apartment, and he immediately throws himself on my couch, opens his bottle of tequila, and takes a gulp. I freeze when his gaze finds my laptop. His eyes narrow as he reads the private messages from Noah and then slams the lid shut.

"You don't need to be looking at that. It'll only make it worse."

"I know." I take my laptop and place it on the coffee table and slump into the spot next to him on the couch.

Without a word, he hands over the tequila.

"Aren't we a pair of classy motherfuckers," I say and drink from the bottle like he did.

The lingering taste of scotch in my mouth mixes with the burning sweetness of the tequila, and for a moment I think this could be a bad idea, but then I throw back another. And another. Then it seems like a *brilliant* idea.

"Share," Wyatt says.

I hand it over. "Why am I an idiot?"

Wyatt winces as he swallows a gulp of tequila, but I don't know if it's from my question or the afterburn from the liquor. "Some people are just born stupid and have no hope."

"Fuck you."

He laughs, and the tequila lands back in my hands. "You fell for someone you shouldn't have. That doesn't make you an idiot. It only makes you human."

"You warned me. Hell, *Noah* warned me." I shake my head. "Idiot."

"While I don't understand how or why you and Noah started fucking around, I do understand falling for the wrong person. Trust me on that one."

My brow furrows. "Where *is* your boyfriend tonight?"

Wyatt doesn't miss the judging tone, but in my defense, his boyfriend is a dick.

"We broke up," he mumbles.

"What, when?" I tell myself smiling would be the asshole thing to do. Wyatt is way too good for Simon, but that doesn't mean he's not hurting right now.

"A few weeks ago." He shrugs. "Around the same time as you and Noah ..."

A thick silence lands between us as we pass the bottle a few more times. I'm hoping he'll provide more details, but after we finish about a quarter of the bottle, he doesn't elaborate.

"What happened?" I ask.

"How about we don't talk about Noah and we don't talk about cheating dickwad fuckface."

I blink at him, trying to figure out if he's being serious or not. *How the fuck could someone cheat on Wyatt?*

"You let me whine about Noah—something that was inevitable—but you've been sitting on that for *weeks*?"

"Not talking about it." He takes the tequila again. "Why do you think I haven't told the rest of the group yet? I don't need the pity stares, thanks very much."

"I'm not—"

"Oh, you so are. Your eyes give everything away. Always have."

"I never knew you realized that shit." I close my eyes tight. "There. Fixed?"

It has its desired effect as Wyatt laughs and shoves me, but then that ugly silence comes back.

"We should go out," Wyatt says. "My ass deserves to dance."

I groan and throw my head back on the couch. "I don't want to dance."

"We can even go to a het bar if you wanna pick up a chick. You need a rebound, and I want to go out. Preferably somewhere we won't run into he who shall now remain nameless."

"Running into Voldemort would be bad juju, bro."

But joking aside, he's brought up something I haven't really thought about in years. After breaking up with my college girlfriend, I swore off women forever and decided to only date men. If I couldn't make it work with the greatest girl in the world, it was never going to work with another woman. We meant a lot to each other, but what we had was something I wasn't ready for.

The humorless laugh that escapes is drowned by accepting the tequila once more. "You remember why I stopped dating women to begin with?"

"Because they tend to want something more."

"Right. And now look at me. *I'm* the one trying to cling onto a person who doesn't even want me. I was convenient, and I regularly dropped everything to run over to his place whenever he called, even though I knew he was using me."

In the beginning, I was okay with that, because I was using him just as much. I don't know when that changed—there was no defining moment, no thoughts of the future, and then suddenly there were, and I couldn't get him out of my head.

That should've been the time to end it, but that's the problem with infatuation—it makes you accept any scrap you're given because you hope and wish he'll change his mind.

Wyatt shifts awkwardly next to me. "I don't know what to say to that."

"Nothin' to say," I mumble. "It's just … ironic, I guess. It's like, full circle. Skylar wanted me to commit, I wanted Noah to commit, and now I feel like I should be committed. Like psychiatrically."

"Dramatic much? Maybe you're done with this." Wyatt inches a little closer and reaches for the tequila again. After a swig, he leans forward and puts it on the coffee table.

I wave him off. "I know I'm being melodramatic. Just need some time to get used to it. I've spent the last few weeks knowing he didn't want a relationship, but to find out it's just *me* he didn't want? Kinda stings."

Wyatt huffs. "Try finding out that your unemployed boyfriend spent his days fucking people in your bed instead of looking for a job."

My hands ball into fists. "Wy … you deserve so much better than that bullshit."

"So do you."

I lie back, resting my head on the back of my couch and close my eyes to soak in the light buzz in my veins and the thumping of my accelerated heart rate.

Wyatt sits up straighter and turns to me. "Can I ask you something?"

"Mmhmm."

"What is it about Noah that you actually want?"

My brain is too out of it to know what he means. "Wha?"

"Do you want *him* or a relationship? You kept running back to him knowing it wouldn't get anywhere, but you never said no. Were you hoping he'd change his mind, or could you not stay away from him?"

"You're sense not making," I slur. "Wait … no, I said that right."

Wyatt laughs. "I make total sense. If you couldn't stay away from *him* and he consumed your every thought, then it's a Noah issue. If the only reason you kept going back was because you wanted to be with someone—have that connection—then it's a relationship issue."

I close my eyes again and try to really think about it, but everything is muddly right now. Muddy. Murky? Fuck, words are hard. "I have no idea how to answer that question."

"Then we should find the answer. I could totally be your life coach. I'd be awesome at that."

"Mmm, that's true. Out of all of us, you're probably the one who's got his shit together the most."

He scoffs. "Cheating boyfriend proves otherwise, but I meant because I'm good at bossing people around."

I snort. "That too."

"So, we're gonna get up, you're gonna go put on jeans so tight everyone can see your impressive dick print, a sexy-ass shirt, and then you have to decide if we're hitting up a gay bar or going looking for pussy. I vote for the latter, but I'll even risk a Voldemort sighting for you if you wanna hit up that new fuckboy bar in the Village."

I wince. "Please don't say pussy. Or fuckboy."

"Pussy, pussy, puss—wait, is pussy one of those words where if you say it three times in a row one will climb out a bathroom mirror and come kill you?"

We burst into simultaneous laughter, and I have to hold onto my stomach to keep it from hurting. "Fine, I'm in. Err, I mean I'm up for going to a bar, not so keen on killer body parts."

Wyatt laughs so hard, his head lolls on my shoulder. Guess the tequila's kicking in. He looks up at me, and I get stuck in his gaze. "Wait … are we really talking about killer genitals? Because I think that's a new low, even for us."

"Unfortunately for me, it's probably a new medium."

He laughs again and tries to stand but can't seem to get off the couch. "Okay. As soon as I find my feet, we'll go find you a rebound, and then maybe you could try dating someone who won't treat you like a rentboy."

Wyatt finally manages to stand and holds his hand out. When I take it in mine, I miscalculate my strength, and instead of him helping me up, I pull him on top of me. We fall from the couch onto the ground in a fit of drunken laughter with tangled limbs everywhere. When he tries to scramble off me, he somehow elbows me in my stomach.

"Ow, fuck."

He stills, his body pressed against mine and his face just inches away. "Shit. Are you okay?"

His blue eyes hold genuine concern which makes me laugh some more, but it fades when he stares at me in a way he's never stared at me before. Or at least, I've never noticed before. I've always known he was hot, but right now, with his breath so close to mine, his petite but firm body on top of me, the way his long blond hair falls in his face …

Fuck, I'm drunk.

My gaze falls to Wyatt's full lips, and my hand moves on its own to push his loose hair behind his ear.

"Aron?" he asks, and his brow scrunches in the most adorable way.

"You're kinda beautiful," I whisper.

He breaks into laughter and buries his head in my shoulder. "You're *so* drunk. Maybe we shouldn't go out."

"I'm totally okay with not leaving this apartment," I whisper.

His body, which is still pressed against mine, starts sliding down as he's going to climb off me, but I wrap my arms around him and hold him close.

"Wy …"

"This is a bad idea."

"What is?" I ask, acting coy.

"You know what. You don't think I can feel …" His hips make the smallest motion against mine, and I become aware of how fucking hard I am. Him too.

"You said I needed a rebound, but don't you too?" I ask.

This time when he tries to get away from me, I let him. Hitting on him certainly isn't my intention, but now that I've thought about it, fuck, the idea of rubbing against him, all hard and naked … I want that.

He climbs back onto the couch with his elbows on his knees and his head in his hands. "You know I don't do the hookup thing."

"Why is that?" I pull myself up so I'm sitting at his feet.

"Look at me." He leans back and gestures to his tight little body.

"I don't understand."

"When we go out, have you never noticed I only attract the guys who are all dominant wannabes? Because I'm smaller, they think it's a given that I'll bend over for them."

I frown. "But don't you? Bottom, I mean? Simon—"

"God, he's a dick. What did he say?"

"I can't remember his exact words. It was at one of our group things, and I think you were roughhousing with Noah. Simon was all 'As long as that guy knows it'll be me fucking that hole later.' I dunno … something to that effect. I wanted to tell him to fuck off, but we don't get involved in each other's shit."

Wyatt sighs. "I wish you'd said something. At least to me. Who the fuck does that?"

"Assholes."

"Exactly! I had a right to know my boyfriend was a dick."

Maybe he did have a right to know, but just like I ignored Wyatt when he told me to stop with Noah, he probably would've ignored me about Simon.

"Would you have believed me?" I ask. "In my experience, if you meddle with friends' relationships, you're the one who ends up friendless."

"I trust your judgment. Although, the Noah thing kinda thins out how reputable that judgment is."

I chuckle. "You don't have to do that, you know."

"Do what?"

"Bitch about Noah to make me feel better. He's your friend too, and this is why it was a bad idea to hook up in the first place."

"I'm mad at him for hurting you. I know there has to be a human being deep inside him somewhere."

"There really is. He just doesn't let anyone see it. Whenever I caught glimpses, he'd school his features and go distant for a few days." I shrug. "I think that's the way it is with him." I frown. *Was.* Was with him. Apparently, Matt Jackson fixes all his problems, somehow."

"I give them a month. Tops."

"I dunno about that," I say. "He's already doing things with Matt that he refused to do with me."

"Dude, he tells you about the kinky shit he's getting up to with his boyfriend?"

I nudge his knee with my elbow. "No, smartass. He's doing things like giving him a boyfriend label."

"That's rough." Wyatt runs his hand over his hair, and his long locks fall around his shoulders.

"I'm sorry I never told you," I say. "About Simon being a dick."

He waves me off. "It's okay. Maybe you're right and I would've been pissed at you instead of the one who deserved it."

I pull back and meet his eyes because something he said before suddenly clicks. "Wait, can we back it up for a sec here? Are you telling me you're like some power top?" The idea of that causes a stirring in my groin.

"No. I like to give and take, but that's not the point. It's the assumption and the shitty attitude when I ask to fuck random hookups. It's unequal, and that pisses me off. I don't bother because of it."

"I'd let you fuck me." Was that out loud? And *let*? More like *beg*.

He shoves me again and laughs. "Stop it. You'd think you would've learned your lesson after Noah."

I wince, because I should've learned my lesson years ago. Skylar and I were able to remain friends, but I know I hurt her.

"Sorry, too soon?" he asks.

"No, I was just thinking I should've learned after Skylar too."

Wyatt cracks a smile. "I totally forgot about that. Feels like she's been with Rebecca forever."

"I set them up after Sky and I broke up because she wanted something serious and I wasn't ready."

"Wow, you're really making your way through the group, aren't you?"

I know he's joking, but for some reason, I hear it as a challenge. I inch closer, and I lower my voice. "Wanna help me cross another one of you off the list?"

It's true hooking up with another friend would be stupid, but either the alcohol, my dick, or like Wyatt says—the need for a rebound—wants me to go for it. Not to mention how it felt to have him on top of me a minute ago.

"Funny."

Pulling myself up onto my knees, I slowly make my way in between his legs and run my hands up his thighs. Wyatt holds his breath, and his legs widen the tiniest bit as if he has no control over them.

"I'm serious," I murmur. "We both need this. You said so yourself."

He releases a loud breath, and my gaze travels down to his lap where he's sporting a major bulge in his jeans.

"Looks like you're up for it." I bite my lip to try not to smile.

He groans and adjusts himself. "You're so drunk you're talking crazy. Even if I said yes, you probably wouldn't be able to get it up."

I push up off him and stand, showing off exactly how wrong that statement is. With me standing and him sitting on the couch, I'm at the perfect height for him to be face to dick with my crotch. "Now you're lying. You were rubbing up on this not a few minutes ago." My hand trails down my stomach and grips my aching shaft through my sweatpants. "I'm not *that* drunk. I mean, I'm drunk, for sure, but not so drunk I don't know what I'm doing."

I totally don't know what I'm doing, apart from maybe trying to fuck up all my friendships. When I go self-destructive, I do a good job of it.

"I'm trying to be a good guy here, Aron."

"You wanted to take me out so I could fuck someone else. Let's cut out the middleman." Even in my semi-drunken state, I can rationalize anything to go my way. Especially if it involves sex.

"The reason we're here right now is because you fucked a friend and it ended badly. You're kinda a mess."

"You're a mess," I say like a petulant child.

"Love you too," he quips.

I sigh. He's doing the right thing, and I can respect that even if I don't like it. "All right then. Let's go out and make me work for it."

Instead of staring up at me though, his eyes lock on my crotch. My sweats aren't hiding anything, and I'm still hard.

He clears his throat and stands, bringing the top of his head close to my chin.

I have to resist the urge to wrap my arm around his waist and pull him against me. "Just tell me one thing."

"What's that?" Those blue orbs look up at me through thick blond lashes.

I cock my head. "Why *have* we never hooked up? Because right now, I can't think of a single reason."

"Because we're friends."

"Hasn't stopped me before. *Clearly.*"

"I've been with Simon for the last two years."

"We've known each other for eight."

He rubs the back of his neck. "You're going to make me say it, aren't you? Bring up that night from freshman year and spell it out for you."

I literally have no idea what he's talking about, and I guess my face reflects that because he keeps talking.

"You told me it was a shame I'd hooked up with Damon because that meant I was off-limits."

"Wait … you hooked up with Damon?"

I mean, it'd make sense. Our friend Damon has a thing for blonds.

He looks confused. "How do you not remember any of

this? It was the pivotal moment where you friend-zoned me forever."

It might be that I've had both scotch and tequila tonight, or maybe it's all the alcohol I drank during college which was more a four-year party than any form of an actual education, but I have no idea what the fuck he's talking about.

If I'd said that to him, I've obviously thought about hooking up with him before. And it'd make sense if he'd slept with Damon that I'd think going out with him would be wrong. Bro code and whatnot.

Wyatt smiles. "I remember the very first time I saw you. You were with Damon at that café in the middle of the quad. You and he were laughing at God knows what, but the sun hit your face in a way that made you all ... shiny."

I screw up my face. "Like Edward from *Twilight* shiny? Eww."

"No, you idiot. Like ... I dunno, you looked all godlike. I'd already met Damon at orientation, so I used my connection with him as an excuse to go talk to you guys, and then—"

"Oh, I remember that now. I thought you were cute. Actually, I'm pretty sure I thought you looked too model-like to be in college."

Wyatt laughs. "Thank you?"

"You're welcome," I say, pretending not to pick up on his sarcasm.

"Anyway, after a few minutes, some girl came up to you and kissed your cheek, and Mr. Flirt came out. I was devastated thinking you were straight. Hence hooking up with Damon later that night."

"Did you really have sex with Damon? Because that's weird. Really weird."

Wyatt shakes his head. "We kissed. That was it. He said

something about me looking like a guy he had a crush on all through high school. Kinda put an end to things pretty fast."

"So, you refuse to hook up with friends ever since?"

Wyatt looks away as he says, "Something like that."

I relent, because he has a valid point, and I like him too much to fuck things up between us. "Okay, if we're going out, I need to shower and get sexy."

"In that case, all you have to do is shower." Wyatt winks.

"Hey, if I'm not allowed to hit on you, you can't flirt with me." I'm only teasing; I secretly like him flirting with me.

Wyatt throws his hands up in defeat. "I was trying to make you feel good about yourself."

"Like I need that?"

"True. In that case, hurry up, you ugly fucker, and try to look semi-decent."

I flip him off while I laugh my way into the bathroom.

2

WYATT

Ooh, this is a bad idea. I know that now. I'm self-conscious of running into Simon because Aron ended up choosing a gay bar.

When we first walk into the club, Aron sits by my side at the high cocktail table and pretends he doesn't find a single guy attractive. When you're as hot as Aron, guys practically fall over themselves trying to get to you. He's got this pretty boy thing going on but with a masculinity that's also sexy. His floppy brown hair is silky, and his blue eyes shine. He can look preppy or badass depending on what mood he's in, and he's always been this laid-back guy who's fun and up for almost anything.

That's probably how he got himself involved with Noah. They're similar in that way. Act now, think later, and fuck the consequences.

Hence the reason I turned him down earlier even though I spent most of my freshman and sophomore year fantasizing about him.

Aron's approached by numerous guys, but he sends them all away, even if he watches their asses as they retreat.

"Go for it," I yell over the music.

He shakes his head. "I'm not really feeling any of them."

"Maybe try your luck on the dance floor."

Aron stares at me out the corner of his eye, takes one last gulp of his drink until it's all gone, and then nods. "Yeah, all right."

I watch his ass as it weaves through the crowd, and less than two minutes later, I sip my beer and watch as Aron becomes sandwiched between two guys.

Of course, jealousy decides to taunt me by reminding me I've had ample chance to take him up on his offer tonight.

Be strong. You said no for a reason.

I could see a future with him without even thinking about it too hard. If he deals with all the crap he's going through, I wouldn't hesitate, but he doesn't want me for the right reasons. I don't even know if he wants me at all. I think it was more an accessibility thing. He's after a rebound, and I was there.

I've always been a relationship guy. Always. If we were to hook up, it'd be my heart on the line because I'd inevitably want more. He's too busy trying to get over Noah to even think about getting involved with someone else.

Right now, watching his long and lean body grinding against one bigger guy and one around the same size as him, I'm getting hard. I'm also wishing I was the one grinding up against him and that the other two would fuck off.

Will watching him fuck every guy in the Tri-state area really make me feel better than if I let him use me to get over Noah? Probably not, but it'll make me ragey instead of heartachy, and that's better in my opinion.

As I think that, my chest plummets to the floor when the smaller dude reaches around Aron and palms his ass, while the bigger guy behind nuzzles into Aron's neck.

Yup. Really fucking bad idea to come here with him.

Instead of continuing to sip my beer, I throw back the rest of it.

"Hi," a deep and rumbly voice says as a large body lands on the stool next to me.

I try to hold in a sigh. The guy is in his forties, at least. No doubt looking for a twink to call him Daddy. Looking young for my age is more a hindrance than a blessing. I'm twenty-six and look barely old enough to drink.

"Hey," I say, because saying *fuck off* usually tends to encourage these assholes.

When did you become so cynical, Wyatt? He might be a decent and lovely man. Rich, lonely, and just looking for companionsh—

"Do you have a name, or can I call you mine?"

Ooh boy, but I guess it's not the worst thing he could've said. "Does that ever really work?"

The guy smiles, and I have to admit, he is hot for an older guy. Dark hair, a few grays that make him distinguished, but he's not exactly geriatric. There's about a weeks' worth of stubble on his jaw, and he's wearing a sexy, well-tailored suit. "Not as many times as I'd like." His chuckle is self-deprecating which makes him even more attractive.

I smile. "Maybe you need a new tactic."

"Wanna dance?"

"Well, that's an improvement, but …" My glance goes back to Aron who's enjoying his manwich, and I realize how sad it is sitting here on my own watching like some type of creeper. The older guy nods, getting my hint, and goes to walk off when I grab his wrist. "On second thought, yes."

Aron's right. I probably need a rebound too. Although, I was pretty much over Simon the minute I found him cheating. I guess that says a lot about our relationship if I could not care so quickly. Maybe I was waiting for an excuse.

"Yes?" this new guy asks.

"Yeah, let's do that." I have nothing to lose.

Sound more enthusiastic, why don't you.

I follow him out to the dance floor, and it takes zero-point-three-two of a second for his hands to latch onto my ass.

With a push and a grunt, I shake out of his grip. "Just dancing."

Gone is all the self-deprecation and charming smile as he grabs my wrist and spins me, my back to his front, and he grinds his cock against my ass.

What the fuck is up with these dom wannabes?

A hand snakes around my front, and a disgustingly hot breath lands near my ear. "Come on, baby boy, you know you want this."

Baby boy? Eww, eww, eww. What in the ever-loving fuck—

The weight behind me is suddenly gone, and so are the grabby hands. They're replaced with arms I could melt into. They're strong. Comforting. The arms of a really good friend.

Even though I could've gotten out of that myself, it doesn't stop the relieved sensation of Aron doing it for me. I should hate the hero act, but it's fucking hot coming from Aron. All that's left for him to do is throw me over his shoulder and carry me out.

Damn, that could be fun.

"I had that covered, you know," I mock.

Aron grins. "I see trying to make you reassess your decision worked a little too well then. Really? *That* guy?"

"Huh?" I pull back.

Aron tips his head in the direction of the two guys he was dancing with who are currently in the middle of carrying my daddy off the dance floor. "I asked them to help me out a little, but you took it too far, man."

"I took it too far? You were practically in a three-way on the dance floor. All I was trying to do was dance."

"With a handsy motherfucker."

"Takes one to know two. Your guys were all over you."

"Because that's what you said you wanted for me!"

"Huh? Wait … and …" I stare after them. "What?"

Aron laughs. "They're friends of mine and a totally monogamous couple. There was no chance of that becoming a three-way. On either side. Because I've decided something."

I cock a brow. "That's dangerous."

Aron cups my face. "I've decided that even though we're both in really shit places, this could ruin our friendship, and we have exes we need to get over …"

He doesn't finish his sentence, and I want to punch him. He can't leave me hanging like that.

"Tell me," I beg.

"I want you."

"Until you're over Noah?"

Aron lowers himself to a knee, in the middle of the fucking dance floor, and my eyes widen, but before I can have a panic attack, he holds my hand and yells, "Wyatt Black, will you be my rebound?"

I can't help laughing, and I shove him as he stands. "You're an idiot."

"But I'm adorable, right?"

I sigh. "Something like that."

Aron pouts and blinks those big puppy dog eyes at me.

"Fine, let's go home."

Aron's face lights up as if he wasn't expecting me to give in. "Really?"

"As long as you know that if this backfires, it's all your fault."

"I will take full responsibility."

That's great, but I don't see how that will mend my broken heart when it all turns to shit.

If I think the walk home is awkward, with us barely talking and our hands in our pockets, it's nothing compared to when we get back to Aron's place.

"Umm ..." He shifts from one foot to the other, and I stand stiff and frozen as if I'd never been in his apartment before. I glance around the small space, looking anywhere but at him.

I throw my hands up in defeat. "See, it's already weird between us, and we haven't even done anything yet. Maybe this isn't a great idea. I should just—"

Aron crosses the room in the blink of an eye. Without warning, his mouth is on mine, and holy mother of God, I thought I was a strong man. I may look small and meek on the outside, but I have strength in other areas. Like my willpower.

Aron's gone and fucked that right up with one kiss that sets my body on fire. His tongue teases mine, and suddenly my eighteen-year-old self is cheering with glee, while I melt under a tempting mouth that's determined to make me cave.

I've thought about doing this since freshman year of college but had given up the idea well before graduation. Doesn't stop me from wanting more now though.

He angles his head, pushing mine back farther because he's so much damn taller than me. And when his hold tightens around me as his hand goes to my ass, I can't stop the groan I've been desperately trying to keep in.

My hands roam over his chest and stomach, the ridges hardening under my fingers.

Dayyymn.

"You're a really good kisser," he murmurs, and I laugh.

"Did you assume I had no skills?"

"No, but fuck, I need another taste." His mouth comes back down on mine, and it's hungry, powerful … the type of kiss that makes toes curl and clothes fall off.

As if on cue, Aron's hands go to my button-down shirt, and he starts undressing me. His touch is tender and slow, unlike his mouth, and when my shirt opens, exposing my chest and stomach, he runs his large hand down to my abs.

My fingers thread through his hair as I continue to kiss and grope his hard muscles.

He moans into my mouth, and without warning, he grips the backs of my thighs and hoists me in the air as if I weigh nothing. My legs go around his waist as he carries me to his bedroom.

When he drops me, I land on the bed with a bounce, but I don't even have time to steady myself when a large weight climbs on top of me.

And then I'm there, laid out for him, expecting him to undress and fuck me, but instead, he straddles my hips and sits up, staring down at me with what can only be described as confusion marring his handsome face.

"What's wrong?" I rasp.

"I don't know whether to suck you or bend over for you."

Hearing him offer himself to me does things to me. Not

only does it set my body to fire on all synapses, but my chest warms at the sentiment. Most guys assume that I'm a bottom, when in reality, I prefer to top. I'm good to go either way, but some guys have issues with a smaller guy topping them—like it's emasculating or what-the-fuck-ever. Those guys are losers.

And Aron's not. He's willing—encouraging even.

My cock leaks, and I'm about two seconds away from blowing. "I don't know why we'd have to choose. We can do both. How about we start with getting rid of the rest of our clothes first. We can improvise from there."

"Improvising can be fun." Aron reaches back and takes off his shirt, showing off golden tanned skin and his lion tattoo over his impressive biceps.

I run my fingers down his tattoo, remembering when he got it in college.

Aron laughs. "God, that stupid tattoo."

"It's sexy."

He shakes his head. "I wanted to be badass."

"And lions are totally badass," I mock.

"Shut up and kiss me."

We get lost in each other again, but it's not long until he pulls back and stands at the foot of the bed. His hands go to the fly of his jeans, and he expertly gets rid of them in record time considering they're tight enough to be painted on.

My breath gets caught in my throat. My mouth goes dry, and my fingers itch to reach out for him and his awe-inspiring cock. It's long and thin, just like him, and he's perfectly proportioned.

His shaggy light-brown hair falls in his eyes, making him blink rapidly. "Thought we were getting rid of our clothes." His eyes trail down my exposed abdomen to my jeans which are still fastened.

"Sorry. Got distracted by a fucking gorgeous guy getting naked for me."

"I wouldn't know what that's like. The gorgeous guy in front of me still has damn clothes on."

I'm unable to stop staring. Aron fully clothed is something. Naked … it's like a whole other level of want.

"Okay, now I'm getting self-conscious," he says.

"Undress me," I croak. "I mean, I want you to do it for me."

Aron smiles. "Lazy ass."

"Saving my energy for when I'm fucking you."

"In that case," he says dryly. One knee hits the mattress and then the next. He stalks toward me on his hands and knees, and instead of going straight for my jeans, he blankets my body with his and kisses me hard.

He doesn't even try to undress me and just keeps kissing me as his hard dick presses against mine.

A sudden hate for zippers makes me growl, and Aron chuckles. I want my clothes gone. I want to explore every inch of Aron's body which I fantasized about a million years ago. And then I want to push him down and fuck him so hard he won't be able to do anything but lie there, take it, and love every fucking second of it.

He finally reaches for my jeans, while I sit up and lose my shirt off my shoulders. When we manage to get me completely naked and I lie back, my long hair splays out above my head.

"Wy … you're so Goddamn beautiful." Aron's tone is raspy, and when he closes his mouth over one of my nipples, I feel the vibration on my skin as he moans.

Aron moves south, slowly, torturously. It's agonizing to the point my hips lift off the bed, pushing my leaking dick against his chest.

He looks up at me. "Didn't your mother ever teach you patience is a virtue?"

"Dude. Do not bring up my mother right now."

Aron chuckles. "I just figured you might need a little something to calm you down." His hand reaches for my cock and gives it a hard pump. "You're leaking for me, and we haven't even gotten to the best part."

"Maybe you should do something to fix that."

With a wicked grin, Aron lowers his head and sucks the tip of my cock into his warm mouth.

"Holy fucking Jesus," I whisper.

"Mmm, and you taste good too," he murmurs and then licks more precum from my slit. "How the hell did I not know how big your fucking cock is?"

I laugh. "It's a proportion thing. Us small guys all have big cocks compared to the rest of our bodies. It's like we need extra help with our center of gravity."

Aron breaks into full-on laughter. "Right. Maybe that's my problem. My height makes my dick look smaller."

"Trust me, I just saw what you're packing, and there's nothing small about it."

"Not in comparison to you. I can't wait to have this thing inside me." His hand strokes my cock, slowly.

I groan and writhe beneath him, which amuses him.

"Not funny. You're killing me," I complain.

"Best way to go out. Death by blowjob. Sign me up." He lowers his head again, this time taking the whole thing into his mouth and adding just enough suction to drive me fucking mad.

He sucks me hard and starts bobbing his head, moving over me fast and on a mission.

"Aron," I warn but it comes out like a breath. "Aron."

Great, now my voice sounds garbled. "Fuck, stop or I'm gonna come," I yell.

With a chuckle, he slowly pulls off my dick, and I sink back into the bed, trying to catch my breath. I wrap my fingers around my cock and squeeze to bring me back from the edge.

"Where are your supplies?" I ask.

He reaches over, and his sweat-wet hair falls across his forehead. I watch him pull out lube and a condom, and the way his muscles tighten and move, the way his long and toned body looks naked … this isn't doing anything to help calm me down.

Aron opens the condom with his teeth and starts rolling it down my cock, but when he catches my gaze, he must mistake my concentration frown for concern. "You still with me?"

"Get on all fours," I rasp.

He grins. "I like bossy Wyatt."

"I'm bossy all the time."

"Good point, but you've never had this growly thing in your voice before. It's adorable."

"If by adorable you mean manly and all alpha-like, then yes, it's adorable."

I ignore his laughter as he gets on his stomach. Grabbing a pillow, I lift his hips and place it under him.

Starting slow, I cover his body with mine, my dick fitting perfectly in his ass crack. My lips caress the base of his neck and then his shoulder blade. When my hips do tiny thrusts, he lifts his ass off the bed for more friction.

He grumbles into his pillow something about delayed gratification.

"Sorry, what was that?"

"Need to come already."

"We haven't even gotten started."

"If I recall, you were two seconds away from coming down my throat, and now you're saying we've only just started? I want a refund."

"I'm sorry, when did I become a hooker in this situation?" I laugh.

"Ooh, roleplaying can be fun. If, you know, you hurry up and get to the fucking, anyway."

"I was kinda thinking I could do something else first."

I kiss my way down his back and grip his ass cheeks in my hands to pull them wide, exposing a tight little hole I can't wait to get inside.

When my tongue lands on him, he groans so loud I'm pretty sure his neighbors can hear it.

"Fuck yes, Wyatt. Oh my God." He breathes heavy and his hips rock.

I can't believe I'm doing this with *Aron*. My dick pulses and leaks precum at the thought.

My college crush.

I'd long given up on the idea of us. By college graduation, he'd turned into one of my closest friends.

Forcing myself to go slow so I can savor every moment, I rim him until he's breathless and rasping for more.

I lean back on my heels and grab the lube. The second I leave him, he lets out a whine.

"I'm not going anywhere." My hand lands on his hip reassuringly, and he covers it with his.

He turns his head, and we lock eyes.

Something passes between us, but I don't know what it is.

"Roll over," I order.

Aron lands on his back eagerly and raises his legs.

I have to bite my knuckles and grunt, because holy fuck

that's hot. Long, hard dick pointing up to his stomach and his hole spit-slick and ready to be stretched.

"If you don't hurry up and do something, I might have to take things into my own hands." Aron reaches for his cock and strokes it long and slow.

I knock his hand away. "That's mine." *At least for tonight, anyway.*

"Then hurry up and make it yours."

With slick fingers, I push into his ass at the same time I bend down to take his cock in my mouth. I want to make the most of whatever temporary, drunken act we'll chalk this up to tomorrow.

I'm still so achingly hard I want nothing more than to bury myself inside him, but he's insanely tight, even just around my fingers.

Aron's hand wraps itself in my long hair, and I wait for the inevitable tug and hard grip that I'm used to.

My hair is a masterpiece, not handlebars, assholes.

I'd let Aron do it though. Fuck, I think I'd let Aron do anything to me. And here's the thing—all he does is caress and cradle the back of my head. There's no hair pulling and no forcing my head down farther to choke on his dick.

He's sweet and attentive even though I'm the one pumping three fingers inside his ass.

I pull off his cock with a wet pop. "I so hope you're ready, because I can't hold back anymore."

Breathless and already sweaty, Aron says, "Ready. Fuck, I'm so ready."

I force myself to ease inside him, because I'm not convinced he's had enough prep, but his body relaxes after only a second or two. Being inside Aron is better than I'd ever fantasized about. The snug fit of his tight channel has my heartbeat throbbing in my dick.

He gives me an encouraging nod, and when I start to move, my whole world shifts. Everything I thought I knew becomes a lie, and existence as I've known it no longer exists. There's only me and Aron and his insanely tight ass.

I roll my hips, taking my time as I thrust in and out. Between heavy breaths, I reach down and rub my hand over his chest, his pecs, and his stomach. I tweak a nipple, and he throws his head back and curses. My lips trail down the center of his chest until he grabs me around the back of my head and pulls me up so they smash against his mouth.

His tongue fucks my mouth in rhythm with my hips, and that's all it takes for me to lose my mind. I don't have control over my body as I thrust harder, deeper, faster.

Aron raises his legs more, holding them open for me with his hands bracing his shins. He writhes beneath me and lets out a round of expletives. "Touch me," he begs. "I need you to—"

My hand goes to his cock, furiously tugging on it.

Our breathing and the slapping of our bodies together become the only sounds to fill the apartment until Aron shouts through his orgasm, coating both of us, but mostly my hand, in cum.

His ass tightens around my cock, and I'm so close to the edge. All I have to do is …

"Oh fuck!" I yell as my orgasm slams into me like a freight train.

I collapse, still shuddering inside him as my head lands on his cum-covered chest.

A hand runs down my sweaty back, we both breathe hard, and then I realize I'm probably squashing him.

I try to move, but my arms and legs are like lead. When I finally find the energy to roll off him, I land by his side, and he looks over at me with the biggest smile I've ever seen come out of him.

"Best. Rebound. Ever."

And even though it's what I'm expecting, my heart sinks.

I'm about to fall asleep into a blissed-out, yet still messy, state when Wyatt shifts beside me, climbing out of bed. I reach for him. "Where are you going?"

"I'm gonna head home."

"Huh?" I turn to my bedside clock. "It's two in the morning. Just stay. It's not like we haven't crashed at each other's place before."

Wyatt hesitates, and I have no idea why. "O-okay. Let me just ..." He gestures to the condom and then points to the bathroom.

I wait for him to get back, grabbing some tissues from my bedside and wiping most of myself clean while I do, but he takes forever. A shower would be good, but I'm still drunk on Wyatt and too sated to get up.

Eventually, my eyelids grow too heavy, and I don't know how much later it is when I feel his body sliding into bed next to mine, but I reflexively wrap my arm around him. "Noah hated cuddling. Please tell me you're a snuggle whore like me."

Wyatt laughs. "I don't mind it."

"Why were you in the bathroom for so long?" I murmur, and then a thought occurs to me. My eyes fly open, and I'm suddenly not tired anymore. I lean up on my elbow to face him. "Am I that shitty in bed you needed to jerk off afterward? Because if I'm not mistaken, you totally came."

He laughs again. "Oh my God, you're an idiot. You want the truth? Like the real truth?"

"Yes. Unless it's that you were taking a dump, because you know, need-to-know basis and whatnot."

Wyatt shakes his head. "I was … I was kinda freaking out."

My brow furrows. "Why?"

"We've been friends for almost ten years. *Ten years.*"

"Eight. You're totally rounding up."

Wyatt sighs and stares at the ceiling.

"If you want to walk out of here tomorrow and pretend it never happened, I understand, but I'm not gonna lie and say I regretted it, because I don't. We both needed this."

I really hope he doesn't want us to forget tonight, because I don't think it'd be possible even if I wanted to, but I don't want this to come between us, and if he thinks he can't be friends with me after it, I'll force myself to forget.

"I don't want to pretend it didn't happen," Wyatt whispers, "but, I mean, where do we go from here? This was a one-time thing, right?"

"We can make it whatever you want it to be."

"It'd be smart to make this a one-time thing."

I cock my head. "Did we ever claim to be smart people?"

Wyatt laughs, and for some reason, it sounds so much more melodic than it ever has before, and it warms my chest … and other areas.

I roll into him, placing my hardening cock against his

thigh. "We could make it a one-night thing, if you really want."

One night, two nights, eternity ... right now, I think I'd take anything Wyatt offered me.

"You wanna fuck me this time?"

"Oh, hell yes." That's all I need to get me to reach for another condom in my drawer.

"He shoots from the three line ... and he scores!" I yell and throw my hands up.

"Congratulations, you beat a girl," Skylar says and chases after the basketball.

"I thought feminism meant we should treat you all equally, so suck it, because I kicked your ass." I dance around the half court like the goofball I am, which only makes Skylar laugh.

"That was a lucky rebound," she protests.

I know she's talking about the game, but my brain gets stuck on the word *rebound,* and then all I can think about is Wyatt.

I've been thinking about him for the last week.

"What's with the face?" Skylar asks and throws the ball at my chest.

I catch it easily and smirk. "My beautiful face that you regret letting go?"

She rolls her eyes. "No, the moronic one that's staring off into space as if trying to cure cancer."

"I ..." I want to confess everything to her, but she's gonna be mad. She'll hate the Wyatt thing more than the Noah thing, and she'll hate even more that I didn't tell her about either. "I need a hug."

She smiles, and it still makes my chest flutter with affection even though it's been eight years since we were together. Her short, black, pixie haircut is wet with sweat, her tank top shows off her sleeve tattoos, and her nose piercing glints in the late Sunday afternoon light. Skylar's not only my ex but probably my best friend. We ended on relatively good terms, and we've only grown closer as the years pass. I should tell her what's going on—I basically tell her most things anyway—but I hate when she yells. It's all high-pitched and mean mommy-like.

"If I hug you, will you tell me?" she asks.

"Nah, it's fine. I can work it out." I drop the ball as she steps into my arms anyway.

The way I feel about Skylar is the same kind of love I've always had for Wyatt. We're friends—great friends. But the potential for more with him is there now, and it makes me wonder if I've had these feelings for him this whole time lying dormant, just waiting for the right moment to hit me over the head.

Wyatt's always been a relationship guy, and he's so fucking gorgeous he can have any guy he wants. And I want him desperately to want me. Which is stupid. Because we're friends.

Friends who fucked.

Then again, so were Noah and I. Now that situation's messed up, and I'm trying to get over that too.

It's confusing though, because I don't know why I'm upset over Noah. I don't think I actually want him anymore anyway. I've had a month to get over it, and I thought I was, but then … then he gets this new boyfriend and seems so *serious* about him. I have to ask why him and not me?

"Your thinking is hurting my brain," Skylar says and steps back. "Are you sure there's nothing I can help you with?"

"Positive. Thanks. I've just been thinking lately about what I want."

"A million dollars, a gallon of lube, sixty-nine condoms, and a week on some orgy island somewhere."

"Holy shit, can you read my mind?"

She laughs.

"But why sixty-nine condoms?"

"Best. Number. Ever."

I pull her in for another hug. "I love you."

"Okay, now I'm really worried."

I sigh. "I should get going. You and Bec coming to the bar tomorrow night?"

"Yup. So are Damon and Maddox. Their cruise gets back in the morning."

"And Noah?" I ask and try not to let my voice croak.

"Dunno about him. Isn't he with that football guy now? How long do you reckon that'll last?"

I want to say not long, but I don't know if that'll be true. "Noah's already labeled him his boyfriend, so it must be serious."

"Are you sure it's not just the media saying that? Noah hasn't had a boyfriend, like, ever."

"He texted me some bullshit about being swept off his feet."

"He did not."

"Okay, that's paraphrasing but it's true. He's in a legit relationship with the football player."

"No. Fucking. Way."

Sounds about right. "That was pretty much my reaction."

"H-how do you feel about that?" Her voice is quiet and cautious.

I narrow my eyes. "What do you know?"

"Oh, hon, if you think I didn't know you two have been going at it for months—"

"Almost a year, actually."

Her eyes widen. "Damn, I'm slipping. I only picked up on it that night Damon and Maddox hooked up at Noah's and he was talking to Matt, and you were shooting daggers at both of them."

"Ah, yeah. That was kinda the end of us."

Noah noticed my jealousy and freaked out. I tried to get him back, but he flat-out refused.

"Don't worry, I haven't spoken about it to anyone. Not even Bec. I figured you'd either come to me or work it out yourself that you two were a disaster together."

"Yeah, well it ended in spectacular fashion."

"He ran away?"

I nod.

"I'm sorry—"

"I don't need the sympathy or pity. I just wish … I dunno what I wish for. To not feel like a loser?"

She wraps her arm around me. "Aron, I'm only going to say this once. You *are* a loser. You may as well accept it."

I burst out laughing and nudge her.

"Okay, in all seriousness, you may be a loser, but it has nothing to do with falling for Noah."

I run my hand through my hair. "That's the thing though. I don't know if … like, I'm not sure I fell for him. I cared about him, sure. No, I *care* for him. I think I wanted more because I might … I mean, I think—"

"There you go with that evil *thinking* thing again."

"Right. The truth is …" Why's it so hard to say? "I think I'm ready for a relationship. I thought I had potential with Noah, and we were practically in a relationship anyway, but he just didn't realize it. So, when he said no, I think it was my ego that got crushed and not my heart?"

I've been trying to analyze this for the past week, but all it does is send me around in circles.

"*You* have an *ego*? Shocking."

"Gah. I'm totally overthinking this, aren't I? I can't make any sense of what's going on up here." I point to my head.

And I'm totally overthinking Wyatt too, but she's taken this news well. If I throw Wyatt on top, that'll probably push her over the edge.

"I need to get going," I say.

"Are you sure you're okay?"

If I were to answer that question truthfully, it'd probably be a no. "I will be." I kiss her head. "I'll see you and Bec tomorrow."

Leaving the basketball courts, I have the sudden urge to see Wyatt. I want to know if the other night was a fluke or if something else is there. Maybe when I get there, all the confusion will disappear and I'll only see him as my friend and not the guy I fucked last week and can't stop thinking about.

I take out my phone and text: You home? Can I come over?

WYATT: *Will be in about twenty. See you then?*

ARON: *On my way.*

4

WYATT

I wipe my sweaty palms on my jeans when the buzzer for the front entrance to the building goes off. Because the button to let Aron in is broken, I have to physically go out there to meet him.

My legs are jelly from nerves, and I'm scared about what he has to say. Any other time Aron has messaged to hang out, I haven't thought anything of it. Now? All I can think about is being inside him, his loud moans as he comes, and what he looks like naked.

Idiot. Idiot. Idiot.

Never cross that line with friends.

At the door, Aron's smile is easy and natural, while mine probably looks forced or like a serial killer's when trying to act like a normal human being.

"Hey," he says like he would any other day.

"Hi." My voice is not like it is every other day, and I'm pretty sure it could be classed as a squeak. I clear my throat and step aside to let Aron pass.

"How was work?" he asks when we step over the threshold to my apartment.

"Usual. You?"

"Half day Fridays." He does a Godawful Carlton dance, and I can't help laughing at him. "Just got done shooting hoops with Skylar."

"Ah, that's why you're all sweaty." My gaze roams over his wet tank top, his sweaty biceps, and his tattoo, and I try to hold in a moan of appreciation. Damn him.

It's been a long time since I looked at him this way, and with one night, he's brought it all back.

Fucker.

It's not his fault, I remind myself. I could've walked away.

Aron takes off his shoes and throws himself onto my long couch with his legs curled up beside him. "Wanna play some *Halo*?"

Guess nothing's changed for him then. Although, he's kinda avoiding eye contact.

"Sure."

I turn on the console, grab the controllers, and throw him one. When my ass lands beside him, his feet loom close to my thigh, and suddenly I can't concentrate on anything but his feet. The game starts on the screen, but I can't seem to shoot anything. It's like being this close to Aron now turns me into the dumb twink most guys assume I am.

I catch Aron glancing at me out the corner of my eye, but I try to ignore it.

"You okay?" he eventually says when I die in the game. "I usually die long before you do."

Fuck, what do I do? Come clean? Tell the truth?

Nah, screw that. Avoidance all the way.

"Guess your sucky-ness is rubbing off on me." *God, don't*

say rubbing off and mention anything to do with sucking in the same sentence.

As expected, my dick twitches in my jeans. I clear my throat and adjust the way I'm sitting.

Aron's gaze burns into me, and my face heats. There's a beat of silence that goes on just a bit too long, but then he says, "Last man standing wins."

The flirt in me wants to ask "Wins what?" but instead, I take his prize-less bet and say "You're on."

We sink into the game, and it's what we need to relax the charged air between us. That's never been there before, and I don't know how to deal with it.

But as the game goes on, everything between us goes back to normal, even if his feet still brush up against my thigh. I don't know if he's doing it on purpose or is unaware of it, but Aron appears less conflicted about our friendship than I do, so I don't ask him to move.

If we have any hope of remaining friends, I have to swallow the niggly longing feeling that's trying to make an appearance.

All I want to do the whole time I'm at Wyatt's is throw him down on his couch and maul him, but instead, we both focus on trying to settle into some sort of normalcy between us.

But when I go home after hours of gaming, my chest aches with a sense of something missing. Perhaps it's missing all the blood pumping through my heart because it's currently in my dick, telling me I should've made another move on Wyatt.

I don't want normalcy between us. I want him.

The thread holding our friendship together is starting to fray, and I fear it'll snap if I do something to mess it up, but there's no doubt about it; I want more.

The following night, as soon as I walk in the sports bar, my eyes immediately find Wyatt, and I break into a smile. On the outside, nothing's changed, but on the inside, it's like I've woken up. Last night was proof of that.

I make my way to Skylar and Rebecca first, kissing each of them and then lifting my chin in hello to Damon and Maddox.

When I reach Wyatt, my heart stutters. His cologne is sandal-wood scented but all I can smell is sex.

Two rounds of really hot sex.

I quickly sit on the stool next to his to hide my hardening cock.

"Hey," he says with an easy smile.

"Hi." My voice comes out like a breath, and I can't tear my gaze away from him.

"Earth to Aron," Damon says, waving his hand in front of my face.

I shake off my Wyatt distraction. "Wha?"

Damon's green eyes glimmer in amusement. "Drink. You want anything?"

"Oh, I'll come with." I stand and for some inexplicable reason turn to Wyatt. "You good? Want me to get you something?"

His lips quirk as he lifts his almost full beer. "I'm all good."

Ah. Right. With a nod, I follow Damon to the bar.

"You okay?" he asks when we're waiting in line.

I startle. "Wha?" Apparently, this is the extent of my ability to create words now.

"Where are you tonight? You're here but not really here."

"I'm fine. Just distracted. How was your cruise?" I almost choke on the words, and I pray to God that he doesn't bring up Noah and Matt. There are bigger, more confusing things I'd rather think about than them.

Damon grins as he stares over his shoulder at his boyfriend. "The best."

"You and Maddox the real deal then? Living together already?"

"Yup. Real deal. If he can survive living with me for the next year, we're gonna buy a place."

"Whoa. That's not just the real deal, that's like … Rebecca and Skylar real deal. Like a future and promises of forever and shit."

Damon shakes his head. "Maddox doesn't do marriage, but I'm okay with what we have. It'll still be forever."

"What's that like?" I wonder, and it takes me a second to realize it comes out aloud.

"What's what like?"

"Having someone you know will last?"

"Awesome."

Is this what longing feels like? My chest aches, and I don't like it. The conversation I had with Wyatt the night we hooked up replays in my head, and the longer I've had to think about it, the more I realize he's probably right.

I haven't been hung up on Noah. I've been hung up over the relationship I thought we could have. I want someone in my life. Someone important. The fact he went out and found it so fast makes me wonder if I'm just not relationship material.

When we're served our drinks and go back to the table, Wyatt smiles at me again, and it's a cocky, knowing smile that says, "We've totally seen each other naked."

And I really want to see it again. If the way Wyatt's gaze roams over me says anything, he wouldn't mind seeing it again too.

If that were to happen, though, I have no idea what it'd mean for us.

We agreed that one night was smart so things wouldn't get messy.

Fuck, I wanna get messy with him.

But then my last mess walks through the door with his next mistake hanging off his arm.

Wyatt's brow furrows as my face falls, and when he sees why, he purses his lips.

Noah stands there, tall and smug like normal, only this time he's talking to a giant of a guy with a thick beard and a body like a fucking God. Okay, yeah, I have to admit the football player is hot.

Gah, why do I hate this so much? I was literally drooling over Wyatt twenty seconds ago, and now I'm mad the football player is here?

I haven't been this confused since I watched my first ever porno at fourteen and wondered why both the male and female turned me on.

While Noah and his boyfriend take a seat, I lose myself even more. The conversations float around me as if I'm underwater. Damon thought I was weird at the bar, but it's nothing compared to now.

Wyatt follows Noah to the bar, leaving me alone … well, Skylar and Bec, Maddox and Damon are here too, but sitting just a few seats away from me is Mr. Perfect himself.

I can't help checking him out, trying to figure out what he has that I don't.

A multi-million-dollar paycheck maybe?

Ugh. Right. That.

Not that Noah needs the money. He's a gajillion-flippty-floppity-aire. His money has money, and then that money has lots of little baby money running around.

I just don't get why this new guy changes everything Noah stands for. It makes me wonder why I'm not good enough.

That's a dangerous thinking path. One I don't really want to take.

"Hey, guys, I'm …" I shake my head. "Yeah, I'm gonna go. Drink ain't sitting right."

"Aron," Skylar says with sympathy in her eyes.

"I'm okay," I try to reassure her, but I don't think I pull it off.

When I walk up to Noah and Wyatt at the bar, my palms sweat, but I don't know which one of them is causing it.

"I'm out."

I stare at Noah, waiting for him to say something, respond … anything, but I know I'm wasting my energy. This is *Noah*. It's what he does. I knew that all along, and yet here I am, still hoping he wakes up to himself and stops being a dick—give me an explanation, an apology. *Something.*

Not that it'd make a difference.

When I realize it's futile and won't change anything even if he did say something, my feet move as fast as they can out to the street, and I don't slow down and take a breath until after a few blocks.

Running footsteps and heavy breathing catch up to me soon after, but I know it won't be Noah, and for the first time since we ended things, I don't wish it to be him. There's only one guy I want it to be, and sure enough, when Wyatt appears at my side, I can't help breaking into a smile.

"Holy fuck, that's so not fair. Your legs are way longer than mine."

"You didn't have to follow me. I'm a big boy."

"I wanted to."

"Adopt a loser day?"

He pinches me. "Call yourself a loser one more time and you might actually become one."

Wyatt's right. I've never let anyone make me feel less than worthy before, so I don't know why I let Noah get to me. Maybe I just need time to get over the crush to my ego.

"So, I'm guessing our little rebound didn't work," Wyatt says.

I think it worked too well, I want to say, because I still don't know how I can be looking at Wyatt right now wanting to undress him and fuck him here on the street, when I just left the bar because of another guy.

That doesn't stop "Dunno. I might need a repeat" falling from my mouth though.

Wyatt's eyes widen, but he covers it with a tight smile. "I'm all for playing wingman this time 'round."

My brow furrows.

"One night. No complications. You know, the smart thing to do."

"I'd totally be willing to call myself a dumbass if I got to take you home again."

"I don't want"—Wyatt points in the direction of the bar—"that to happen to us in a few months. Because we both know if we had a repeat it wouldn't be long before we had another and another and—"

"I'm waiting to see the problem with that." I've been thinking about that every day for a week now.

"You know why that would be a bad idea."

"I really don't."

"Because you will do to me what Noah did you."

I cock my head. "How do you figure?"

"I told you last week I'm not a hookup guy, you won't be ready until you stop pining for Noah, and I just got out of a shitty relationship. We can't go down the casual sex route. We'll end up hating each other."

"What if I don't want just casual?"

"You don't know what you want."

I hate he has a point. "Are you in my brain now?"

"I refuse to be someone's second choice."

He's so far from my second choice, but I do kinda wish we happened at a different time, when we both weren't so fucked up.

When would that have been though? It's taken this long to even get this far. All I know is I want Wyatt again. For another night, for a week, a month, forever, I don't actually know.

"I want to go on a date with you," I say.

"What?"

"Hear me out. We are both in really shitty places right now —I get that—but last week also made me realize that I'm ready for a relationship. Like the proper, full-on, serious relationship. I've never had that before, but when I think of who I'd want it with, it's not Noah."

Wyatt looks down at his feet. "Is it me though?"

"I want it to be."

"Are you really in a state of mind to know anything you want?"

"I'm not professing my undying love for you here, but I want to take this step with you. We're friends, and I think that's a good start to have something more."

God, how unromantic does that sound?

I try again. "Ever since last weekend, all I can think about is *you*."

Better.

"To me, it sounds like you've decided you want a relationship and I'm convenient."

Okay, he still needs some convincing.

"If I just wanted the randomness of a relationship, I could go out and find one pretty easily."

Wyatt smirks. "Think highly of yourself, huh?"

"It's easy meeting people. You know that. You're barely ever single."

He laughs. "Oh boy. Now I want to say no just so I can see you struggle out there. Okay, no, that's mean. You're right, it's easy to meet people. Holding on to them is the hard part."

I shake my head. "I think we're going off track here. This thing, between you and me, I want to explore it. If it was just a relationship I craved, I wouldn't put our friendship on the line to see where this could go. I had fun last weekend, and last night when I was with you, all I kept thinking about was how much I wanted you again—that the one night wasn't enough."

"What if it's too soon?" Wyatt whispers.

"Is it too soon for you? You just broke up with someone you'd been with for two years. We're in the same situation, and all I'm asking for is a couple of dates. If you don't think it'll work out, we end it before we're in too deep. But I'm serious about giving us a real shot. Shitty situations and bad timing be damned."

"We'd have to go slow."

Yes. Progress.

"We can go at any pace you want," I say.

"So, you want to date me." Wyatt says the words as if he's trying to make sense of them, but he doesn't need to make sense of it all right now.

"Yup. And I think we should start tonight."

I grab his hand and start dragging him toward a diner I love, but it also happens to be in the direction of my apartment.

"I thought we were gonna take it slow," Wyatt says.

"Unless you wanna fuck in an old fifties diner in front of everyone, I think milkshakes and burgers is taking it slow."

"Oh." He lowers his head, and if I'm not mistaken, his face reddens.

"I mean, I'm up for it if you are, but I'll probably be kicked out of my favorite burger joint and banned for life. That'd be pretty shitty but well worth it."

"Okay shut up. I thought—"

"You thought I was just bullshitting you to get you into bed again?"

Wyatt avoids eye contact and stares out at the busy street.

"Well then, first thing we're going to work on is trust. You need to trust me that I'm not just fucking around here, and I need to trust that you're going to give me a fair shot."

"When did you get all mature and sensible?"

"I have no fucking idea, but it's scary, huh?"

"Almost as scary as you and I dating."

I purse my lips. "I feel like I should be offended."

"Come on, you have to admit this is crazy."

I lean in. "You know what they say: there's a fine line between crazy and genius."

"I don't think that's a real saying."

"Come on, this could be the best decision we've ever made. Take a leap of faith."

Wyatt still seems skeptical.

"Stop thinking about what'll happen if it ends badly or why this is crazy. Think about it. This could be the beginning of our future." Look at me, being all romancey.

"Sounds kinda hokey, but okay."

Just like I did a week ago on a crowded dance floor, I lower myself to one knee on the busy and dirty street. Some people stop and stare, one woman screams, but they all sigh and move on when they hear me say, "Wyatt Black, will you go on a date with me?"

6

WYATT

Once I make Aron get up off his damn knee, he drags me into the diner. I focus on his words and his sentiments because my brain keeps wanting to tell me that Aron and I together don't make sense. At least, not right now.

But fuck, I want it. I want everything he's saying to be true, and I want to give us a real shot, even if a big part of me thinks it'll be a mistake.

There's affection that has never been there before in the subtle way he touches me, the way his hand runs down my side and clasps my hand, and the way he takes a seat next to me in the booth instead of across from me.

Instead of normal first-date conversation where we try to get to know each other, Aron and I already know everything. Even down to embarrassing stories about ex-boyfriends.

"You know what's the sad thing?" he says. "Simon wasn't even your worst."

I groan. "Aren't exes like a first-date topic no-no? The only ex of yours I can really ridicule is Noah, and it's probably not best if we bring him up any time soon."

Aron ignores me. "Ooh, what about the guy in sophomore year who was total goth and made you wear that spiked collar?"

"I chose to wear that collar because it was cool."

His laugh, while taunting, gives me a sense of comfort, and I can't help laughing along with him.

"Okay fine. I wore it because *he* told me it looked cool."

I'm hoping he drops it, but it turns out he's on a roll.

"You know who I thought you'd end up with? That guy senior year. What was his name?"

"Jai."

"Yeah, him. He was cute and sweet and—"

"Heavily into the BDSM scene," I finish for him.

Aron pulls back. "Really?"

"Yup."

"Sooo, that's not your thing?" It's cute how he's trying to ask coyly.

"Not really."

Aron sighs dramatically. "I was wrong. This isn't going to work *at all*." He goes to stand, but I pull him back down, and he breaks into laughter.

"Funny. And it's one thing to add a little kink like bondage or edging, but I draw the line at humiliation and pain."

Aron screws up his face. "Yeah, that's not my jam either."

"It kinda became a problem in the end. Basically, he said he didn't want to lose me, but if I couldn't do what he wanted, he'd have to go elsewhere for his … 'needs.'"

"You're like an asshole magnet, huh?"

"Understatement."

His hand reaches for mine on top of the table. "I promise that even when I'm a dick I won't be an asshole."

I want to believe him, but it's hard with my past history

and taste in men, but I cover my insecurities with a joke. "I don't know what that means, and I don't know if we're talking about actual anatomy or—"

He snorts. "I don't want to be like those other guys. Ever. No matter what happens between us."

"Can you promise me something?" My voice is small, and I kinda hate it.

"Anything."

"That we're always honest and open with each other. All of those guys had one thing in common. They weren't completely honest about who they were or what they wanted until we were in the middle of a serious relationship. It's like they waited for me to fall for them before showing me their true side."

Aron leans in. "I could promise that, but I really don't have to. You already know everything there is to know about me."

That's true. "A perk of dating one of your friends, I guess."

"I'm sure there's a whole list of perks to justify us being on a date right now."

I shake my head. I'm on a date with Aron Roe.

Nope, still makes no sense, but we're here now, and I wouldn't change it for anything.

I never thought it possible, but the best date I've ever been on included a diner selling greasy and disgusting food that's surprisingly delicious. I don't think the food has anything to do with making the date great, though.

Aron is surprisingly flirty and funny, dropping innuendo every chance he gets. It's a side of him I've never seen before, other than last week. It's like he's giving me a piece of him that's only privy to those he's with. He's never shown me this part of him because he's never looked at me like he is right now.

On our way out of the diner, I stop just outside the entrance because our apartments are in opposite directions. "I guess this is goodnight?"

He cocks his head. "You think I'm not the type of date to walk you home?"

"Am I a seventeen-year-old girl?"

"No, but you look like one," he mumbles.

"Oooh, and just when I was thinking about inviting you back to my place."

Aron shakes his head but gestures for me to lead the way. "We're taking it slow, but that doesn't mean I won't walk with you. If not to be gentlemanly, then to just be with you a little longer before I go home and jerk off."

I bark out a laugh. "That was *almost* romantic."

"Mediocrity at its best. It's how I make sure I'm not setting my dates up for disappointment."

I nudge him, and he throws his arm around my shoulder as we continue down the street.

I thought it might be weird to have Aron's arm around me or to be affectionate, but it comes as second nature. It's reflexive for me to wrap my arm around his waist and fit against his side.

But those mushy, first-date nerves shatter into a million pieces when we arrive on the stoop of my apartment and find Simon waiting for me.

He stands from sitting on the front step, and he runs his hand over his crew cut. "Can we talk?"

"Nope," I say.

Simon's dark gaze goes from me to Aron as if only now

noticing him. "Who are you?"

Aron rolls his eyes. "As if you don't know who I am, dick."

Simon steps closer to Aron and puffs out his chest. Aron's got a few inches on him, but Simon's stacked. He had all the time in the world to go to the gym in between pretending to look for a job and fucking other people in my bed.

I expect Aron to cower or back down, but he doesn't. He shoves me behind him protectively, and instead of getting pissed at it like I would've had Simon done it when we were together, I secretly love it.

"Seriously, Wyatt?" Simon asks. "*This* guy? Talk about a step down. Not even worthy of a rebound."

Aron scoffs, probably because he knows Simon's full of shit. Aron's one of the hottest guys I know.

"I'm not a rebound," Aron says, and his words sound sincere. "You fucked up, and now Wyatt's mine."

Again, if Simon had said something like that while we were together, I would've called him a possessive dickhead, and we would've gotten into a fight. When Aron does it? I want to let him claim me right here on the street.

Those thoughts should scare me after only one date.

Don't get ahead of yourself.

"Just like that you're moving on?" Simon asks, tilting his head to see me behind Aron.

"You moved on before we were even broken up."

"That didn't mean anything. Can we please have an adult conversation without your new"—Simon's gaze rakes over Aron who folds his arms across his chest—"toy in the way?"

"I'm good here, thanks," Aron says, and I try not to laugh.

"There's nothing left to say." I step beside Aron and wrap my arm around him.

"Can I at least come inside and get the rest of my things?"

"Give me a forwarding address, and I'll send them. You're not stepping foot inside my apartment ever again."

And to think we were talking about moving in together. Although, he'd practically lived with me anyway, because he was still living with his parents.

Yeah, he's a real winner. Why did I stay with him for so long?

Simon's glance flits between Aron and me until he finally gives up and stalks away.

"God, he's a dick," Aron says.

"As we've already established, nearly all my exes are."

Aron's arms wrap around me from behind, and he nuzzles my neck. "So … we're together, huh?"

I laugh. "I'm yours, am I?"

"Sorry about getting all possessive and shit. I know you don't like it, but it's just … I really hate that guy."

"So do I. And the idea of belonging to you isn't so bad."

Aron's lips graze my neck and lead up to my ear. "Maybe one day soon, you'll belong to me for real instead of this possibly, maybe, kinda dating but still have doubts thing you got going on."

I turn in his arms and grip his shirt, pulling him closer to me. "Well, if our first date is any indication, I'd say it could be a possibility."

"*Could* be? I'm giving you all my charm, and the best you can come up with is *could be*?"

I start dragging him up the stairs to the entrance of my apartment building. "Maybe if you come in, you can convince me to upgrade to *it might be*."

"Mmm, I love it when you talk dirty," he says dryly.

His hand covers mine when I get my key out to open the

door. "I thought we were taking things slow." His voice is more curious than stern, which is perfect for me.

I lean in, touching my mouth to his and teasing him with the lightest kiss until he caves and sinks against me and forces his tongue into my mouth. I let him devour me until we both can't stand it anymore.

I smile as I pull back. "Fuck going slow?"

Aron nods. "Fuck going slow."

7

ARON

EIGHT WEEKS LATER

W yatt wrings his hands together. "I'm nervous. Why am I nervous? It kinda feels like coming out all over again."

I snort. "It's not that dramatic. We're just telling our closest friends that we're official."

We're finally in a place where we're both confident in what we have. We knew if we'd told everyone right off the bat that it would add pressure to an already rocky beginning. Wyatt didn't trust I was truly in it for him and kept thinking he was a prolonged rebound. I knew differently though, and even though his asking me to keep this thing on the downlow while we worked it out reminded me of how Noah treated me, I also knew it was different this time.

Wyatt would hold my hand in public and didn't care if we ran into our friends. If it came out, it came out, but we just weren't advertising it right away. He called me his boyfriend early on, we'd go on dates, we'd stay at each other's houses … it's been more than just dating for us from the beginning. I didn't need him to tell the world to prove that.

And now we both feel we can tell people about us with confidence. When our friends express their concern about changing the group dynamic yet again—which they probably will—we're both comfortable in defending the relationship.

"Aren't you nervous about telling Noah?"

"Who's Noah?" I ask. It's become a running joke between us. Wyatt said one night he was going to fuck me until I couldn't remember Noah's name anymore.

Little does he know, he pretty much did that the night we first hooked up.

Wyatt shoves my shoulder. I like it when he gets pushy. "I'm being serious."

"Why should I care what Noah thinks? According to Damon, he's moving in with the football player."

Wyatt's eyes widen. "Seriously? But he's … Noah."

I shrug. "Matt's the guy he was supposed to end up with. I … I'm actually thinking about, you know …"

"What?"

"Calling a truce with Noah and me? Try to be friends again … Would … would you be okay with that?"

Wyatt purses his lips as if needing to seriously think about it. "Why? I mean, I don't want to be the type of boyfriend to say you can't do something, but we've had this whole honesty thing from the beginning, and I guess I want to know why you need him."

"I don't *need* him, but I realize that the reason he didn't want me was because we were completely wrong for each other and better off as friends. Our breakup had nothing to do with me. It's just that we weren't supposed to end up together." I step forward and grip Wyatt's hips, bringing them against me. "I'm with the person I'm supposed to end up with."

Wyatt's cool eyes stare up at me. "Really?"

"I love you, Wy. You have to know that." I pretty much fell in love with him on our first official date.

Who knows, maybe I fell for him years ago and just didn't know it. We've both settled into the relationship so easily it feels like we've been together for years. Maybe being friends for so long beforehand has helped with that, but I like to think it's because we were made for each other.

"Well, I do now," Wyatt says. "But that's the first time you've said it."

"I didn't want to scare you off. It's technically only been two months."

"I knew I loved you about six weeks ago." His voice is soft and warm, and I love it almost as much as I love him.

I smile. "Me too. So much for being completely honest with each other, huh?"

"I didn't want to seem crazy."

I lower my head into the crook of his neck. "Aww, babe, you are crazy, but I already knew that, and I love you anyway."

"If I'm crazy, you're a loser."

"Match made in heaven."

My hand cups his face, and I cover his mouth with mine. I'll never tire of the sweet little moans he makes while I kiss him. I love sharing my bed—or his—with him. We're trading off on places right now, but I hope one day soon to ask him to move in. It's super-fast which is why I've held off, but after a couple more months, there won't be anything stopping me from getting down on one knee and asking him to move in with me.

If I were ever to propose for real to Wyatt, he'd probably never believe me, because I basically get down on my knee for every little thing. It drives him crazy, but I'm convinced he secretly loves it.

Wyatt pulls back, and I groan. "We need to get going or we'll be late."

"Can't we be a little late?" I rock my hips against his.

He stares down at my half-hard cock tenting in my jeans. "I guess ten minutes of waiting for us won't kill them."

"Ten minutes? Fuck, better make it fast."

Wyatt merely sinks to his knees with a confident smirk on his lips.

Yup, I definitely love this guy.

Okay, I totally understand what Wyatt was nervous about now. As we sit with our friends, silently debating on when exactly to do this—to tell them all they basically haven't seen us for two months because we've been too busy fucking—Noah walks into the bar and heads straight for me like he's on a mission.

Fuck.

"Hey, have you got a sec?" Noah glances around the table where our friends stare on wide-eyed, and if I'm not mistaken, Wyatt looks a little worried. Or wary.

I guess now's as good a time as any to put it out there and reassure my boyfriend in the process. Leaning in closer to Wyatt, I cup his face and kiss his lips softly. "I'll be back soon, okay, babe?"

His eyes widen even more if possible.

The others are in a similar state of shock.

I'm the first one out of the bar, and Noah trails after me.

Then we're both on the street, staring at each other awkwardly.

Fun.

Noah's always been this guy who has more confidence than anyone could need, more arrogance than anyone likes, and a self-absorbed attitude. The guy standing in front of me, with his head down, his blue-green eyes dull … it's not the Noah we hate to love.

He says "I'm sorry" at the same time "I want to thank you" falls out of my mouth.

Noah cocks his head and lets out a tiny laugh. "Thank me?"

"It took you walking away for me to see what was right in front of me the whole time."

"You and Wyatt?" There's no condescension in his tone like when we ran into Wyatt's ex, just pure curiosity. He breaks into a smile. "I can actually see that. Like, it makes sense."

I run a hand through my hair. "Yup. We, uh … I dunno. We just work."

"How long?"

I look away. "Couple of months."

His eyebrows shoot up. "Oh, wow. So when you say it took me walking away, you literally mean as soon as I did …"

My eyes narrow. "Is that jealousy I hear, because I'm pretty sure you moved on well before I did."

"No," he says quickly. "It's just … shit, I've been feeling guilty about the way I handled … our whole situation. I went about it the wrong way, and until recently where I personally experienced that kind of heartache—"

"It was rejection," I say. "I thought it was heartache, but it wasn't. I was never in love with you. I thought I was, but with Wyatt …"

Noah's smile becomes blinding, it's so wide. "It's totally different. I understand. A couple of months ago, I wouldn't have, but then I met Matt, and …"

"Everything fits."

He nods.

It sucks we had to lose what was once a decent friendship, and while I'd lecture myself on being foolish and an idiot for doing it in the first place, I have to wonder if Wyatt and I would've happened had I not gone through all the shit with Noah.

I shove my hands in my pockets. "Does this mean we can go back to being friends?"

"Really?" His voice, uncharacteristically quiet and exuding a vulnerability I didn't know Noah possessed, shows off the guy I thought I fell for—the one who lets people in and isn't a dick for the sake of being a dick. If Matt's got him to open up this way, I'm happy he's found someone who can tear down his frustrating walls.

"Even though your attitude can be annoying as fuck, I've actually missed you."

"Fuck yes." He lets out a relieved breath. "Can we please hug it out?"

"You, Mr. I Don't Cuddle?"

"Shut up," he grumbles, and I smile.

I step into his arms, and that zing I used to feel when he touched me doesn't even make an appearance.

"I'm sorry for hurting you," he whispers. "I really am. I didn't—"

"I'm sorry for making you feel guilt over something that wasn't even your fault."

We stand holding each other a few seconds longer until Noah pulls back.

"Did we just have, like, an adult conversation?"

I screw up my face. "Fuck, what's next? Marriage? Kids? God, I don't want to grow up."

Noah laughs. "I think that's why we always got along so well."

"Our shared Peter Pan syndrome?"

"Exactly."

"We better get back in there," I say. "Apparently, it's the last catch-up you'll make for a while. Moving to Chicago, huh?"

"If Wyatt was relocated to Chicago, would you go?"

I don't hesitate. "In a heartbeat."

"That's how I feel about Matt."

I smile, and it's not even forced. "If you need any help moving, hit me and Wyatt up."

His brow furrows, as if he thinks my gesture is empty.

"I'm happy for you. I mean that."

And as my gaze lands on Wyatt when we enter the bar, Noah grips my shoulder and squeezes. "I'm super happy for you guys too."

Wyatt stares at us, and I don't miss the cute concentration line on his forehead. We don't break gazes as I approach the table, and when I wrap my arms around Wyatt and nuzzle into his neck, everyone at the table breaks into awws.

"So, you told them?" I ask, kissing his neck before settling on the stool next to his.

"Technically you did," he says with a wry smile.

"Nah, I kiss all my friends. Everyone should know that by now."

"Well, you have kissed fifty percent of the people at this table," Wyatt says.

"Who wants to make that percentage higher?" I joke, but Wyatt reaches over and covers my mouth with his hand.

"Not on your life."

I lick his hand, making him pull it back.

"You're gross," he complains and wipes his hands on his pants. I want to tell him he's had a lot worse things of mine on his hand than saliva, but I refrain.

"You still love me."

"Yeah, I do."

Skylar looks as if she's about to cry from happiness, her fiancée looks confused, and Maddox and Damon have matching grins.

It's Noah, though, who appears at the table with a tray full of drinks. "Well, this was going to be my goodbye present to you all, but now it's gonna be a celebration. To Aron and Wyatt."

We each raise a glass just in time for Noah to finish his sentiment.

"Two blind motherfuckers who didn't realize their perfect partner had been by their side for eight fucking years."

I have to laugh. There's the Noah we're all used to.

As we clink glasses, our other traitorous friends say, "To two blind motherfuckers."

THANK YOU

Thank you for reading *Rebound.*

IT'S COMPLICATED

FAKE BOYFRIEND 3.5

PREMISE

Max:

I thought watching my best friend and brother be together was hard enough. Then they had to go and break up and all those feelings I've been harboring for Ash have resurfaced with a vengeance.

But I can't do anything about it, and I've been trying to squash my ever-growing need for him, unsuccessfully.

I can't chase after him, and here's why:

One, he's engaged to another man. Two, he's my best friend and business partner. Three, he has no idea I'm not straight. And four, he's my brother's ex-boyfriend. That's a massive bro-code violation.

Ash and I can't happen.

Ever.

Ash:

Why are men such dicks? No, really. Why?

Closeted NHL players, corporate A-holes who are using me … relationships shouldn't be this hard.

Why can't there be a gay version of my best friend, Max, who's perfect for me in every way except for the fact he's not into guys?

At least, that's what I think. Walking in on him and another guy turns my entire world upside down.

Now all I want is for us to have a real chance, but Max will never let that happen. He won't disrespect his brother that way, and I understand it. I do.

I just wish we could find a way.

It's Complicated can be read as a standalone but is best read in conjunction with _Deke (Fake Boyfriend book 3)_. While it belongs in the Fake Boyfriend universe, it does not contain a fake boyfriend trope.

PROLOGUE

ASH

The first time Max Strömberg broke my heart was when we were fourteen years old. I'd known for three years that I was head over heels in love with the boy next door. While he was talking about girls, I was thinking about *him.*

Part of me always hoped that he was putting on a front like I was when I'd say a girl in our class was cute, but deep down I knew it was wishful thinking.

No one knew I liked boys, and that was probably because I hung out with the jocks of the school. For being a scrawny, short dude, I was never picked on, and I can only thank the Strömberg brothers for that. All five of them.

Even at three years younger than us, Ollie, the youngest Strömberg brother, was bigger than me.

I don't know what possessed me to do it that day—to out myself to my best friend. Maybe I was sick of holding in the secret I'd figured out when I was eleven. Maybe I wanted him to stop talking about the group of girls across the cafeteria who were staring and whispering about us.

"If you had to pick one, who would you go out with?" He'd asked me this five times by that point.

My answers of: "I don't care," "Any of them," and "I dunno, it's too hard to choose" weren't good enough until I finally said, "None of them."

Max's gaze flicked to mine, and he held my stare.

I lowered my voice and glanced at the mac and cheese in front of me. "I think I'm into dudes."

Okay, so I knew I was into dudes, aka *him*. I didn't know why I was playing it down like I wasn't confident in my words. I might've been hoping he'd confess to his own confusion because that'd be more likely than the off chance he'd been pining for me all that time too.

"That's cool." Max shrugged. "We don't have to talk about girls."

"What, you want to talk about guys?" I scoffed and played it off like I wasn't hanging all future hopes on his answer.

"Well, no, but you're still my best friend, Ash. Always will be." Then the asshole flicked some of his mac and cheese at me.

That may or may not have resulted in a food fight which we got in trouble for. We had to clean the floor of the cafeteria during detention. All the while we were cleaning, I waited for a shift to happen. A change. I waited for him to act differently around me, but he never did.

And that's what broke my heart.

Nothing changed between us because there was nothing but friendship coming from his side.

I immediately wished I hadn't told him.

Ignorance and hopeful wishing didn't make my chest ache the way longing for my straight best friend did.

So I forced myself to move on.

And I did. Eventually.

It took a few years, but as soon as we got to college, there was no holding me back.

Max was always still a constant in my life, in my mind, in my heart … and in my dorm room. We roomed together all four years.

The second time Max broke my heart was junior year. His girlfriend's name was Laura, and she was perfect, and they were perfectly perfect with all their coupleness.

He'd had girlfriends before. I'd been kicked out of our dorm room countless times while he was hooking up. That was different.

We were at the student cafeteria on campus when he'd said the words he'd never said before.

"I'm in love with her."

I blinked at him. "Whoa."

He stared at me like I was supposed to say more.

"I mean … congrats? I don't know what I'm supposed to say here." I began to hate cafeterias.

Max scrutinized me to the point I was paranoid about having done something wrong. "That's all you have to say?"

"I like her. She's … nice." That was true, but it didn't make me hate her less.

"That's it?"

I threw up my hands in defeat. "Why don't you tell me what you want me to say?"

"I thought maybe you'd say the same about that Jordan asshole you're seeing."

"Jordan is not an asshole." He was kind of an asshole, but in a cute, cocky way, not in the genuinely mean way.

"Do you love him?"

The answer to that was a resounding no, because I'd only

ever been in love with one person, and that guy was sitting right in front of me.

"I think we'd be better off as friends. We're not ... compatible." Which was also true.

In my years of hooking up and exploring, I'd come to one giant conclusion. I didn't like bottoming. Honestly, it was too much work and prepping for little reward. Jordan and I both lacked versatility in that area. If we were in love and I could see a future, it wouldn't be a big deal. I knew lots of gay guys who didn't do anal. But I didn't feel enough for Jordan to compromise on that. The longer Jordan and I were together, the more I realized he fit more a best-friend label than boyfriend. Maybe not on Max's best-friend level but close.

"Oh." Max's brow scrunched. "I thought ..."

"Thought what?"

"I thought things were different with him. You seem ... close."

I had to be reading into the jealousy I was sensing. Unless ... "Aww, are you scared Jordan's going to take your place as my best friend? You know that won't happen. You promised we'd be together forever."

Max nodded. "I know I did. Forever and ever. Forget I said anything. We'll always be best friends. No one can take that from us."

It was the reminder again that friends was all we'd ever be.

It was the same reminder that flashed through my head eighteen months later when Max's little brother asked me out.

Max and I would never happen.

But Ollie and I could.

1
___

MAX

I walk back into the tattoo shop after my lunch break, never failing to get that *welcome home* feeling in the pit of my gut. This place is what Ash and I built from the ground up. It's home. It's where both Ash and I belong.

Kids may have dreams of being a cop or a hero or an NHL star like my stupid brother, but Ash and me, this has always been our dream. And we're not only succeeding, we're fucking nailing it. We've never been busier, and our social media following gains more fans every day.

We're booked solid, the shop's making a name for itself, and while we'll be paying off student and business loans for what seems like forever, we've put a major dint in them since we started the business five years ago.

I take a look at the rest of my bookings for today but pause at the blacked-out block for the afternoon. It's the same for Ash. I swear it wasn't like that this morning.

"Ash?" I call out.

He doesn't answer. Maybe he's still with his last client.

Although, he was almost done when I left to get food. I check his workroom, but he's not there.

Noise from the other side of the shop catches my attention, and I follow it to my room where I find Ash setting up my workstation just the way I like it.

"What's happening in here?"

Ash doesn't look at me as he says, "Tattoo cover-up."

I narrow my eyes. "*Your* tattoo? Which one?"

I know which one. Not long after getting together, my knucklehead brother and Ash got matching tattoos.

Mi Vida: My life.

They're both idiots. Never tattoo something that will remind you of a boyfriend or girlfriend, people. Otherwise you end up here.

Ash levels me with a look—one I've seen many times on him before. It means to stop playing dumb. *Even if it's hard for you.* I snort at Ash's voice in my head, and he glares at me more.

"Are you sure you want to do that?" I ask. "I know you're not with him anymore, but—"

"I'm ridding myself of reminders," Ash says. "I need to."

"Is this because of the press conference?"

I feel for Ash. I really do. He and Ollie were together for four years. All of which Ollie said he couldn't come out because of hockey. Now, a year after their breakup, my brother's on TV coming out to the world, and he has a new boyfriend to boot.

"It's not because of the press conference. Although, I might've sent an impulsive text when I saw it. And now I feel shit about that too."

I approach my best friend and run my hands up his arms,

from his elbows to shoulders and back again. "You're allowed to be mad, you know."

Ash shakes his head. "Nah. He's not my life anymore. I don't have a right to him."

"That's not true at all. He—"

"I don't want to talk about it. I want to not care. Ollie and that Lennon guy—"

"Clark," I correct. When Ollie introduced us to his boyfriend, Lennon, it turns out they didn't even know each other. They'd literally just met in a public restroom. We'd been on Ollie's case about coming out so he and Ash could get back together, so he lied and said he had a new boyfriend. He didn't know Lennon's real name, so he introduced him as Clark. It took over six months for them to tell us the truth, so the name has stuck with our family. It's a weird punishment for lying to us.

Us Strömbergs put the fun in dys*fun*ction.

Ash rolls his eyes. "I want to be able to see them in tabloids or on the news and not wonder why him and not me. I want to not send myself crazy."

"And you think erasing your tattoo will achieve that?"

The reason he's never gotten a full sleeve on that arm is because he didn't want to detract from the very thing he now wants to cover up.

Ash grits his teeth. "I don't know, but it's something. I need to not think about him for a while."

"Healthy," I say dryly.

Ash accidentally drops a container, and it falls to the floor, spraying black ink all over the linoleum. "Shit." He scrambles to pick it up, but his hands shake, and his whole body trembles.

With a sigh, I grab his arm and pull him to me.

"Ink," he croaks.

"Hug." I hold him close even though he's stiff against me. I wrap my arms around him tighter until he gives in and buries his head on my chest.

My heart pounds hard like it always does in Ash's proximity, and I pray he can't feel it. I don't think my usual "I just went for a run" excuse will pass this time.

"Why is your brother an asshole?"

I huff. "He's adopted."

Ash laughs. "No, he's not. Out of all of you, you're the one who looks adopted."

Ash's hand runs over my brown hair. We've always had an affectionate relationship, so the move isn't weird, but it does things to me now that it never used to.

I'm the only Strömberg who's not blond. I'm totally thinking Ma had an affair or I was switched at birth or something. That'd totally be a legit argument if I didn't have my dad's eyes and the trademark Strömberg height. Ollie's literally the shortest at six four.

Ever since Ash and my brother broke up, I've struggled to keep Ash in the best-friend box.

"Are you sure you want to do the cover-up?" I ask again and step back.

"I do."

I swallow hard. "Do you still love him?"

I honestly don't know what I want his answer to be. It's been a year since they broke up. He always tells me I'm like the child of a divorced couple, pining and wishing for them to get back together, and he's right because it was so easy to squash the need I have for Ash when he was with my brother.

Now, he's like this possibility who's not actually a possibility. He's engaged to someone new, first and foremost, and he's crying over Ollie like he isn't over him. Not to mention even thinking of him this way breaks all sorts of bro-code. Ollie would have my head.

"Of course not. I have Taylor." Ash swallows so hard, I see his Adam's apple bounce.

"That doesn't mean you can't still have feelings for Ollie."

In fact, I'm sure Ash and Taylor's relationship was an act of rebellion at learning Ollie was dating Clark. They have nothing in common, and the guy's a twat. Pretentious, snooty, and … so fucking boring.

"I don't love Ollie anymore. I'm still heartbroken and sad it didn't work out, but I can't go backward, you know?"

"Just know that I'm always here for you, Ash. And I'll be here if you need to talk about any of the shit going on in your head. I know he's my brother so you're reluctant, but I love you just as much as I love him." *Just in a totally different way.* "I'll always be here for both of you. *Forever and ever.*"

Ash smiles. When we were kids, we vowed we'd be best friends forever and ever. It became a thing and now mostly doesn't make sense. *Want to catch up next week? Forever and ever.*

"We should clean up the ink before it stains the floor." He goes to bend down, but I don't let him.

"Ash …"

"What?" he snaps.

"I'm only going to ask you this once, and then I promise to drop it. Are you happy with Taylor? Truly, one hundred percent happy? Because it's not too late. It's gonna be a whole lot harder once you're marr—"

"I am."

I'd believe it more if his eyes weren't cast down, his voice soft and croaky, but a promise is a promise. "Okay then. Let's get this cleaned up, and then I can stab you repeatedly with needles."

"Totally cathartic."

"You got sketches for me?"

"Even better. I've already stenciled it."

I prefer to sketch and stencil my own work, but I trust Ash and respect him as an artist. I step over to my work bench. "Holy shit, man. This is amazing."

It's done over two pieces of stenciling paper because the piece is so large, but it's a picturesque landscape of pine trees and a lake, and—

"Wait. Is this Camp Frottage?"

During our summer breaks in college, Ash and I were counsellors at a summer camp. Had we not gone into tattooing, I so would've become an art teacher.

"Remember how disappointed I was when I found out it was an art camp for kids?" Ash laughs. "The title had so much promise."

I can't help laughing too. "You'd think they'd change it after you so helpfully told them what else it means in the non-art world. Can I *please* tattoo the camp name on your arm?"

Ash laughs. "No. Just the lake."

"I miss that place."

"Those were the best summers of my life," Ash whispers. "It means a lot to me, so …"

"Don't need to explain. I don't ink shame."

Ash smiles, because okay, I've totally been known to ink shame. But for real, ink should represent something. Even if it's a drunken night where you get the word *stupid* in Sanskrit down your ribs, at least that has a story. And a lesson. It's memorable and *means* something. Getting something because it's "cute" makes tattoo fairies die a slow and horrible death. True story.

Ash and I work together in getting everything set up, but as he settles in my chair, I can't help feeling hesitant about it.

Ash's left arm is completely bare except for the one tattoo running along his forearm. It represents his life with Ollie, but just because my brother's not in the picture anymore, that doesn't mean he wasn't important to Ash.

"Are you sure?" I ask again as I glove up. "Getting an entire half sleeve to cover up one tiny tattoo is extreme."

I expect more dismissiveness, perhaps getting yelled at for babying him, but instead, he lets out a shaky "I'm sure."

"All right. Never argue with a client, right?"

Ash smiles, but it's forced.

I apply the stencil and admire the intricate lines of Ash's artwork. The tattoo gun starts the familiar hum that I associate with new ink, and the buzzing matches that in my veins. There's no doubt I was born to do this. It's better than meditation. Better than sex.

As I settle in to work and examine Ash's face for any more hesitance, I'm reminded of why I've never told him about my feelings for him.

Ash has been my best friend, my business partner, my go-to person since forever, and I didn't want to fuck that up. It was in college when I first knew I liked him as more than a friend.

We grew up together, ever since he moved next door when he was five, and we've been inseparable ever since. But there was a defining moment in college where I knew I loved him more than I should. I realized I was attracted to him in a way I hadn't been attracted to another man before.

I thought all those times I got jealous of Ash going on dates was because he was my friend, and growing up with four brothers, I've always hated the sharing concept. But no, the night he and our friend Jordan thought I was asleep junior year and they fooled around in the bed not six feet away from me was the moment I realized I wasn't just worried about losing my friend. I wanted to be where Jordan was. In Ash's arms, wrapped around him, and laughing like we always did but with the added bonus of orgasms.

By the time I'd gotten over my confusion stage, Jordan and Ash were officially together.

Then I met Laura, the only serious girlfriend I've ever had, and we lasted a lot longer than Ash and Jordan's short-lived romance. They realized they worked better as friends, but by that point I was in deep with Laura. That lasted about a year.

The timing for Ash and me was never right. Before I could build up the courage to tell my best friend that I had a thing for him and was willing to risk our friendship, our newly founded business, and basically our entire childhood of memories growing up together … *Bam.* Ollie came home from his first year in the AHL, and Ash fell in love. Ollie was no longer the little kid three years younger than us, following Ash around like a puppy.

Ollie has always been big—it's a Strömberg trait—but his first year playing pro hockey made him fill out like the fucking Hulk.

He and Ash went from being flirty at a family gathering to dating to living together in a span of *weeks.*

I'd lost my chance. And for a long time, I was surprisingly okay with it. I told myself it saved us the risk. My life with Ash is everything to me, even if I don't get to touch him. I'd rather take what we have than have nothing at all.

And my brother made him so damn happy.

Until he didn't anymore.

It seems like a complete waste of a relationship, because not only are they not together now, but any remote chance I had with Ash was crushed the minute he and Ollie got together. I can't go for one of my brothers' exes. I really don't want to be with someone who can say "Your brother did it differently."

I often think no one will ever compare to Ash, but I also know if I ever want a successful relationship, I need to let him go.

Maybe when he walks down that aisle and marries Taylor, I'll get closure and will be able to see him as just a friend again like I managed to do while he was with Ollie.

My hand finds Ash's forearm, and I grip the tattoo gun tighter as I move in to start the piece.

"Wait," Ash croaks before I get anywhere close to his skin. "I can't. I just … can't."

When I meet his gaze, a tear slips down his cheek.

"Fuck, Ash." I put the gun down and push the tray with the ink and supplies out of the way so I can pull him in for a hug.

The perfect way he fits against me usually has me on edge, but as I breathe him in, the scent of his aftershave makes me keenly aware of something not being right. It's not his usual woodsy scent I can smell but something spicier. Taylor's, I realize. Then I hate myself all over again for pining over a taken man. A man I claim sometimes to have been mine first, but even that's not true. Ash has only ever been mine in friendship.

I force myself to pull away. "You need more time, and that's okay."

"God. More time, more time, more time. It's like that's my

motto right now. How much time? How long until I feel like everything is right again?"

"I can't answer that for you. I wish I could."

"I … I need to go think for a while. Sorry I fucked up our schedules for no reason."

I take a hold of his hand. "It's okay."

"I'm sure you could call the clients I canceled and get them back in."

"I could do that, yes, but how long has it been since we've had some time off? We're both working six days a week. The shop's always busy. We can afford to take the afternoon off for once."

Ash hesitates.

"I'll clean up here," I say. "You go."

He runs his hand over his dark hair. "You sure?"

"What, like it's super far for me to get to my place?" It's literally up one set of stairs.

The shop lease comes with the small two-bedroom apartment, and seeing as Ash and Ollie had their own place, I decided to take it. When Ollie and Ash broke up, Ash lived with me until he moved in with Taylor a few months ago.

I miss him. I miss living with him and sharing a space with him. We've been a team for so long and have worked together so well that when he moved in, I worried we wouldn't be able to live in sync like the rest of our lives. We managed during college, but we were older now.

I had nothing to worry about, because living with him had been the highlight of my last year.

Then he went and met … Taylor. Ugh.

"Hey, I got a message last night saying Jordan's in town," Ash says. "Maybe we could go catch up with him."

Ugh at Jordan too. He and Ash never became serious, but the guy still grates on me.

Yet, I still find myself agreeing, because I know Ash is struggling, and I want to be there for him even if it's killing me slowly.

———

And Ash is drunk.

Fun. Yay, day drinking.

I don't even know what he's laughing at. He and our friend Jordan have been reminiscing about old times, and apparently, the memories are a lot more humorous to those who were there for them.

There was a time during college where Ash and Jordan were inseparable. During a time of exploration and having fun, Jordan had a lot more going for him than I did—mainly, he's gay and I'm not.

Ash can barely contain himself and hunches over, using my shoulder as a headrest as he continues to laugh. My arm goes around his back to make sure he doesn't fall off his stool, because he's three sheets to the wind right now.

At least, that's the excuse I'll use, because any excuse to touch him, I'll take.

With Ash so close to me, his phone vibrates against my thigh. I've trained myself to hide my reactions to his proximity, but as I stare at the side of his tattooed neck and shoulder that's peeking out from his tank top, I tell myself the lie I always do when I look too closely at him: it's my artwork I'm admiring. Not *him.*

Minus a few pieces, every inch of tattooed skin was done

by me. I've left my physical mark on him, and the same goes for me—most of my tats were done by Ash—but no one knows the chunk of my heart that's been marked as his for years.

I nudge him and move my lips closer to his ear to speak over the noise. "Your phone."

He lifts his head, his green eyes glassy. From alcohol or laughing so hard, I'm not sure. "What?"

I roll my eyes and put my hand in his pants pocket.

"You're about two inches too far to the right." Ash winks.

My best friend, ladies and gentlemen.

I hand him his phone. "It's been ringing, jackass."

I get a glimpse of the screen and am surprised to find Ash's laughter fade and his face fall at his fiancé's name.

"I've gotta take this." Ash runs off with his phone to a quieter part of the bar so he can hear.

I hate watching Ash be with someone who isn't even his type.

He says he's happy with Taylor, but he's usually vibrant and lively. That's been missing lately.

I don't know if it's because of Ollie or Taylor, but watching him suffer makes me want to punch Ollie out. He may be a hockey player, but I'm bigger and I work out with two of our older brothers who are MMA trainers. I could still kick little bro's ass.

I don't realize how long I've been staring at Ash across the bar until Jordan's deep laugh appears next to me as he moves to the stool next to mine.

"Well, at least *that* hasn't changed since college."

I break my gaze from Ash and frown. "What?"

"You never got the balls to tell him you're in love with him, then?"

My mouth drops open. Then closes. Then opens again. "I

don't know what you're talking about."

Jordan takes a sip of his beer. "Mmhmm."

No one knows about my feelings for Ash, and the idea of Jordan telling him has me sweating. "You can't say anything—"

Ash appears at my other side. "I'm out. Taylor got off work early and is out front waiting."

"He's not even going to come in for a drink?" I ask.

He shrugs. "Not his scene."

Ash spent four years not going out because of my brother's closeted status. He says he needs to make up for lost time, but then this new guy makes him leave because it's *not his scene*?

If it was a nightclub or something, that'd be one thing, but it's a practically deserted bar in the middle of the afternoon.

This is what I mean. It's like Ash is ignoring all of Taylor's incompatibility because he's willing to offer Ash the one thing Ollie couldn't. He's replaced my brother with another guy who won't let him be who he wants to be.

"Fuck him, then," I say. "If he doesn't want to be here, he doesn't have to be."

Ash frowns at me.

Jordan downs the rest of his drink. "If you're taking off, I'm gonna go piss and head out too."

Ash's hand lands on my shoulder once Jordan's gone. "I know you don't like Taylor, but I need to cling onto any little happiness I have in my life. Okay?"

It's these moments and words he says that makes me want to wrap my arms around Ash's smaller frame and protect him from the heartache. I want to feel him against me and have him melt into the security of knowing I'd never do anything to hurt him.

But that can't happen.

Instead, I nod.

"See you at the shop on Monday." Ash ruffles my hair, because even though I love him, he can be an asshole, and bounds his way to the exit.

I can't do anything but watch.

I keep my eyes on the doors for a while, just hoping Ash gets the balls to tell Taylor where to fuck off and come back in, but after a few moments, I remind myself why that would never happen.

Jordan catches my eye across the room as he comes back from the bathroom.

Not much has changed since college. The tall, dark-haired model turns heads wherever he goes, and he gains the attention of the few people who are here on his way over to me.

"Leaving?" he asks.

"Aren't you?"

He purses his lips. "I was going to, but …" Jordan eyes me from head to toe slowly in a move that could not be more obvious.

I laugh. "Not interested, man. I'm not gay—"

"You're in love with a guy. You're a little bit gay."

"Ash is different. And you can't say anything. To anyone."

Jordan leans in close to my ear, and I can smell his Tom Ford cologne. He probably bathes in an endless supply of it seeing as he models for the brand. "I didn't say anything when we were in college. Not gonna say anything now. Your issue."

"Thanks." I relax a little but hate knowing Jordan, of all people, can hold something over my head. "I'll catch you again before you head back to L.A."

Mr. Fancy Pants is making a name for himself on the West Coast. He's a pretty successful model, but he's trying to become an actor. He certainly has the looks for it, and I have no doubt it's only a matter of time before it happens for him and he hits it big.

Then Ash and I can watch his movies or sitcom or whatever he lands and be all "We went to college with him!"

I pull away to slip on my jacket and leave, when Jordan grabs my arm and pulls me against him. He's almost my height, which is impressive considering I'm six five. Ash is a tiny thing at five nine. Jordan and I are pretty evenly matched. Chests together, hips, a bulge in his designer pants pressing against me …

I have to admit, it feels different than any other time I've been groped by a guy. I've played the straight best friend a long time—that involves going to gay bars. A lot. Especially after he and Ollie first broke up. So I've had my fair share of grabby hands from men.

I have no idea why this feels different with Jordan. Whether it's because I've known him for six years or we're kinda friends, I dunno.

"Are you telling me you've never been with a guy even though you've been in love with one for …" He brings one hand up and starts counting on his fingers.

"Ooh, look at that, the model can count."

His other hand comes up and gives me the finger. "Eight years? Although, you guys have been friends since you were kids, so it might be longer than that, and—"

"Six."

"What?"

I sigh. "Junior year. When you and he first started hanging out and got together. That's when …" I wave my hand in a "you can fill in the rest" gesture.

"Wow, no wonder you hate me."

"I don't hate you."

"Anymore, maybe, but you definitely did back then." Jordan smiles and his hand moves down to my ass and squeezes.

I remove it for him. "It's just *him*. No other guy has ever done it for me. I'm not in denial. Like, I realize that means I'm bi or pan or some label under that umbrella, but I just don't see it happening with any other man."

"Have you even looked at other guys?" Jordan asks.

"Well, no, but if you think about it, it took me years to really notice Ash. Maybe I'm just slow."

Without warning, Jordan's mouth's on mine. Warm, soft lips send a surprising jolt down my spine. A strong tongue pushes its way inside. The stubble throws me for a second, and then a large hand cups my face, but instead of pulling away, a loud moan escapes me. Before I can really get into it, Jordan pulls back and looks smug. It's really not that much different to how he always looks.

"All I'm saying is, maybe you haven't given it a chance."

"And you're volunteering?" I ask dryly, our breaths mingling.

"I'm here for three weeks." He cocks a brow. "Could be fun."

I narrow my eyes. "You could literally throw a dart in here and hit any person willing to fuck you. And trust me, they would." I may be mostly straight, but I'm not blind.

"As fun as it sounds injuring a potential hookup before dragging them back to my lair like some sort of caveman"— his thumb trails down my cheek, and I feel absolutely no need to pull away—"breaking in noobs is a favorite pastime of mine."

I snort. "Shocking."

"You're not just a tiny bit curious?"

It's my turn to run my gaze over him, and I can't lie. I can't deny the arousal in my groin or drown out the voice in my head telling me this might be a solution to my Ash problem.

I can't keep doing this to myself.

I can't handle the self-inflicted torture.

Maybe Jordan is what I need.

My hand fists in his jacket. "Yeah, I am."

"Then let's get out of here."

2
———
ASH

Something niggly at the back of my mind bugs me the entire drive home from the bar, but I don't know what it is.

It's in the small things Taylor does. The way he clicks his jaw, as if his teeth are permanently grinding together.

His thumbs tap the steering wheel to an imaginary beat because he hates listening to the radio.

I'm happy with him. I am.

Right?

Gaaah. I don't know why Max's words from earlier today are playing on a loop in my head. *Are you happy with Taylor? Truly, one hundred percent happy?*

What Taylor and I have is the exact type of whirlwind romance that I wanted when I ended things with Ollie. Taylor and I have a future. He's asked me to marry him … okay, well, he didn't really ask me, but it's the sentiment that counts, right?

When we met, he was straight up in telling me what his intentions were. He was ready to settle down and didn't want to date someone who'd waste his time. He's seven years older than me and knows what he wants, so that's been the goal from the beginning.

When it came time to proposing, he slid a ring across the dining table and said he chooses me. Not the most romantic proposal, but it still made me feel special. Because finally, someone loves me enough to put me above all else.

Then why couldn't I cover my tattoo today?

Why is Ollie's coming out getting to me so much?

Why is it that when I look at Taylor, I don't get that feeling I thought I'd get when I looked at my fiancé?

Butterflies. Eternal love.

There's … nothing but mild fondness.

Taylor's a great guy. He's got a good head on his shoulders.

He's a perfect on paper kind of guy.

When Taylor parks the car and helps me upstairs to our apartment because I'm still a little drunk, we stumble through the door with a laugh.

Or at least, I'm laughing.

Taylor's kind of sighing like I'm a giant child.

Which, I guess compared to him, I probably am. He's always so straitlaced and put together.

Actually, now that we're inside, there's other things I'm only now noticing.

The apartment's filled with Taylor's furniture and knick-knacks and doesn't have a touch of me anywhere.

Taylor's classic chic, and I'm … urban rustic.

He's neat, and I'm more lax about the state of our apartment.

Taylor meticulously places his briefcase near the door and hangs up his jacket, silently moving through the space before making his way into the kitchen.

I watch as he pours himself a cup of water from the jug we keep in the fridge and slowly drinks it down.

Only when the glass is back on the counter does he give me eye contact again, and he must see something in my expression. "What's wrong?"

What's wrong? Only *everything.*

What the fuck am I doing here?

It hits me with such force I feel like an idiot for not realizing sooner.

I'm not in love with Taylor.

I've just been holding on to something he could give me that Ollie couldn't. I overlooked everything wrong with this relationship because I thought it was filling a void.

Taylor is somehow mixed up with all my unresolved resentment toward Ollie, and it wasn't until today when Max asked me to be completely honest that I allowed myself to see the complete truth.

I've been lying to myself for months.

My brain told me I was where I was supposed to be even though it never … clicked.

Ollie led me to Taylor, so I thought it was fate.

It wasn't fate.

It was overcompensating, pure and simple.

I take a deep breath. "I'm so sorry, but I can't … I can't do this."

"Can't do what?"

"This … us. We're … I don't know what we are. I care about you so much, I truly do. I just …"

"You don't love me."

I shake my head, but it's subtle.

"I was giving you everything you wanted." He sounds so pained, and I feel like the worst human in the fucking world.

"I know," I whisper. Tears prick my eyes, because I wish everything was different. I wish I could make myself feel more for him. I wish our relationship was something that it's not.

"I thought we were on the same page. I chose you because we wanted the same things."

"Can you hear your own words though? You *chose* me. What we have isn't an all-consuming type of love. *That's* what I've always wanted. Not the marriage or dream, but … *the one.*"

"The one doesn't exist, Ash. The truth is, marriage is work. A life with another person takes compromise and sacrifice and even settling. I know you have your head in the clouds sometimes, but I didn't think you were this naïve."

Naïve.

Settling.

I almost break into laughter. Taylor's not in love with me just as much as I'm not with him. He chose me because he wanted a marriage, not a partner.

"Why did you ask me to marry you?"

"I thought we could build a life together. And I do love you."

"What kind of life?"

"The kind of life an executive manager leads."

I stumble back. "What?"

"The firm likes stability in their team leaders. All the top execs are married. It's why I told you when we started dating not to waste my time."

And here I thought it was because he wanted the same life as me—being so disgustingly in love. I left one guy for choosing his career over me, and now I'm with someone who's doing the exact same thing.

I can't believe how *dumb* I am.

He's been using me this whole time.

This is why he's never raised his voice and we've never fought. Not because he's always calm and put together, but because he doesn't care enough to fight. He doesn't care enough to come to the things I'm interested in—like hanging out or having a few drinks with my friends.

He. Doesn't. Care.

I should be mad, but all I am is relieved.

"Don't you want true love?" I ask. Guilt over breaking up with him has vanished, but now it's replaced with the same achingly low self-worth that Ollie left behind.

"The last guy you thought was your true love chose his career over you. If that isn't proof *the one* isn't out there, I don't know what is."

"What you're doing isn't any different. You chose me to advance your career. Not because you wanted *me*."

"But I do want you," he says simply. "That's the point. I want the life we agreed we'd have. I want it all."

"You want it with *anyone*. I'm just the one who agreed to it." Because I was so desperate for someone to love me.

"I don't see what that has to do with anything."

"Ollie was never the one. I wanted him to be, just like I wanted you to be. But the one would always put me first."

"Good luck trying to find that. It doesn't exist."

It has to exist, right? And it's not like I expect my partner to *always* put me first or that I wouldn't do the same for him. The point of finding your soul mate is to be there for each other. To support each other. Forever and ever.

Something pings in the back of my mind, telling me I already have that with someone.

My forever and ever.

But that someone is in the body of a straight guy, and how

is that fair? Is that the universe's way of having a laugh at my expense?

I have to believe a gay Max is out there waiting for me.

"You might be right," I concede. "But I'd rather spend my life trying to find it instead of settling for the wrong person."

I only make it two steps before Taylor stops me.

"Please, Ash. I do want a life with you. What we have can grow into the type of love you're looking for."

"You're speaking as if our whole relationship to you has been like an arranged marriage, and that's not what I want from life. I'm sorry."

Apparently, that's all the amount of fight Taylor has in him.

It's nowhere near enough for the love of my life.

My guy will fight for me a hell of a lot harder than that.

I have to Uber it to Max's because even though walking out on Taylor sobered me right up, legally, I'd still be over the limit to drive.

I'm exhausted both mentally and physically, and all I want to do is crash in my old bed and sleep for days.

I haven't knocked in forever because the keys for the shop are the same for the apartment, so letting myself in isn't anything out of the ordinary.

Neither is finding Max on the couch making out with someone.

It is, however, weird that the person on top of him is not female.

What. The. Fucking. Fuck.

I'm frozen in the entryway, staring at my two best friends kissing and grinding, and—

The door shuts behind me, breaking Max and Jordan apart.

They stare at me wide-eyed, but Jordan doesn't make a move to get off Max.

I have no idea what to say. Or do.

I can't fucking move.

This isn't happening. I blink, hoping Jordan will magically disappear, but nope. He's still in front of me. Shirt open, model abs on display ... on top of my best friend. My *straight* best friend.

"Ash," Max croaks. "This isn't ..." Max's skin turns pasty white.

Apparently, that's what I need to get my feet moving.

I run back down to the street as fast as my short legs will carry me and am relieved to find my Uber still sitting there. The guy is scrolling through his phone.

I open the back door, and he jumps. "Sorry. Didn't mean to scare you. Can you accept another job?" I'm surprised to find my voice emotionless.

He nods. "Sure. Where do you need to go?"

Now there's a question I don't have an answer to. I can't go to Taylor's, I can't be here ... There's really only one place I can go.

I sigh. "Milton."

The guy pulls onto the road just as movement in the corner of my eye catches my attention.

Max stands on the sidewalk, watching the car pull away. The forlorn look on his face kills me, because anytime he looks stricken like that, I'm the one to console him. Just like he does for me.

I still can't believe it.

Max.

And Jordan.

All throughout junior and senior year of college, Jordan would incessantly talk about how hot and unobtainable Max was even when he and I were together. In the long run, Jordan pining for my best friend didn't matter anyway because Jordan and I worked better as friends. There was always something missing with us.

The sex was fine, we got along great, but there just wasn't any spark.

Guess he saved the spark for Max, who, as it turns out, isn't as unobtainable as Jordan thought.

I blink away tears, but my cheeks are already wet. I hadn't cried when I walked out on Taylor. I should have. He was my fiancé, for fuck's sake. Yet, here I am crying over yet another Strömberg brother.

Only, I don't know why I'm crying. Is it because he was always this awesome guy who was straight, and now he's a liar who isn't? Or is it the fact he went gay for Jordan but not for me?

It's always somebody else.

Traffic is a bitch, and there must be an accident or something along the way because it takes twice as long to get to Milton as it usually does, and by that time, I'm all out of tears, patience, and maybe sanity.

If the Uber guy notices my meltdown, he doesn't say anything.

Five stars to the dude who pretends I'm not slobbering all over his back seat.

And then, of course, the universe decides to really put me through the wringer when we pull up to my parents' house. There, on the porch of the Strömberg house, right in the line of sight of my mother and father's driveway next door, is Ollie with his boyfriend, Lennon ... Clark ... whatever the fuck that guy's name is.

For someone who lives in New York now, I've seen Ollie more these last few months than the six months after the breakup where we lived in the same city.

So when I climb out of the Uber, I hold my head high and smile tight, pretending I'm just home for a random visit with the folks.

Here's the thing about Ollie though. He's known me just as long as Max has known me. For four years, I was this guy's partner and we knew each other's tells. We knew when the other was upset with one look, and when Ollie's face falls as he meets my gaze, I know I'm not covering my hurt enough.

He says something to his boyfriend, who nods and squeezes Ollie's hand before Ollie ambles down the steps of the porch and heads in my direction.

Great. Just great.

I contemplate running into the house and locking the door, but you know, I'm supposed to be three years older than Ollie, who's clearly going to be the bigger person right now and make sure I'm okay.

Damn it. Why can't he just be an asshole so it's easier to hate him?

"Everything okay?" are the first words out his mouth.

"Of course," I croak and then fucking break down and start crying again.

"Shit."

I'm engulfed by Ollie's big, tattooed arms.

"I'm not your problem anymore," I mumble into his T-shirt. "You don't need to deal with all"—I wave my hand around—"this. Why are you home anyway?"

"Just visiting the parentals." Ollie pulls back but keeps his hands firmly on my shoulders. His hazel eyes, that match his mom's but are nothing like Max's, stare at me in pity. Or maybe concern. I don't know. I guess I can't read him as well as he can still read me. "Just because we aren't together, it doesn't mean I don't care. We're practically family, Ash. Have been since we were kids. I will always care."

I nod behind him toward his boyfriend. "He have anything to say about that?"

Ollie turns toward Clark, and the smile that lights up his face doesn't do tingly things to me like it used to when he smiled at me. It just reiterates that he has someone else now, and I have … no one.

"Lennon's cool," Ollie says. "I promise."

If we were still together, I'd hate for him to care about an ex, but I guess that's the point, isn't it? In true relationships, the type of love I'm looking for, there's a thing called trust and the blind reassurance that your partner is the only one for you.

I sigh. "I don't suppose you left our old apartment to sit there empty when you moved to New York, did you?" I already know the answer, because I was there to get all our furniture in storage when he was traded to New York. I had to vacate the apartment of all our belongings so other people could move in, but I figure telling him that way is easier than blurting out Taylor and I are no longer engaged.

"Why—aww fuck. You broke up with what's-his-face?"

"Yeah." The ground is super interesting to look at right now. "But it was my decision. It wasn't … right, and as soon as I said something, I learned he felt the same way." My eye catches on my ring. "Fuck, I should've left this with him."

Now I've noticed it, there's nothing more I want than to get the damn thing off, but as soon as I start tugging on it, the fucker gets stuck.

"Ash." Ollie gives me a little shake, but I don't stop trying to get the symbol of my stupidity off my finger. "*Ash*," he says again.

"What?" I snap.

"What's really going on?" Ollie's voice is soft and tender, reminding me of the guy I fell for—you know, before we started resenting each other.

It makes me want to pour my heart out to him, but I can't. Because out of everything that happened today, the only thing I'm truly upset about is Max, and no way am I going to out Max to his brother. Especially when it wasn't his choice to come out to me.

I shake my head. "It's nothing. My friend Jordan did something stupid. On top of the Taylor thing … Seriously, Ollie. This isn't your problem anymore. One good thing about breaking up is you don't have to deal with my flair for the dramatic." I manage a smile, which he matches.

"Turns out I'm a bit of a drama queen myself."

I mock gasp. "No way."

He chuckles. "I know we can't be friends or whatever because that'd just be too …"

"Weird. The word you're looking for is weird."

Ollie smirks. "Right. But that doesn't mean you can't come to me when shit's too hard, okay?"

I nod, but it doesn't take the sting away from the truth. It turns out there *is* a less-than-straight version of Max out there, and he still doesn't want me.

I'm always someone's second choice.

Even my best friend's.

3

MAX

S hit, shit, fucking shit.

I barely remember chasing after Ash without so much as a goodbye to Jordan. All I remember is running for my car. But now I'm driving around aimlessly, because when I rushed to Ash's apartment, all I found was a pissed-off Taylor telling me I'd won. Ash had left him.

I was back in the car before I could ask why or what he meant by I'd won.

If Ash couldn't go home or to the shop, there's only one place he'd go.

I make a U-ey, and head for Milton.

The radio says the I-93 is backed up because of an accident, so I take an alternate route, but I am so not prepared for what I find when I pull up outside my childhood home.

Ash. With Ollie.

This past year, all the times I've thought I wanted Ash and Ollie to get back together because it's easier for me if they are? Seeing them now makes me realize they can't go back. I don't want them to go back.

I want Ash to see me. To choose me. To be with me.

But then I look at my brother, and I know I can't hurt him that way.

I throw my head back on the headrest of my seat.

Even though I can't be with Ash, I want to explain Jordan. He's owed at least that much.

With a deep breath, I get out of the car and approach them.

"Max," Ollie says with a furrowed brow.

I ignore him and focus on Ash, but I don't know where to start. Or finish. "Jordan and I didn't mean anything. At all."

Ash's eyes bug out of his head as his gaze flits from mine to Ollie's and back again.

"Didn't mean to do what?" Ollie asks.

God, this is not the time for this, but I turn to my brother. "Ash found me … uh, with a guy."

"With my other best friend," Ash supplies unhelpfully.

"Can we have a minute to talk this out?" I ask Ollie.

He doesn't move. Only looks confused. "You're not straight? Since when?"

"Since, I dunno, when-the-fuck-ever. Didn't realize I had to make an application to join your club. Can I please just talk to Ash?"

Ollie glances between us, and I see the hint of accusation without him having to say anything. He doesn't voice it though. Instead he brings up something much worse. "You know Ma's gonna throw you a ridiculous coming-out party, so please come out to her while I'm here to witness it."

There's going to be our brothers' taunts, our parents' inappropriateness, and yes, an over-the-top coming-out party, but hey, at least it's one thing I don't have to worry about when it comes to finally expressing this side of me out loud. My family will accept me no matter what.

"Fuck," I hiss. Because he's so right. Eh, I'll deal with that later.

He backs away with a giant grin. When Ollie's finally out of earshot, I turn to Ash and hate what I see. Hurt, betrayal, and confusion all rolled into that pouty face he gets when he's upset.

"Ash, I—"

"You don't owe me an explanation."

"I *want* to give you an explanation."

"Why? It's your life, and clearly you don't think I have any right to it."

"Because I didn't tell you this one little thing about me? That's not fair."

"You know what's not fair?" Ash yells. "Being hung up on a straight guy for *years*, letting him go, and then finding out he's not so straight, he just didn't want *me*."

I stumble back as if his words physically push me. "What?"

"I accepted we were never going to happen. I accepted that I was the sad, cliched gay guy in love with his straight best friend, and I moved on. And I was happy. Now, everything is fucked-up. Everything I thought I knew is wrong, and I don't even know what the hell is going on anymore. I was sure Ollie would choose me. That Taylor would be upset if I ended it. That you would be there for me through it all. But you're just like *them*."

"Ash, wait. Just … wait. *Please*."

"For *what*?"

I run my hands through my hair. "How do I explain six years of swallowing my feelings for you?"

"I … wait, what?"

"I didn't want to risk what we had, and you were in love with my brother. How do I explain that I've been hurting for so long but had the silver lining of you getting everything you ever wanted?"

"Y-you—"

"I hate myself for not telling you in college how I felt about you."

"C-college?"

This is a lot to put on him at once, but I don't stop. I'm on a roll now. "I can't look you in the eye, realizing everything could've been different if I'd told you sooner. Then I was too late, and now it's still too late. We can't be together, Ash, no matter how much I fucking want you. No matter how pathetically depressed I've been over you finding Taylor and planning a future I could never have with you. Jordan … he—"

Ash holds up his hand. "I don't want to know."

I ignore him. "He was a substitute for the guy I actually want. He knows it, and I know it. It didn't mean anything. All we did was make out a little. It was the first time with Jordan —with *any* guy. We just both got sick of me pining over you, and I thought it'd be a solution to getting over my inappropriate feelings. It was a mistake, because while he was kissing me, I still couldn't stop thinking about *you*."

Ash closes his eyes. "You never told me," he whispers. "This whole time … and you never … *you never told me!*"

"Ollie. He's still my brother."

As if finally realizing my dilemma, he slumps. "Fuck."

"Exactly."

Ash glances up at my parents' house. "What are we supposed to do now?"

Dejected, I sigh. "What we've always done. Swallow our shit down and pretend it doesn't exist."

That's what we *should* do. What I *want* to do is throw Ash against the nearest surface and show him how much I've wanted him for six years. Show him that he's worthy of a guy who thinks the fucking world of him and will always put him above all else.

Then I look at the house where my brother disappeared into not mere minutes ago and know why I can't do those things.

"Well, this sucks," Ash says.

I snort. "Understatement."

"I'm … I'm gonna stay with my folks for a while."

"You don't have to. Move back in with me."

I can't lose Ash. I'd rather be forbidden to touch him but still have him in my life than lose him completely. I'll hate it, but it's better than the alternative.

Ash shakes his head. "I think that'd be too hard. I kinda need to … process. Not just you and Jordan, but Taylor and all that other bullshit."

"What happened with that?"

"I realized I wanted what he was offering, not him."

I want to reach for him, and it kills me that I can't. This morning, I wouldn't have hesitated. Now? It's all weird and awkward, and even though we haven't crossed any lines, it feels like we have.

"I'm sorry he didn't end up being what you were looking for. That's all I've ever wanted for you."

"Guess I know why you haven't had a serious girlfriend since college."

I laugh. "God, my family is gonna have a field day."

Ash grins. "Yeah, they are. I hope I can be there for it."

My face falls. "I want you there for my torment."

"Max … I … need time."

"How long?" My heart stutters, anticipating the very thing I was afraid of when it comes to having these feelings for Ash.

Ash shakes his head. "I don't know."

Fuck.

I amble up to my childhood home, hating that Ash is in the house next door, not wanting to see me.

I'll walk into this house, I'll tell my overbearing family that I'm into guys as well as girls, and I'll endure their weird quirkiness. That doesn't worry me, though I'm not looking forward to it. It's that I have to do it without Ash by my side that I'm dreading.

We've literally done everything together since grade school. I was the first person to find out he's gay, and I was there when he came out to his parents. He was the first person I told when I'd lost my virginity, and the only person who knows my irrational fear of clowns. If I'd ever told my family that, I could guarantee all my brothers would turn up to my birthday dressed in clown masks.

Ash has been by my side through everything, and it's only taken a day to tear all of that down.

A moment.

All because I was with Jordan.

Shit, Jordan.

I get out my phone and find a string of texts from him.

JORDAN: *OKAY, THIS IS A NEW ONE. I'VE DRIVEN GUYS AWAY BEFORE BUT NEVER ONE FROM HIS OWN APARTMENT.*

HELLO? ARE YOU COMING BACK?

UH ... WELL THIS IS AWKS.

OKAY, SUPER WEIRD NOW. AT LEAST LET ME KNOW YOU'RE OKAY AND HAVEN'T BEEN KIDNAPPED BY A GANG AND SOLD INTO SEX SLAVERY?

As I reach the porch, I detour to the sitting area and hit Call on Jordan's number.

"Max?"

"Nah, this is the, uh, Booty Cartel. Max's ass belongs to us now."

"Well, shit, I was totally planning on paying a ransom, but by the sound of that, Max will have the time of his life. Give him my well wishes."

"Asshole." I laugh.

"But really, dude? Booty Cartel? Worst fake gang name ever."

"It's all I could come up with on the spot. So, listen, I'm kinda cleaning up the Ash mess at the moment."

"How pissed is he?"

"I think you're fine. He's more mad at me for not telling him I'm not exactly straight."

"Which is still entertaining to me considering you've been in love with him *forever*."

"Yeah, yeah. Some people aren't as perceptive as you."

"I'm one of a kind. It's true."

"And so humble."

Jordan chuckles. "You gonna be okay? You need moral support or anything?"

"Nah, all good. I'm at my parents' place now. Kinda outed myself to my little brother, so I guess the rest of the family is next."

"Whoa, for real? You sure you don't want me to come, then?"

"Thanks for the offer, but this has been a long time coming. I'm ready."

"Well, uh, I would apologize for being the catalyst that made you take this step, but you're right. It has been a long time. So instead, I'm going to say you're welcome."

I laugh. "Of course you are."

The line goes silent.

"Are we cool?" Jordan asks.

"I'm good if you are. I mean, what happened—"

"It was nothing. I get it. If all I had to do to get you to stop hating me was make out with you, I would've done it years ago."

I scoff. "Like I would've let you years ago."

"I definitely would've tried."

"I know you would have. In fact, I'm pretty sure you did? Why do I have a sudden memory of going to the movies with you and Ash, only Ash mysteriously didn't turn up, and when I asked him, he had no idea what I was talking about?"

There's a quick silence before Jordan's laugh breaks through. "You're delusional. I don't recall that at all. Maybe in your dreams?"

Of course Jordan wouldn't admit to it. He's got too much ego for that.

"Well, it was eye-opening to say the least," I say.

"Glad I could help. Now go get your man."

"Don't think that's gonna happen either, but thanks."

Jordan grunts. "Now it's all out there, don't fuck it up by keeping your mouth shut. Taylor doesn't compare to you."

Oh. Right. Jordan doesn't know. "Uh, they broke up."

Another warm laugh. "Can I be best man at your wedding?"

I roll my eyes even though Jordan can't see me. "It's not that simple, Jord."

"It really is."

"No. It's more complicated than algebra."

"That's pretty fucking complicated, but I don't see how."

I sigh. "There's something you don't know about Ash. About his ex-boyfriend … the one before Taylor."

"The big secret that wasn't so secret?"

"Huh?"

"What NHL star has a roommate?"

My mouth dries. "A few actually. Especially those who come up from the AHL. They don't start out on a lot of money."

"But I'm right, aren't I? Ash was with your brother? I knew something was up when I'd come to visit and Ash would be all vague about the guy he was seeing and why I couldn't meet him. For a while there, I thought he was lying about having a boyfriend so we wouldn't cross lines like we did in college, but then when he said he was moving in with your brother, it all clicked. Because if Ash needed a roommate, why wouldn't he live with you? I stopped asking after that, and he never told me the truth. He never needed to."

"Well, yeah. Hence complicated."

"Does your brother know how you feel?"

"Fuck no. I'm not stupid."

Jordan huffs. "That's debatable. But if you want to uncomplicate things, talk to your brother."

"It's not that easy."

"Yes, it is."

The front door to my parents' house opens, and Ma pops her head out.

"Jordan, I gotta go."

"I guess catching up while I'm still in town is out of the question?"

"Umm, at this stage, probably."

"Figured. Hopefully next time I'm in Boston, Ash won't hate us and we can pretend today never happened."

"Let's hope."

We end the call, and then Ma approaches, eyeing me suspiciously.

"Why are Ollie and Clark in there staring out the window like two little gossips? What's going on?"

And so the fun starts.

Something twinkles in Ma's eye as if she already knows what I'm gonna say. "Oh, honey. I'm so happy you're finally addressing your repressed feelings."

I shake my head. "What?"

"Please. You and your brother both have the same look of longing when you want something. Ollie has always stared at Ash that way. Well, until recently. You didn't start until after college. Right around the time he got together with Ollie."

"You have way too much time on your hands, woman."

There's that evil chuckle again. "No, hon, I have to make sure my five boys turn into respectable men. That's a full-time job."

"Your youngest is twenty-four. Maybe it's time to retire?"

"Pssh. Bite your tongue. You boys will always be mine to torture."

"I'm sure we're all grateful."

She glances back at the window my brother and his boyfriend were no doubt watching Ash and me from, and then she steps closer to me. "Just promise me one thing."

"What's that?"

"Talk to Ollie before anything happens between you and Ash … if it hasn't happened already?" She raises an eyebrow.

"Ash and I will never happen, Ma. I wouldn't do that to Ollie."

"Then what was"—she gestures to the curb where Ash and I were talking—"that all about?"

"He … kinda … sorta … walked in on me and another guy."

"Oh." Ma blinks, and I think I've genuinely surprised her.

"Oooh, Queen Know-it-all didn't see that coming, did she?"

Before Ma can kick my ass for sassing her, a car pulls into the driveway. My brother Nic and his wife get out of the car with their two kids.

"Saved by my big brother." I grin. "Wait, were they already coming over, or do you have telepathy now?"

"They were coming over to see Ollie, but this conversation isn't over," Ma promises.

I bet it isn't. "Can you just promise *me* something?"

"Anything."

"Can you let this thing settle between Ash and me before you go pulling any big parties or announcing this to the whole damn family?"

Ma smiles. "Of course, hon. Take all the time you need. But just so you know, the minute you're ready …"

I nod. "Huge coming-out party, I know."

"The biggest. Ollie didn't let me throw him one."

"Can't imagine why considering he's a public figure and all."

She pinches my cheek. "Well, lucky for me at least one of my sons is an underachiever."

"Ma!"

"Oh, stop it. You know I'm joking."

"You're the worst mother ever."

"I know! The reason we had so many kids was because we wanted to keep going until we found one we liked."

Yep. We're definitely dys*fun*ctional, but in the best possible way.

———

The following day, I head downstairs to the shop and find Ash already inside. He's … cleaning. Which is weird, because we recently hired someone to do that for us so we don't have to.

"Uh, Ash?"

He looks up from where he's wiping down the glass display where we keep our line of jewelry for piercings.

"What are you doing?"

"Being neurotic. What are you doing?"

I laugh, but it's awkward. I hate that it's like that between us now. "I'm wondering if we're okay."

"I just don't get it."

"Get what?"

"Why didn't you ever say anything? I know what you told me last night—why you never told me—but what about your ma? Your brothers? You don't think Ollie would've understood?"

"Ollie? Did you see the way he looked at us when I turned up yesterday? He's probably already assumed we've fucked behind his back or whatever. The last person I was going to tell was Ollie. And I never told anyone else because there was literally no point. Until Jordan came along, I thought you were like … a magical, sexy unicorn. No other men did it for me the way you did, and I assumed it was a *you* thing. It just turns out, I wasn't seeing past you to notice other guys. Kissing Jordan made me realize I definitely am bi."

"Shame."

I cock my head at him. "Shame?"

"Yeah, because if it was a me thing, I'd totally create a new sexuality called Ash-sexual."

"I'd sign up."

We both chuckle, but then Ash looks pained again like he did last night.

"What's wrong?"

"We should get to work setting up. Our first clients are due any minute."

"No, what's wrong?"

"I think … I think I need time to get used to this. Like, we've always joked around, and normally you saying something like you'd turn Ash-sexual wouldn't make my chest burn. But now it does, and …" Ash shakes his head.

"And what, Ash? Please talk to me." My heart stutters.

"It's all too much. Everything is *too much*. Taylor called this morning wanting to talk. He wanted to see if I'd come to my senses and would take him back—"

"You can't," I say, my voice stern.

"Oh, I can't, can I? You know how I love being told what to do."

"No, I'm serious, Ash. Take time away from me, clear your head, but not with him."

"What?"

"He's all wrong for you."

Ash rounds the counter. "Did everyone think Taylor was wrong for me? Why is it when you're with someone, and you think everything is great, no one tells you how ungreat they think it is until you break up? All Mom and Dad did last night was tell me how wrong Taylor was for me."

"You want to know why I never told you Taylor wasn't good enough for you? Because *no one* will ever be good enough for you. I thought my brother could be, but not when he chose his career over you. Constantly. The person you end up with should not only encourage you, but push you to be the person you want to be. They should hold your hand while you drag them to gay bars. They should take you places you want to go even if it bores them. They shouldn't be scared to claim you. You deserve so much more than that, and neither Ollie or Taylor could give it to you."

Ash takes two steps back. "That's just it, Max. Neither can you. Otherwise you would've said something *years ago*. It's too complicated. You're … you, and I'm me."

"I don't know what that means."

Ash sighs. "Neither do I. I know it's going to be hard—staying away from each other when we work so close, but I can't … I need to …"

I nod. "I'll give you whatever you need, Ash."

Everywhere aches as I go to my workroom and shut the door behind me.

I didn't know it was possible for my heart to break more

when it came to Ash, but apparently I'm wrong, because I realize there's a lot more obstacles blocking us than just my stupid brother.

This is why I never said anything back in college.

Years of unexplored and repressed feelings were bound to explode like this.

It was inevitable, and now it's finally here.

I don't think either of us are prepared to deal with that.

4

ASH

The idea of working with Max day in and out is daunting at first, but I underestimate the power of busy days. Before I know it, Max and I have gone three weeks with barely speaking.

Our shop has been doing well, picking up momentum, and we've been making a name for ourselves ever since we opened five years ago. Ollie's fame helped—being the brother of the co-owner, he was able to plug us whenever he could without anyone being suspicious of him and me as a couple—but since he came out and has become a massive role model and public figure, our business has exploded even more.

Being busy with clients is a good distraction from Max but exhausting with the long hours. Traveling back to Milton every night to stay with my parents makes it harder; I'm used to living five minutes away from work, but my only other option is to move back in above the shop.

That's not going to happen. I need time away from Max, not to push us together and share a nine-hundred-square-foot box.

Working in the very room next to his is hard enough. I can hear his laugh, his polite banter, and the buzzing of his tattoo gun as he does what we were born to do. I swear I can hear us syncing as we put ink to skin.

I miss him already.

This is so fucked. I'm fucked. It's not going to be possible to stay away from him.

I thought packing my feelings back into the box where I kept them all throughout adolescence would be easy. I've done it once before; I could do it again. But it's completely different now, because he was never a real option before.

Knowing my childhood crush, my best friend, the first and only guy I've ever pined for is in the room next to mine, close but not close enough, far but not far enough, and now knowing he reciprocates my feelings … it kills me that I can't go in there and just be with him.

I *hate* this.

After saying goodbye to my last client who I called Dragon Left Ankle because I forgot her name, I hear Max finishing up with his, so I hightail it back to my room and close the door.

I would've run out the front seeing as I'm done for the day, but I still have cleanup to do.

My phone buzzes on my desk, and Jordan's name pops up on the screen.

I grunt. Guess I can't keep ignoring his attempts to get in touch with me. For some reason, Max and Jordan hooking up felt like a betrayal on both their parts—Max for keeping his sexuality a secret from me, his supposed best friend, and Jordan because … I dunno … possessiveness and jealousy maybe. He always asked if Max and I had ever hooked up, and I'd have to tell him repeatedly that Max was straight, but he had to have heard the hurt in my voice. We were both crushing on Max, and I guess I'm pissed that he was the one to crack him. Which is ridiculous, because I know that's not what happened, and I know that's not how sexuality works. No one broke Max. No one turned him.

I answer the phone before I lose my nerve. "Hey."

"Yes, silent treatment broken."

"Don't make me hang up."

A long sigh comes through the phone. "I don't know why you're pissed at me. You can have Max now. I was nothing, and you're his everything."

"You don't know why I'm pissed? Seriously?"

"What, because you and Max still hadn't gotten your act together after how many years of friendship? You were engaged to be married. I figured he was fair game. Okay, and I also didn't think he'd cave, but he did, and this might make me an asshole, but I don't regret it, because you know how much I wanted him in college."

Gah, I want to stay mad, but I don't have a right to be. I have no claim to Max. Ever. Being with Ollie closed that door for us.

"But for what it's worth, I am sorry if it hurt you," Jordan says. "I know 'it meant nothing' are just annoying words that mean about as much as the gesture, but it's the truth. Nothing is a giant wake-up call like being ditched right after kissing someone."

I can hear the rejection in Jordan's voice—a rarity for him.

"Do you know how easy all of this shit would've been had you and I had any romantic chemistry at all?"

I laugh. "Right? We'd be married with kids and a happily ever after."

"Shame you kiss like a dead fish."

"Fuck you, I do not."

"Feels like it," Jordan mumbles, and then the line goes quiet. "Are we cool?"

The need to be mad at him dims, because it's not his fault Max and I are both idiots. "We're cool."

"Good. Because now I can yell at you. You're avoiding Max? Why? And don't use Ollie as an excuse, because you guys haven't even spoken to him and been up-front."

I'm stunned silent for a second. "Y-you know about Max's brother?"

"I'm a perceptive fucker."

"Wait, how did you know I've been avoiding Max?"

"Max told me."

For years, I've been the middleman between Max and Jordan, because they never really got along.

"What, one make-out session and suddenly you're best friends?"

"Not even close. All we talk about is *you.* He keeps asking if you're talking to me yet. If I know anything. If I think you guys could even remain friends after this. You both need to pull your heads out of your asses and fucking *talk.* Why are you avoiding him?"

"It's complicated."

"God, you sound like him. It's not complicated at all. What do you want, Ash? Forget consequences with family drama, forget your business, forget all outside things. What. Do. You. Want?"

"Max," I blurt. "It's always been Max. Forever and—shit."

"Forever and shit? Might I suggest you work on your speech before making a grand gesture?"

He's been there in front of me forever and ever. We've already promised our lives to each other, but we've just been too dumb, preoccupied, or stubborn to fucking say up front what that means.

I want Max to be *mine.*

But it can't happen. Max has made it super clear he won't go behind Ollie's back.

"Jordan, we can't go there. This could tear his whole family apart."

There's a knock at my door, and Max's voice makes my heart stutter. "Ash?"

"Jord, I have to go."

"Please don't hurt him? I'd hate for him to have to fly to L.A. to mend a broken heart by worshipping my co—"

"It's time to hang up. Bye." I end the call.

With a deep breath, I pray for the courage I need to do ... something. I don't know what.

When I open the door, my eyes lock on his lips. They look so damn kissable. So inviting.

His black wifebeater highlights his tattooed muscles and amazing physique, but the sweet look of innocence on his face is my Max. The Max I fantasized about every day from when I was eleven until I told my poor heart to give him up.

Only, I didn't give him up. My heart didn't move on. It's as if a protective layer trapped Max inside so I could delude myself into being happy, but it has only taken one day of unfortunate events and then three weeks of it simmering at the forefront of my brain to uncover those feelings I thought were lost long ago.

"So, uh"—Max runs a hand through his hair—"I held Ma off as long as I could, but tonight's the night."

"Your big coming-out party?" I ask.

He nods. "I'd really like for you to be there."

"I ... uh ... umm ..."

"Think about it?"

"Yeah, o-okay, I can do that."

"Come?"

"Uh, no. I mean, I'll think about it."

I hate the disappointment in his gaze and the way he holds his head low as he walks away.

We need to learn how to act around each other, which is so fucking weird, because it has never been like that between us. Even when all that shit went down with his brother, even when we both went through those awkward teen years and I was popping boners whenever I went near him.

It's never been like this between us, and it hurts more than any breakup, fight, or disagreement with anyone I've ever dated. Including when I walked away from Ollie.

I need Max in my life like I need my next breath.

Which is why I can't go to his coming-out party.

There's no way I'll be able to hide that from his brother. Ollie knows me too well.

———

"You coming next door for some typical Strömberg antics?" Mom asks from the guest room doorway. Unlike the Strömberg matriarch, my mom converted my childhood bedroom into a guest room the minute I went off to college. Max's mom has kept the guys' rooms pretty much the same except the room in the attic. It's weird but kinda cute at the same time.

"Uh, I dunno if I'm up for that."

"It'll be a good way to forget about Taylor."

"Forgetting about Taylor isn't really the issue," I say.

"I guess spending the night with one ex to forget the other

isn't the best idea," Mom says. "I'll let them know you can't make it."

That's not why I don't want to go over there. I can't get Max out of my head.

It's torture.

This is the guy I followed around like a fucking puppy since adolescence. While Ollie was following me, I was following Max, and Max was chasing anything in a skirt.

It's the circle of puberty. Fun times. Heartache and unrequited love all around.

It was only when he got together with Laura our senior year of college that my heart finally caught up with my brain. Max didn't want me, and he never would. I reminded myself of that even after he and Laura split and he was heartbroken. And when that stopped working, I turned to someone I shouldn't have.

That summer, something clicked. Max would never love me, but Ollie could. And I could love him.

I huff a humorless laugh. I spent four years being mad at Ollie for putting me second, when in reality, I did it to him first.

It's not that I didn't love Ollie in that way. I fell hard for him. Once I'd let Max go, it was amazing how fast I was open to being with Ollie.

We had the real deal. We cared for each other. But he was never the guy I was supposed to end up with, and I hate it took us so long to figure that out. The idea of our relationship ruining my chance with someone who could be my soul mate … it makes it worse. Makes every happy memory with Ollie tainted. Which is unfair. To me, to Ollie, and to our relationship.

Fuck, I can't do this to myself or I'll go crazy.

My phone pings, and I don't want to look at who's messaging me. Taylor, Ollie, or Max—all of who I don't want to deal with right now. But with an unhealthy need to know who it is, I look anyway.

Max: Please come save me. No shit, Ma has put out a penis piñata …

I bite my lip to stop from laughing, but it breaks free. Poor Max. I contemplate going over there to rescue him, I really do. But I just can't. Everything is so messed up. As if reading my mind, Max sends through another message.

Max: I know it's super weird now, and the last few weeks have been shit, but you're still my best friend. It's your job to make these torturous events less painful. Maybe if we pretend things are as they've always been, we can go back to normal faster?

I don't want that though. I don't think I'll ever want to go *back to normal*. I reread the text and then notice something …

Me: Fuck, you're drunk, aren't you?

Max: How'd you know?

Me: You can spell when you're drunk. That text is too perfect for you to be sober.

Max: XD

Me: I don't think it's a good idea. If I go over there, I'm probably gonna make a scene, and I don't want to ruin your party.

Max: Please make a scene. Ruin my party. Please, please, please.

This is the thing with Max and me. No matter what we're going through—breakups, money problems, just pure bitchiness at the world because let's face it, sometimes the universe sucks—bottom line is, we've always put each other before ourselves. Where all my other relationships have felt an uneven balance of power, things between Max and me have always been equal. Always.

Forever and ever.

Damn it.

ME: *I'LL BE OVER IN FIVE.*

I can do this. I can go over there and try to see Max in the same light I always have—as the unobtainable guy I need to swallow my feelings for. Easy peasy. Been doing it since I was eleven years old.

Rolling out of bed, I amble downstairs and head out, not bothering to freshen up or even fix my bed-messed hair. The street is packed with Strömberg cars, and it looks like the entire extended family turned out for this.

Most likely, everyone's in the backyard, so that's why I go through the front door and not around the side of the house. I might be here to support Max, but I don't really want to face a mob of Strömbergs. They're gonna stare at me. I wasn't good enough for Max when we were teenagers, and now he's out and I'm still not good enough for him.

After making my way through the dark and empty living room, I hit the dining area only to find Max and one of his brothers, Leo, in the kitchen leaning against the counter and talking.

"I see you escaped on your own," I say, startling them apart.

"Ashy!" Max yells and his face brightens.

Leo laughs and claps me on the shoulder. "Good luck, buddy. I lost count of his drinks after the penis piñata came out."

"No way, there really is a penis piñata?" I go to the bay windows overlooking the backyard.

Max stumbles over to me and throws his arm around my

shoulders. "Ma bought it when Ollie came out publicly. The only reason he convinced her not to use it for him is because he said he couldn't risk those types of photos being leaked because he's the biiiig, important hockey player. I'm not famous enough to have to worry about that."

I snort. "You're not famous at all."

"Hey, we're famous in our own world. People pay us a shit ton of money to tattoo them. Because we're awesome."

"We are pretty badass," I agree with a smile. "But I'm pretty sure none of our clientele will care if you're photographed whacking a dick with a stick."

"Heeey, that rhymes!"

My smile drops when I see my dad step up to the low-hanging penis … And there's a sentence I never thought would enter my mind. I groan. "Oh, God, I can't watch."

"I can't tear my eyes away," Max says.

We stay like that—Max's arm around me, although, I think it's more to hold himself up than an embrace of affection—and watch my dad. This is the guy who gave me the silent treatment for three days after I came out. He accepts me and loves me and all that, but he admitted it took a while to adjust to the idea. He talked about the way he was raised and realizing how his generation needs to start thinking differently. Still, compared to the Strömbergs and Mom, he's straitlaced and a tad conservative. And right now, he's beating the shit out of a papier-mâché cock. He's come far in ten years.

Yet, watching him makes the reality of why we're here that much more apparent.

A pit of want, longing, and anger settles in my stomach.

Max is acting like nothing has changed between us. His hand on my shoulder isn't out of the ordinary. His warm smile and natural glow aren't either. But there's definitely something different in the way I look at him.

I haven't had the shiver run down my spine when Max has touched me in years, but now there's no holding it back. There's no pulling it in.

Max kissing Jordan opened Pandora's box, and now all hell's breaking loose on my insides. I'm back to where I was as an awkward teenager, realizing I had a crush on my best friend.

You'd think the sixteen years of telling myself *no* would've cured me of it. Nope. It's like my teenage hormones have taken over, and all I want to do is throw myself at him.

Which, of course, I can't. And I won't. Because I won't disrespect Ollie that way.

When Max meets my gaze, my stomach does a flip. From his brown hair, tanned skin, and the edges of his ink sticking out of his shirt collar, he's more man on the outside than the last time I had this crush, but those warm, brown eyes … they're the eyes of the boy I fell in love with when I was eleven years old.

Why did it take him so long to figure out? Why didn't he say something sooner?

Everyone has a right to come to terms with their sexuality at their own pace, but … gah, it's just so frustrating that timing has fucked us over.

Max's brow furrows. "Why do you look mad?"

"Still pissed you didn't tell me."

"You were with my brother, Ash." His tone has lost any sign of inebriation and only holds defeat.

"So? You still could've told me. And to tell Jordan first? You don't even like him."

"Why do you and he keep saying that? I like Jordan fine."

"Plenty fine, it turns out." Yeah, can't keep the bitterness out of my tone even if I tried.

"The only thing I've ever held against him is he got to have you in a way I didn't. And it turns out he's known about me since fucking college. He knew from the way I stared at you."

All this time …

The unease hits harder. "Maybe we shouldn't talk about this. It's not making me feel any better."

Max turns and grips my shoulders so we're facing each other and he's leaning over me with his stupid tallness that's tall. "I am so sorry. I didn't plan on you finding out that way. Hell, I hadn't planned on you finding out at all, because I knew this would happen. It's all weird, and it's like … I don't know. Now that it's been said out loud, I can't put it back in, and all I want to do is show you how much I've cared about you and wanted you for the last six years. I can't have you as just my best friend anymore, but I can't have you as more, and it's already killing me. It's only been a few weeks."

His breath smells like he's brewing alcohol in his mouth. Normally that'd be a turnoff, but all I want to do is taste it. Taste him. "I shouldn't have come here."

When I step back, a throat clears behind us, and we both freeze, expecting the worst.

I let out a breath of relief when it's not Ollie or his boyfriend as Max and I step apart. It's Max's cousin, Cruz.

"You guys aren't allowed to get together for two more weeks," he says. "So back away."

Max and I share a glance. "Huh?" we say in unison.

"There's a pool going."

"On us?" Max asks. "Just because I'm bi, that doesn't mean I'm going to fuck the nearest gay guy."

Ouch. I know he's saving face and trying to cover, and it's not true, but … *ouch.*

"And you only bet two weeks?" Max asks. "Dude, he's my brother's ex-boyfriend."

Cruz shrugs. "Not a big deal. Did you know Lucy and I went on a date before she married my bonehead brother?"

"A date isn't four years together," I point out.

"Have you even spoken to Ollie about the possibility? Because seriously, everyone out there just thinks it's a given you two are gonna end up together now."

"There's nothing to discuss," Max says. "There's no way Ollie would be cool with this."

Cruz smirks. "So there is something between you two. Awesome. Just remember though"—he waves a finger between us both—"two weeks. Got it? The prize money is up to like a thousand bucks."

Cruz takes a beer from the fridge and goes back outside.

I scoff. "Your family is the coolest."

"And the weirdest," Max mumbles. "You don't really think Ollie would be okay with us, do you? I mean, it's just always been a firm no in my head."

"Honestly? I don't know. I'm an only child, so I have no idea what having a brother feels like."

"Not true. You have all of us. You practically grew up in this house with us. What if, say, Ollie wanted to hook up with Leo?"

I burst out laughing. "Apart from the whole incest thing, you mean?"

"Pretend we're not related. If Ollie was to date someone as close to you as Leo, or Nic, or Vic, how would you feel?"

I sigh in defeat. "Pretty fucking shitty." Even so, I don't think I'd stop him. We have no right to each other anymore.

"Exactly. Cruz is wrong." Max goes to walk off, but I catch his arm.

He spins back toward me, our bodies pressing against each other.

My question hangs heavy in the air. "Max? What if he's not?"

Ash is so close. So fucking close yet still out of my reach. Not physically—I could literally drag him against me, press his smaller body to mine, and ravish his mouth without even a step.

His lips part, and my cock stirs as if urging me to go for it.

My heart pounds. From the alcohol, from adrenaline, or from being pressed against Ash, I don't know, but I want him so bad.

The last six years have shown me that no one could live up to his mere presence, and I've hated myself every day, because I let him get away. I let him chase my brother instead of having the balls to tell him how I felt.

This past year has done nothing but test my strength. It's like the minute he broke up with my brother, my heart's been beating a rhythm that keeps repeating Ash's name. I hoped when he'd got together with Taylor, my brain screaming about us being platonic would come back—like it did when he was with Ollie. All it did was complain about Taylor being so wrong for him.

Here, right now, there's a chance. It's the closest I've ever been to getting him, and I *can't* let it go.

"I need to find Ollie" falls out of my mouth, and before I can stop myself, I force myself away from temptation.

I charge into the backyard and look in every direction, but I can't see him anywhere. Or Clark.

My aunt, Ma's sister, cuts me off before I can weave my way through the hordes of Strömbergs to find them.

"I'm looking for Ollie," I say before she can get a word out.

"Oh, umm, I think he and Clark left already."

"Wait, what? Weren't they staying here the night?"

"Umm, I don't know … I didn't think so."

My heart sinks.

My brother's gone, and I can't have this conversation with him over the phone.

I glance back toward the house and see Ash on the back porch. His arms are folded, but his face looks hopeful.

I shake my head, and I see the moment all that hope deflates.

If I wasn't too drunk to drive, I'd chase after Ollie. If we didn't have a full schedule at the shop for the next few days, I'd get Ash to drive us to New York.

Ash points to his parents' house, and I give him a nod. It's probably best he leaves before I'm tempted to cross lines I refuse to before being able to talk to my brother.

I'll go see Ollie next weekend.

I've waited over six years for the possibility of Ash. I can wait a few more days.

———

I don't think I can wait a few more days.

My brother Leo dropped me home last night, and after the room stopped spinning, all I could think about was the possibility of Ollie being okay with Ash and me. It was on a repeating loop all night. I kept thinking of course he wouldn't be okay with it … but what if he was?

I owed it to Ash, and owed it to *us*, to try.

Tired, hungover, and looking a little worse for wear, I drag my ass downstairs to work.

The second Ash steps into the shop, my eyes track his every move. He's wearing a loose white tank top and black ripped skinny jeans, and the colorful tattoos stand out along his pale skin.

Fuck, I want him.

My gaze snaps to his when he laughs.

"How hungover are you?"

"On a scale of one to ten? Spring break senior year."

Ash winces. "Ouch. I'll go for a coffee and bacon run as soon as we're set up for the day."

This is why I love you almost runs off the tip of my tongue, but that holds too much weight between us now. It's not the same way it's always been between us—the I love yous and worshipping of friendly actions like getting me a bacon-and-egg sandwich to cure my hangover. Extra bacon. Because, hello, it's bacon.

Ash and I share a look, and I wonder what he sees in my gaze. I imagine he can see the kind of hope and possibilities that are running through my head, but instead, he smirks.

"You're totally forgetting about the penis piñata, aren't you?"

I groan. "Oh my God, that actually happened?"

Ash laughs again.

I haven't heard that sound in weeks, so I close my eyes and

breathe it in as if his laughter is something I can swallow and keep forever.

"Feeling sick?" he asks.

I step closer to him. "Feeling helpless. I can't stop thinking about Ollie and—"

Ash shakes his head and steps back. "We can't. We both don't want to hurt Ollie that way, so until we get a chance to talk to him, I think we should still keep our distance. We have to. Because even though I really want Ollie to be okay with this, I don't think he will be. And if that's the case … we *can't* let anything happen."

Damn it. I know he's right.

That doesn't stop me from dwelling on it. All day.

Time slows so much that I have to ask one of my clients if I'm moving at a sloth's pace. They think I'm joking.

Ironically, my next client wants a sloth tattoo.

I think I'm being punked.

The entire day is agonizing, only made worse by knowing I can't get to New York until next Sunday because that's my next day off.

When it's finally time for my last client to leave, I can't wait to get upstairs and go to bed, but when cleaning up my work-station, I come across Ash's sketches in my drawer—the one of the lake at Camp Frottage. The same image he wanted to cover his Ollie tattoo with.

"They were the best summers of my life." His words ring through my head.

The best summers he had were with me.

Not my brother.

Ash and I deserve this chance because we never got it when we were younger.

If something as small as bad timing is what has kept us apart all these years, I'm going to be pissed.

Ash and Ollie never belonged together.

Ash belongs to me.

And I need to fight for him the way he deserves to be fought for.

Suddenly I'm not so tired anymore. I need to see Ollie, and I need to see him now.

I leave a giant mess in the shop for Ash to clean up so I can drive three and a half hours in traffic to ask Ollie for permission to date his ex-boyfriend.

Doubt starts to creep in somewhere in Connecticut.

With one tattoo stencil, I was out the door ready to plead with my baby brother to let me have this one selfish act.

Granted it's massively selfish and a big deal …

Shit, maybe I shouldn't?

This is for *Ash*, I remind myself.

That's enough for me to hit the button on my steering wheel that's connected to my phone.

"Call Ollie."

"Calling Polly. Is that correct?" the voice says back at me.

"No. Cancel." When I get confirmation they're not calling some chick named Polly—I don't even know what a Polly is doing in my phone—I hit the button again and speak clearer. "Call *Ollie*."

"Calling Grammy. Is that correct?"

Motherfucker. "No."

How did it get Grammy from Ollie?

"Call *Ollie Strömberg*."

"Calling Leo Strömberg. Is that correct?"

I huff. Close enough. "Yes."

"What's up?" Leo answers immediately.

"Can you message Ollie and get him to call me?"

"What? Why?"

"My stupid voice thingy isn't working, and I'm a little over an hour out from New York."

There's a pause. "Why are you going to New York?"

"Why do you think?"

"With none of us there to referee the fight? I dunno if we should let that happen."

"This is between Ollie and me. Just get him to call me." I hit End before he can protest more.

Knowing my family, they'd want to turn this into a spectator sport and add their own comments.

The call from Ollie comes in a few minutes later.

I hit Answer. "Hey."

"Why exactly do I have to call you?"

"What'd Leo say?"

"That your phone is broken and that I need to call you, but that didn't make sense if your phone was broken."

"I'm on my way to New York and I'm driving, so I couldn't reach my phone. I'm coming to see you."

He's silent for a beat. "Coming to see me? Why?"

"Brotherly chat?"

"Mmm. What about?"

I sigh. "I think you know, but I want to do this face-to-face. Where are you?"

"At home."

"Yeah, great. You do realize I haven't visited you in New York yet? Send me your address."

"'Kay."

"I'll see you soon."

The nerves build the rest of the drive, settling in my stomach and setting up permanent residence.

Before I hit the city, I punch his place into the GPS so I know where the hell I'm going. I've only ever been to New York a couple of times, and it's as confusing to navigate as I remember.

I notice I have a slew of notifications from Ash wondering where I went. So after I find a parking garage near Ollie's apartment and balk at the cost, I message Ash back and tell him I'm sorting this once and for all.

It's almost eight, and the thought of having to drive back to Boston tonight makes me want to gag. Maybe after my brother punches me out, he'll offer me a place to sleep.

I reach the stoop of his apartment and hold my breath as I hit the buzzer to let me in.

Climbing the stairs in his building, I have a moment of panic where I want to turn and run away, because my relationship with my brother means everything to me, and I don't want to do anything to jeopardize that.

But then all I have to do is think of Ash and remember that he deserves this. He deserves a man who will fight for him.

Neither Ollie or Taylor were willing to, and if this is my only shot, I'm taking it.

Ollie's door comes into view as I round the last set of stairs, and I pause.

I haven't wanted anything more than Ash. And to get Ash, I need Ollie's approval.

His door pops open, and there's baby bro, looking more intimidating than usual.

I mean, he's a six-foot-four hockey player—intimidation is his career. He's just never intimidated me that much, because he was always the little shithead brother who wouldn't leave me and Ash alone growing up.

"Aww, don't chicken out now after driving all this way," he taunts. It's not a playful taunt, but in a way that lets me know he's not going to make this easy for me.

I trudge up the last of the steps and head inside his apartment.

The door shutting literally sounds like locks on a cell and I'm about to start my sentence.

"Drink?" Ollie asks.

"Definitely."

He smiles. "Don't worry, bro, I'm going to make this as painless as possible." Something in his tone suggests the opposite.

"So you do know why I'm here."

"Surprised you didn't come sooner." Ollie takes out three glasses, the scotch from on top of his fridge, and starts pouring.

"Three …"

"Hey." Clark's voice comes from behind me.

Oh great. I get to do this with an audience. An audience who hates me, because admittedly, I was a dick to Ollie's boyfriend when I first met him.

"Uh, hi."

Clark walks around the other side of Ollie and takes his drink. Ollie's arm wraps around his boyfriend's shoulders, and they wait.

Right. Time to grovel. I go to start when I stare over at Ollie's living room. "Should we sit for this?"

Ollie shrugs and takes a sip of his drink. Then just stares at me.

God, this is already painful.

"We can sit, but it's going to be a short conversation," Ollie says. "You can't fuck my ex-boyfriend. End of story."

Any hope I had disappears with a whoosh.

My mouth drops open, but Ollie remains stoic. The drink in front of me looks mighty inviting. Ollie's too.

I drink mine down and then take Ollie's out of his hand and drink that as well.

"That's it, then? I don't even get to plead my case?" My gaze flicks from Ollie's to Clark's and back again.

Clark nudges my brother. "You promised you wouldn't do that."

Ollie breaks out into a grin. "Come on. It was so easy. And fun. It looks like Maxi's gonna throw up."

I resist the urge to punch him. "Are you fucking kidding me right now?"

"Hey, you're the one who's here to tell me you have a thing for Ash. I'm just trying to deal with it the only way I know how, because if I don't joke, I'll fucking beat the ever-loving shit out of you."

"I'd like to see you try." I step closer.

Clark gets in between us. "Okay. That escalated quickly. Back to your corners." He turns to Ollie. "You said you were going to hear him out."

"Fine." Ollie pours himself some more scotch and heads for his couch. His eyes are cold as he takes his seat. "Convince me why this shouldn't piss me off."

A million excuses run through my head.

You're happy with Clark.

You've been broken up for a year.

He was mine first.

I've been in love with him longer than you.

Though, that one's technically not true. Ollie pretty much

fell for Ash as a kid, he just didn't know it until he was fifteen and realized the infatuation meant he was gay.

None of my reasonings are good enough excuses to come between us as brothers.

"Because five years ago when you started dating, I was already in love with him and I never said anything."

Ollie loses the smugness in his face. "W-what?"

I huff and take a seat in the armchair opposite him. "My junior year of college, I realized I liked Ash more than a friend, but the timing never worked out. When we graduated, we were going into business together, and I was scared of fucking everything up."

"Y-you're in love with him ..."

"You remember the summer you two got together?"

"Duh."

"It was the only year I went to Camp Frottage without him, and the whole summer I spent building the courage to tell him how I felt. And, of course, when I came home—"

"We were already together," Ollie says, his voice quiet. "You never said anything."

"You made each other happy." I shrug. "I couldn't want anything more for my brother and best friend. Saying something after it had already happened was only going to cause shit."

Ollie still appears to be in shock. "You should've said something. He would've chosen you, and then maybe ... maybe we wouldn't have tortured each other for so long to make something that was wrong work." He hangs his head.

"What do you mean he would've chosen me?"

"You know what I always used to think?" Ollie asks.

I shake my head.

"I used to always think, 'Thank fuck Max isn't gay.' If you

were, I never would've stood a chance. It's like you two were complete complements of each other, and I thought it was a best-friend thing, because you were straight. Guess it was more than that all along."

Guilt gnaws at me. "I was never going to act on something that would've hurt you. But when you broke up, it's like all those feelings came flooding back, and I've been ignoring it and pushing it down for so long that I ended up kissing his best friend just so I could try to forget."

"That Jordan guy," Ollie murmurs. "Why can't you just date him?"

I wish it were that easy. "He's not Ash. While you two were together, I could accept that he would only be mine in a platonic way, and I've been telling myself the same thing every day since I found out you broke up. I don't want to disrespect you or what you had—"

"Fuuuck." Ollie runs a hand through his ash-blond hair.

"What?"

"How am I supposed to sit here and tell you not to date him after that? I ... I didn't realize you've been in love with him forever. Though it makes total sense now."

"I'm sorry. I really am. And the thing is, I don't even know if Ash and I will work as a couple, but it's getting to the point where we have to try or we're going to send each other crazy."

Ollie purses his lips. "Have you ... have, you know ..."

"Nothing's happened. But ..."

"You want it to."

"Hence driving all this way to talk to you even though I have to be back at the shop in the morning."

Ollie lets out a long sigh. "I still really don't like it. I mean, I'm in love with Clark"—he smirks at his boyfriend—"and I couldn't be happier, but Ash ..."

Even I see the guilt in his eyes as he stares at his current boyfriend.

Clark steps forward. "He'll always mean something to you, and I understand it. You have matching tattoos, for fuck's sake."

"Uh, about the tattoos. Ash asked me a few weeks ago to do a cover-up on his …"

"He what?" Ollie asks.

"He couldn't go through with it though. I thought, maybe you could talk to him about it?"

Ollie stands. "I'll be back."

I narrow my eyes. "Okaaay."

He disappears into his bedroom.

"What the—" I turn to Clark. "What's he doing?"

"Sending Ash a video of him jerking off?" He shrugs.

I stare at him like he's crazy.

"Okay, that was a joke. Breathe." He sits where Ollie was sitting a moment ago.

"How are you okay with all this?" I wave my hand around.

"I'm not. I mean, not really. But I guess that's why I understand it. I don't like that Ollie still has hang-ups over Ash, but I also know it's not because he still has feelings for him or wants him back or any of that. I may not know what it's like to have a family as close as yours or an ex who I still have to see, but I do know what it's like to be heartbroken, and that never really goes away. I know Ollie loves me and that I'm the guy for him." Another shrug. "That makes it easier."

Ollie's low murmurs come from the bedroom and then stop. Then start again, but I can't hear anything he's saying.

"For what it's worth, I think you and Ash will make a great couple. You're defensive of him and protective, and I know the reason you treated me like shit is because of the love you have for both Ollie and Ash. I hope everything works out for you two."

"Even if it'll be awkward at family gatherings?"

Clark laughs. "Hey, I'm already pretty awkward. More won't get me down."

Ollie reappears.

I narrow my eyes. "What did you do?"

"Sent Ash a video."

After Clark's joke earlier, my eyes widen. "What kind of video?"

Clark smirks.

"Telling him if you guys want to be together, I'm not going to make your lives difficult. And to keep the fucking tattoo, because erasing it won't erase what happened between us, and I don't want to forget anyway."

"Really?"

"Yes. He'll tell you the rest when you go back. Which is when, by the way?"

I groan. "I should probably wait awhile after those drinks. Don't suppose you could feed me dinner?"

Ollie chuckles. "Let's go out to eat."

"Wait, have you guys not eaten?"

Clark looks at me incredulously. "Are you kidding me? He's already had two dinners. This will be his third."

"I'm a growing boy."

"You better watch it, because it's off season and with your lack of training, you'll start growing outwards."

Ollie pulls Clark close. "We'll work it off later."

"Too much information for your older brother," I interject. "Please feed me."

"You two go," Clark says. "I'm not hungry at all, because I eat one meal like a normal-sized human being. Might be a good thing for you two to hang out on your own now I know you're not going to kill each other."

Ollie leans in and kisses his boyfriend. "I'll be back soon."

He nods. "I'll be in bed waiting for you."

I sigh. I want that type of relationship in my life.

Now that I have Ollie's blessing, the opportunity is within reach.

Ash and I just have to take it.

Max has ignored my calls since he walked out of the shop hours ago, and now I feel like an idiot for waiting for him in his apartment.

Or technically, *our* apartment.

We're both on the lease, and up until a few months ago, I was living here with him.

I think back to every time I sat in this very spot on the couch and broke down over his stupid brother. How Max would be there to wrap an arm around me, tell me Ollie was a dumbass, and then kiss me on the top of my head.

Fuck, how did I miss seeing Max had feelings for me? Straight guys don't kiss their gay guy friends on the head … do they?

I always thought it was normal, but now I'm not so sure.

I take out my phone and message Jordan.

ME: *Do straight guys show affection to their gay friends?*

JORDAN: *In my experience, no. They always wanna ride the D. Then again, everyone wants to ride my D.*

ME: *SURE THEY DO. KEEP LIVING IN THAT DELUSION, BUDDY.*

If Max actually wanted me all that time ... Oh my God, how did he put up with me dating so many guys after Ollie? Once I got over Ollie's rejection, I went on the prowl for someone who could give me what I wanted. Some of them made it home with me, only to discover the next day they were full of shit and I never saw them again. But most were up-front about not wanting to settle down and wouldn't make it past the first date.

Yet, there Max was every night, reminding me of my value and telling me I deserve the world.

I never once thought he was offering it. Which, I guess he wasn't, technically, because he thought he couldn't. Now I don't know where he is at all. He said he needed to talk to Ollie, but surely he didn't mean he was going to New York.

I try to call him again, but before I can hit Dial, a message from Ollie takes over my screen.

When I open it, a video-still pops up, and I hit Play without hesitation. Maybe I should've hesitated.

There's my ex-boyfriend, all messy blond hair and hazel eyes staring at me. "Hey, Ash. I thought you should know Max is with me, and we're ... talking some shit out. I'm sending you a video, mainly because I don't think I can talk about it with you yet, and I didn't want to send you a text message."

My heart beats erratically, and my mouth dries. Max told him. He actually told him.

I hold my breath, because the next thing out of Ollie's mouth could go either way, and I don't think I'm prepared for either answer.

If he was okay with it, there'd be an enormous amount of pressure on Max and me. What if it doesn't work out? What if we're wrong? On the flip side, what if it's everything we've both wanted for fucking years? What if it's our time to have a real chance at this?

If Ollie is not okay with it, we're going to have to figure out a way to deal with that. I vote for moving to New Zealand, because the only way I'll be able to stay away from Max now I know how he really feels is to move to the other side of the world.

Ollie runs a hand over his hair, messing it up some more. "I … I'm gonna be honest and say I hate the idea of you and Max."

My heart sinks.

"But you wouldn't be happy with me loving the idea either. If you really think about it."

"True," I say aloud even though he can't hear me. I couldn't imagine how I'd feel if Ollie turned to his brother and said, "Have at it." It'd be like hearing he never actually cared for me.

"I will be okay with it," he continues. "Eventually. Don't let me stand in the way of what you guys could possibly have, because from what Max has told me, it could be everything you've ever wanted. I didn't live up to that, but maybe he could. I just want you to be happy. As empty as that sounds, it's true."

It's more than we could have possibly hoped for, and I have to say Ollie's a bigger man than I probably could be.

"One last thing. Don't get rid of our tattoo, jackass. It means something. We meant something. That'll never change no matter what happens."

My gaze drops to my forearm where our matching tattoo is. I thought getting rid of it would mean I was moving on and forgetting about him, but there's a difference between pretending he never existed and accepting it for what it is.

Ollie's and my relationship taught me so many things—compromise, patience, comfort … It taught me some hard lessons too, like knowing my worth and refusing to settle. It might've taken me a while for those lessons to be implemented, but after Taylor, I know I'll never settle again.

I'm holding out for the guy who gives me the future I want.

All he has to do is come home.

The last thing I remember is working on some sketches while waiting for Max. Next thing I know, I'm flat on the couch clutching my sketchbook with warm laughter rousing me from sleep.

A soft hand cups my cheek. "I'm home."

My eyes open slowly, and my best friend kneels beside me with the biggest smile on his face.

I lean up on my elbow and take in the room. The lights are still on, but I have no idea what time it is.

"It's two thirty," Max says as if reading my mind.

"You went all the way to New York," I croak.

"I had to."

"Why?"

"Because if I had to go another day without doing this, I don't think I could've done it without hurting him."

"Do wha—"

Max's lips land on mine, taking me off guard, but within mere seconds, I melt against him. I throw my arm around his shoulder and pull him closer, moaning when his tongue pushes into my mouth.

He kisses like he's savoring me, like he's been waiting a lifetime for it.

I want to be as cool and calm as he is, but this is *Max*.

Then it actually registers what's happening right now, and I push him off me.

His warm eyes stare down at me, dazed and confused. "What's wrong?"

"You're kissing me."

Max chuckles. "No shit."

"You. Max. My Max."

He nods. "Your Max. Your everything, if you'll let me."

I reach for the scruff on his face, my fingers moving over his unshaven jaw. A small nod is all I can manage, but it's enough.

He kisses me again, maneuvering himself so he's on top of me and pinning me to the couch.

His big body blankets mine, and even though I've been with bigger guys before—who am I kidding, it's my only choice when I'm a short-ass—the way Max feels on top of me is different.

It's as if my soul recognizes his. My heart beats only for him. With our mouths together, our hands exploring, our parallel lives become one and promise to never part again.

Max groans, and his hips grind against mine.

My mind blurs. Between the sensation of Max's mouth on mine, which I'm finding out he really knows how to use, and his hard cock grinding against my hip, it's easy to believe I'm dreaming, because no reality has ever felt this good.

"Bed," Max mumbles.

"Mmm." Apparently, that's all I'm able to say even though I want to tell him to slow down. To savor this. To explore each other in a way we never have before.

Hell, up until I saw him with Jordan, I didn't even allow myself to think of this ever happening.

But here we are, his tender hand running down my side, gripping my hip and squeezing hard.

Next thing I know, I'm being pulled off the couch and up into Max's strong arms as he lifts me. My feet automatically go around his waist and my hands around his neck.

Max moves us about the apartment effortlessly, with his eyes still closed and his mouth assaulting mine.

We move into his darkened bedroom, but the light still filters in from the living room.

He throws me on the bed like I weigh nothing, which admittedly, to Max, I probably do.

Something in the back of my head keeps needing to remind me that this isn't some random guy and it isn't some random hookup.

Max reaches for the hem of his shirt.

"Wait," I blurt.

But his shirt is already over his head and being dropped to the floor.

His brow furrows. "What's wrong?"

"I … I, umm … I'm sure I was going to say something, but now I can't remember what it was." I've seen Max shirtless before. Lots of times. But seeing it and being allowed to look are two very different things.

"Ash?"

I shake my head and force my gaze up to his eyes. Aw, fuck. That doesn't help because it's his eyes that hold the true beauty that is Max Strömberg. "This is weird. You're still Max."

"Does fooling around usually turn your dates into unicorns or something?"

Smartass.

"Yes."

Max smiles.

"No, I don't know. This doesn't feel weird to you?"

"This feels like something I've been dreaming about for six years." His knees hit the bed. A hand lands by my side, and the other above my head until Max is hovering over me but not touching. "You have no idea the things we've done in my head."

"I probably do. My first dirty dream about you was when I was eleven."

"Then how about we make eleven-year-old you happy?" Max screws up his face. "I didn't realize how creepy that would sound until the words were out of my mouth. Eleven-year-olds do not do it for me. Just in case you wanted me to clarify there."

I laugh. "I knew what you meant. But the thing is, I have no idea what does do it for you. We've never talked about sex before. I don't know if you have any kinks or—"

"Hard-core latex fetish," he deadpans.

"I'm serious."

"We've talked about sex before. I told you when I lost my virginity."

"Yeah, and I was totally in love with you at sixteen, so I blocked that out. We don't know each other's preferences, or—"

"Isn't that what we should be doing now?" Max's hand lands on my thigh, and I flinch. Not because I don't like it, but because it's still Max. And this is weird.

Good weird. But still fucking weird.

His hand moves up to my hip. "Exploring? Getting to know each other in a way we never have before?"

I like that. "Who would've thought after twenty goddamn years of friendship, we'd still be having firsts together."

Max leans over me, slowly closing the small gap between us. "I want this to be your last first time ever." His lips land on my cheek. "I want to take care of you. Love you. Claim you and make you mine."

I close my eyes to remember every single part of this moment—the moment my best friend gave me everything I ever wanted. But with one small confession, I'm about to make shit awkward again.

"I don't bottom. Like ever."

Max doesn't say anything, so I start to ramble.

"A lot of people think I do because, well, I'm small and guys still seem to think typical gender roles should belong in a sexual relationship, but—"

Max starts laughing.

"And now you're laughing at me."

"I'm not laughing at you. I promise. I already knew that about you, Ash. We may not talk about sex, but I *know* you. Plus, Ollie might've said something when you two were together. I mean, he didn't come right out and talk about your sex life, but he hinted at your dynamic, and it kinda stuck, because, well, it was about you, and I remember everything about you."

"Y-you're okay with that?"

"I'm willing to explore that. I've done some of my own exploring and don't hate it. Don't know how I'd feel with anything bigger than my finger though. But I want to." Max cups my cheek and lowers his voice to a whisper. "I want to give you everything."

"How in the world did you get to be so perfect?"

He grins. "Easy. I was made to be yours."

In a split second, I fall for my best friend all over again.

Everything happens fast after that. Our clothes are practically torn from our bodies and strewn around the room.

Kisses and more kisses—the best fucking kisses in the world—are shared.

Our naked bodies move against one another and grind, seeking friction and craving heat.

Ash's skin tastes like sweat, and his moans sound like fucking angels singing.

I've wanted this for so long. So fucking long.

We take our time exploring each other, only laughing half the time because while it's so hot, this is also Ash. My best friend from next door.

I remember asking my parents when I was a kid to adopt Ash so he'd have brothers just like I did.

I've wanted to be his forever since I met him. It just took me a long time to realize in what capacity. For a long time, I thought it was brotherly, but I definitely haven't felt for my brothers the way I feel about Ash.

I roll us over so Ash's leaner body is on top, while I continue to nip and suck on his skin.

He runs his hands through my hair and lets out a loud moan of impatience.

Our cocks, trapped in between our bodies, rest against one another, both hard and leaking.

Ash slowly works his way down. Slowly. Agonizingly. Over my pecs, my stomach, then hip until I feel his breath on my cock. "Are you sure about this?"

I chuckle. "If you want to pretend like I've never gotten a blowjob before, we can, I don't care. I just need it. I need you, Ash."

He glances up at me. "You've never gotten a blowjob from a guy before."

"Guys do it differently?" I snark. "Did you learn that in gay school?"

Ash laughs. "No, but …"

"If you don't want to—like, if it's too weird."

"Oh, I want to. So much. I guess I'm worried about you not being ready or somehow taking advantage of you."

I snort. "Sure. Advantage. That's what's happening here."

Ash playfully slaps my chest.

"Now you're beating me up. You're just treating me horribly today. But I totally know how you can make it up to me." My hips shift, bringing my cock closer to his mouth. "Please." I'm so not above begging.

Bright green eyes blink up at me as Ash closes the gap between my aching cock and his lips. The first touch has my whole body trembling. Anticipation fills my veins, and when Ash's tongue sneaks out and licks the head of my cock, the trembling turns to shudders of pleasure.

He teases me with light licks and slow movements as his mouth tortuously covers the length of me.

His light stubble scrapes my skin, adding something I've never experienced before.

How long have I been fantasizing about this happening?

I have to remind myself that Ash Carmichael is sucking my dick.

Nope, that doesn't comprehend correctly in my brain. Over twenty years it took us to get here.

I want him like this for another twenty.

No, thirty, forty, fifty years.

Ash adds a hand, gripping me at the base of my cock and stroking slowly. His masculine, tattooed hand works me over, and who the fuck knew that could be so hot? When his mouth and hand start moving in sync, I know I've reached the point of no return.

My orgasm is coming; it's coming fast.

"Do I need to warn you?"

Ash shakes his head and hollows his cheeks until I spill over. My hand flies into his hair, my hips buck off the bed, and I empty into his mouth.

My whole body uncoils, my muscles relaxing as I sink back into the mattress.

Ash's lips trail my sweaty stomach and chest, and those green eyes pierce straight through me.

Then his mouth is on mine, the salty taste of my release on his lips, and for some reason I find that hotter than any other sexual encounter I've ever had.

I try to think back to another time where a woman has kissed me after swallowing my load, and I don't think it's ever happened before. Is it supposed to be out of politeness or something? Because up until this very moment I didn't realize how claiming it is to taste yourself on someone else.

Ash moves against me, his hard cock dragging against my exhausted one. It wants more of the action that's happening, but I'm too spent.

While Ash continues to kiss me and grind against me, I reach between us and wrap my fist around his cock.

Ash fucks into my hand, but his mouth stays on mine.

Only when he gets close does he break the long and hard kiss. His breathing is ragged, and the tattoo on his neck pulses in time with his rapid heart rate.

"Fuck, Max." Ash thrusts once more before his whole weight drops onto me.

With the hand that's not trapped between us, I stroke up and down Ash's back.

"Well, we've never done that before."

I laugh. "No shit."

He rolls off me and looks around the room with a dazed look in his eyes. I reach for the bedside table for a tissue for him to clean up, and I get what I can off me.

"Stay in here with me tonight?" I ask.

Instead of answering me, he finishes cleaning himself up, tosses the tissue, and curls back into my arms.

Where he belongs.

We wake up late and have to run downstairs to the shop where waiting customers are out front, looking confused.

I thought this morning would be weird, and if I'm honest, I'm kinda glad we didn't have time to dance around each other all morning.

Not that I would. Last night was awesome. I just don't know how he's feeling about it.

Fooling around and confessing feelings that are years old is bound to put some pressure on us. But we don't have time to dwell on it.

Our first break isn't until lunch, but Ash manages to slip out and bring coffee and muffins around ten. I want to pull him close and kiss him, but I have a client in my chair, so I can't.

He leaves it on my bench and gives me a wink as he walks back out.

Concentrating after last night is damn near impossible, but somehow I manage to make it through the day without accidentally tattooing a lifelike cock on someone in the distinct shape of Ash's dick.

Seriously questioning the quality of my last piece that just left though.

Eh, I'll fix it at our next session. It's a big tattoo that will take a few appointments.

All I've been able to think about all day is wanting more of last night. More of Ash. I want to know what it feels like for him to move inside me. I shift uncomfortably as my ass clenches at the thought, but that doesn't stop me from wanting it.

Ash must feel the same way, because when his last client leaves for the day, he turns to me with heat in his eyes. "Do you know how hard it's been to be in the room right next to you all day without being able to walk a hundred feet to touch you?"

"I do know how hard it's been all day. At least, if it's been anything like my day." I step forward and reach for his hand, placing it on my seemingly forever hard cock. "I want you inside me."

"Upstairs?" Ash rasps.

"Cleanup."

"We'll do it later."

We can't run up the stairs quicker if we tried.

Our clothes come off the second we walk in through the front door of the apartment. We paw at each other, removing piece by piece of cloth covering our skin until we're bare and pressed against each other.

Warm mouths exploring.

Hard cocks rutting.

If I didn't want him to fuck me so bad, I could do this until we both came.

"Bed. Fuck. Now."

"Wanna speak in full sentences?" Ash asks.

"I want you to fuck me in my bed right now."

Ash growls and leads me to my bedroom so fast he almost trips over his damn feet. He pushes me down on the bed, and I love it when he acts all strong and bossy.

He makes his way to the bedside drawer. "I assume you have supplies in here?"

"Yup." I lift my arms behind my head and watch as the most gorgeous man ever walks around my room naked. He's lean but toned, and his tattoos practically glow in the dimly lit room.

The way he stares at me, condoms and lube in hand, he owns me with his predatory smile.

I lift my legs so my feet are flat on the bed and spread my thighs.

Ash climbs on the bed in between my knees. His face is intense as he lubes up his fingers and leans over me. It's as if he's studying me for a reaction—good or bad—when he teases my hole.

I can sense his hesitance, just like last night. As if he's corrupting me or some shit. So I reach between us and grab his wrist, pushing his finger into me. I bear down and accept him willingly, my eyes fluttering closed at the initial sensation.

It doesn't take long for Ash to understand I'm okay and he doesn't need to be gentle, and when he adds a second finger and starts pumping them in and out of me, I'm able to let go and just *feel*.

He takes his time opening me, taking extra care to make sure I'm ready.

When his fingers brush my prostate, I cry out.

My toes tingle.

My ass fucking pulses around his fingers.

It's not enough.

"I need all of you," I rumble between heavy breaths.

And when he pulls away to roll the condom on and add more lube, I whine with impatience.

Ash lines up his cock but doesn't push all the way in. Just the tip brings a burn to my ass. I breathe deep, and he sinks inside me a little more.

"You doing okay?" he whispers.

I nod, unable to form words. My eyes squeeze shut.

"Max?"

"Mm?"

"Open your eyes, babe. I want you to see me. What you do to me."

When I do, the completely blissed-out expression makes me relax enough to take a bit more.

"That's it," he encourages.

He pushes in harder, and I call out something so unintelligible I don't even know what it's supposed to be.

He moves in and out of me smoothly. Expertly. He knows how to drive me crazy without pushing me too far.

"Max. Eyes."

I didn't even realize I'd closed them again.

With Ash hovering above me, his cock deep inside my ass, I can't stop myself from cupping his cheek and giving him what he's wanted since he was a kid.

"I want this. You and me."

Ash comes, shuddering inside me. His eyes widen in wonder. He stares down between us where we're still joined and then back up to my face. "Well, that's new."

I can't help laughing. "Coming is new?"

"Coming that early is new."

"Eh. It happens when you're with someone as hot as me. My ass has talents you've never dreamed of."

It's Ash's turn to laugh. "If you say so, but I think we might have to do this again. And again and again and again until I'm desensitized to the amazingness that is your ass. And no spouting shit about giving me everything I've ever wanted. I'm pretty sure that's what tipped me over the edge."

"I'm totally okay with that, but first, do you think maybe …" I glance at my still-hard cock.

"I'm on it." Ash pulls out of me, and I wince, but a second later, he moves down my body and engulfs my cock into his hot, wet mouth and the pain in my ass is forgotten.

"Fuck, yeah. Just like that." I will myself not to come just yet and enjoy this moment, but one look at Ash's wide grin, eyes blinking innocently up at me while his mouth does ungodly things to my cock, and I know I won't be able to hold back.

If he thinks he came early, it's nothing compared to how quickly it takes me to come down his throat.

Moaning and panting, I continue to unload into his mouth while he licks me clean.

When my cock is finally done and it falls from his lips, my grip on him loosens. Ash makes his way back up, leaving small, tender kisses along the way.

"I agree," he whispers, staring down at me. "I want this too."

I wake up to the smell of coffee and cooking bacon and can't help thinking, *Ash is back.* Bacon and eggs for breakfast has always been Ash's way of taking care of me.

When I broke up with Laura—bacon and eggs every morning.

When we first started getting busier at the shop—bacon and eggs every morning. He'd come in early just to make sure I was eating because he knows me, and he knew that if I had stuff to do, I was most likely going to forget to eat.

Ash is fucking back, and not only as my roommate and provider of sustenance, but he's in my bed. With me.

I finally have my Ash.

I untangle myself from the sheets and find some sweatpants to throw on, go to the bathroom, and then head out to the kitchen.

Ash is wearing one of my shirts which is so long on him I can't even tell if he's wearing anything underneath. He doesn't hear me approach and jumps when my hands run up the side of his thighs to find he's not wearing anything else.

I groan into the back of his neck as I plaster my front against him.

"Mm, good morning to you too." Ash relaxes against me.

"Tell me the last two days have really happened," I whisper against him. "I keep expecting to wake up and realize you're still with …" I clear my throat. It's still going to be weird mentioning my brother. It probably will be for a while.

"I would've thought the seven-hour drive to New York and exhaustion from all the orgasms would've tipped you off that it's really happening."

"Hmm, nah, it's the ache in my ass this morning that sealed it." I reach for the burner on the stove and switch it off.

"It's not cooked yet …"

My arms wrap around him tighter, my hard cock pushing against his ass. "We'll come back to it."

Ash spins, and I grip him under his legs. The bedroom's too far, so I lay him down on the kitchen counter.

I stand between his thighs, pushing them apart. Lifting his shirt—no, my shirt—up his chest, I kiss my way down his slim torso.

Never did I ever think I could have this. That this would happen. I want to dive in and take my time. I want to explore every inch of skin I've explored the last two nights all over again, because it wasn't enough. It might never be enough when it comes to Ash.

I move lower. Ash tries to sit up, but I push him back down.

Ash's cock, long and thin, stands tall and hard.

He's already writhing beneath me, moaning small curses as I take it slow and agonizing. Not just for him, but for both of us. I'm loving the way he responds to me but am eager to jump right in.

I tease him, licking the skin below his belly button, over to his hip, down his thigh.

He grunts and whines.

I lift my head. "Stop being impatient."

Instead of being offended, he laughs and mock solutes me. But that doesn't stop him from making impatient sounds or lifting his hips and trying to get his cock near my mouth when I go back to teasing him.

My phone starts ringing in my sweatpants, and normally I wouldn't answer it, but it's so much fun dragging this out. The look on Ash's face when I pull out my phone is priceless.

But then mine probably matches when I see Ma's name flashing across my screen. "Shit. It's the parentals. And it's a video call."

"You can't answer it." Ash shoves my shirt back down so it covers his junk.

"I have to. You know her. If I don't, she'll be here in twenty minutes."

He goes to sit up, but I push him back down.

"I'll be quick. I promise." I hit Answer and hold the phone in front of my face. "Hi, Ma. What's up?" My voice comes out squeaky like it does when I lie or when guilty of something and trying to act calm.

"Oh my Lord, thank the heavens!"

"You don't believe in the Lord or Heaven, Ma."

"Not funny. Are you okay? Is Ollie okay? Where are you?"

"Calm down. I'm fine. Ollie's fine. And I'm at home. Where else am I supposed to be?"

"Leo told me this morning … he told me that you went to talk to your brother two nights ago, and I hadn't heard from either of you yesterday. Where was my phone call? At least you didn't kill each other."

"Dramatic much? You told me to talk to him if anything was ever going to happen with Ash, and I did that. We talked. That's all." I lift my neck and move my face from side to side. "See, no bruises."

"No swings were taken?"

"Thanks to Clark."

"I always did like that boy."

I glance at Ash and grimace. You kinda don't want to hear your ex-boyfriend's Ma prefers the new guy, but I know she doesn't mean it that way. She loves Ash the same as she does me and any of my brothers, but Ash might not see it like that.

"Max?" Ma asks.

My gaze quickly snaps back to the phone. "Huh?" Did she ask something?

"How did the talk with Ollie go?"

"Really well. Umm … actually …" I glance at Ash again, and he nods. "Ash is here with me."

He sits up and puts his arm around my shoulder. "Hi, Mrs. Strömberg."

Her eyes widen in shock, but she recovers well. She especially breaks out into joy when I turn and kiss the side of Ash's head. "Really? You two are …"

We nod.

"We are," I say. "Ollie's not entirely cool with it, but he gave us his blessing." More or less.

Ma's entire face lights up. "We have to have a family gathering. Oh, wait right there, I need to run next door so you can tell your parents too, and eeeeee, this is so exciting!"

So much for getting off the phone fast.

Ma's way too overenthusiastic about this. The picture on the screen wobbles. We get flashes of the floor and then blinding white light. There's the porch. The front lawn.

I shake my head. "She's insane."

"Heard that," she sings through the phone.

She gets to Ash's parents' place and doesn't even bother knocking. "Judith! Where are you?"

A small, tinny voice sounds in the distance. "Kitchen."

"Our sons have news."

"Oh geez," I mumble.

Ash just laughs at the whole thing.

When Ash's mom appears, she stares at us with a confused expression until it clicks. "No. No way!"

"Yes way," Ash says.

"When's the wedding?"

Both of us stiffen.

"Uh, haven't even had an official date yet." My cheeks flame.

"Yeah, but it's not like you two are only dating," Ma says. "You can't. You've been friends forever. This is like starting out in the middle of a relationship."

I swallow hard. "Uh-huh."

Logically I know this, but marriage? My throat closes up at the idea.

There's no rational reason for it. It just does.

But I also know marriage is something Ash has craved for as long as I can remember. He's a romantic. I'm a ... realist.

I guess standing in front of a bunch of people and vowing to love and obey just seems archaic. Why promise something you don't know for sure you can carry out? People change, people grow, and people drift apart. I would never ever think that could happen between Ash and me, but when he and Ollie broke up, I thought there was a possibility I'd lose Ash completely.

I was worried about needing to take sides or Ash being awkward and uncomfortable around me.

That didn't happen, but it would've been easy to.

"No wedding," Ash says. "After Taylor, I kind of have no desire to get married anytime soon. If at all."

My shoulders relax a little at that, relief filling me.

"Exactly," I agree. "So no shoving us down the aisle, okay? We might realize we're better off as friends, or we might not have any chemistry. I love the guy, but maybe we're too close, you know? We need to figure it out without family input."

I'm probably wasting my breath. It's our moms. They're nosy apart and twice as bad when they're together.

"We'll behave," Ash's mom says.

Ma nods in her direction. "She will. I'll try."

It's probably the most I can ask for.

"Thank you. Now we have to go because Ash is cooking me breakfast, and I'm starving." Just not for bacon.

Ma opens her mouth to say something, but I cut her off.

"We love you both, byyyeeee."

I hit End Call, and Ash bursts out laughing.

It's the sound I love the most.

He rests his head on my shoulder, and I can't get over how amazing it is to run my hands over him.

"It wasn't as bad as it could've been," he says.

"You're right. One of us could've had an embolism or something. That would've been worse."

"It wasn't that bad."

"Except they're already planning a fucking wedding."

"Well, yeah, but they were like that with me and Oll—" His mouth slams shut.

There goes the mention of my brother again.

"You can talk about Ollie," I say.

"It's not … weird?"

"Yeah, it is, but I mean, it's bound to happen. And in this context, it's not anything I didn't already know. If you were to talk about sex stuff, I'll probably get a little wigged-out. But it's not as if we can pretend you two never happened."

Ash nods. "Okay, yeah. Well, you know how our moms were with us. I think it put more pressure on us than needed."

"You want marriage though. I know that."

He shakes his head. "With Ollie, I did, but even then … I wonder if I wanted that because he couldn't claim me publicly. Like being married would make our relationship more real when so much of it was hidden. With Taylor, I think I wanted to prove something—that Ollie not wanting to take that step with me didn't mean no one would. I was in it for the wrong reasons. This …" Warm hands take my own and hold them between us. "What we have … or … what I want us to have, is exactly what we've already got. What we've had for years. You're my best friend. You stick up for me. You would go out with me, even to gay bars though you were straight."

"Well, I've never really been straight. Oblivious, maybe. In denial, sure. Never straight."

"My point is you would go outside your comfort zone for me. You once told me that you don't understand marriage, and that you don't think you could ever live up to the perfect couple that is your parents, and I meant what I said on the phone to our moms. After Taylor, I don't know what I want, but I do know what I *don't* want. I don't want a marriage for the sake of being married. I don't want to settle for someone because I think it needs to happen. I want it for the right reasons."

I try to bring him closer, but he stops me by kissing my neck. My cheek.

"I want what you and I have. Whatever it grows into. Right now, I just want to keep exploring this." His hands run down my bare chest.

"Mm, you can explore me all you like."

My skin tingles as his hands move lower, his fingers trailing softly and sending shivers through me. And when his green orbs look up into my eyes, warmth I've never felt fills my gut.

His hand stops at the waistband of my sweats. "I want to suck you."

I push him back down so he's lying flat on the kitchen counter again. "I thought that's what I was doing."

I don't let him fight it. Just lean over him and go back to what I was doing before the stupid cock-blocking phone call. Having Ash under me, in my arms, near me, I can feel his body tremble. I can sense his need. His want.

I want to give it all to him.

I run my tongue down his hard shaft and then tease his balls, licking and tasting him. My experience with guys might be limited, but I don't even care with Ash. I will experiment for as long as it takes to learn his tics, his desires, and everything that turns him on.

My mouth moves back to the head of his cock and sucks gently, just on the tip.

"Fuck, I knew you were a tease, but I didn't realize that meant in the bedroom too."

I pull off him. "Haven't you worked it out yet? It's my life's goal to torture you any which way I can. I'm pretty sure it's the only reason the gods sent me to earth. Operation *Be Friends With Ash For Twenty Years Just To Tease Him For One Blowjob* is almost complete."

He moans. "No more talking. Please."

"Well, seeing as you asked so nicely."

I quit with the teasing because even though it's fun, it's also teasing *me*. My cock wants some action, and I don't know if I'll make it until it's my turn. I reach into my sweatpants and squeeze my dick.

Ash, as if sensing something, lifts his head and looks down at me. "You better not be touching yourself. That's mine when we're done here."

"Then come already."

"Use your hand and work the base in time with your mouth."

Mm, bossy Ash I could get used to.

I do as he says, and everything changes. Ash goes from moaning pleasantly to unable to breathe, letting out needy sounds that only grow with each stroke. Each suck.

A desperate hand grips my hair. "You gonna swallow?"

I nod.

Ash thrusts his hips up once, then twice, and just like that, he crumbles, falling to pieces and calling out my name.

The taste is … weirdly unsurprising, but I can't say if it's good or bad.

When he's done convulsing and I've swallowed everything he's got to give, I kiss my way up his stomach and chest, pulling my shirt all the way back up him again.

He keeps saying my name over and over again like he needs reassurance that I'm actually there. It might take a while for both of us to believe it, but I'm willing to do this for as long as it takes for us to know, without a shred of uncertainty, that we've found our forever person.

"I'm here, Ash," I whisper. "Always here."

"Kiss me?" he asks, and his voice cracks.

"Forever and ever."

ASH

SIX MONTHS LATER

"I can't believe we've managed to avoid this for so long." I nervously stare out at the Strömberg yard from my parents' back porch.

My boyfriend's hands land on my shoulders and run down to my elbows and back up again. The warmth of him against my back helps relax the anxiety growing in my stomach, but it might not be enough.

"You don't have to come if it makes you too uncomfortable," Max says.

"No, I already bailed on going to his hockey game when his team was here. This was bound to happen sooner or later. Maybe we just need to rip off the Band-Aid."

"Or, better idea. We could fake food poisoning and tell them we'll catch them next time they're in Boston."

It's the first time Max, me, Ollie, and Lennon are going to be in the same space together since Max and I got together. Max has seen them on his own, but it's Max's dad's birthday, and his Ma has already ordered we be there.

All of us.

Together.

With the rest of the Strömbergs and my parents.

Fun times.

"Don't tempt me, but you know that excuse won't fly tonight. I suspect everyone thinks you can't cook and that's why I've been mysteriously sick a lot lately."

Like, whenever Ollie happens to be in Boston.

"It probably is time we get it out of the way." Max takes my hand and leads me to the front of the house.

When we were kids, we'd jump the fence between our yards, but we're trying not to draw attention to ourselves. Plus, we're supposed to be adults and stuff now.

We use front doors, my mother's voice says in my head.

Before we can make our way next door, we're stopped by Ollie and Lennon pulling up in a car. Their Uber pulls into our driveway for some reason.

They get out and make their way over to us, each step they take filling the gap between us with tension.

It's like the first time the four of us were in the same space all over again.

It's a four-way standoff.

Max's gaze flicks between me and his brother, I avoid eye contact with all of them and try to pick a spot behind them to focus on, and Ollie's adorably nerdy boyfriend shifts from one foot to the other.

An enema is more comfortable than this.

Ollie's the first to speak. "How are we gonna play this? Go in separately and have everyone staring at us or go in together and present a united front, show them how cool we're pretending to be about this situation, and still have everyone staring at us?"

I meet Ollie's amused gaze. "Tough choice."

"Actually …" Max says. "Ollie, can I borrow you for a moment?"

"And send me in with Clark?" I ask, my eyes wide.

Clark turns to Ollie. "I love that your ex-boyfriend makes me feel so welcome."

"Shit. Sorry. Knee-jerk reaction." I have nothing against the guy other than our abnormal situation.

Clark laughs. "No, I get it. This is fucking weird."

Max pulls me close. "We'll be right behind you. I just want to talk to Ollie for a second."

"About what?" Ollie asks with a furrowed brow.

"About brother shit."

I turn to Max. "Are you really going to make me face your family alone?"

My boyfriend grins. "You'll have Clark."

Ollie snorts.

"Is this some ruse to play a prank on your family?" I ask. Strömberg brothering 101.

Max pretends to think about it. "It wasn't, but *now* it is. You should so turn up with Clark on your arm."

I huff. "Brilliant. Because we haven't caused enough gossip with the Strömberg clan."

"Do we get a choice?" Clark asks.

Both brothers shake their heads.

"There's really no fighting them," I say to Clark and point to Max. "This one is even more stubborn than that one." I point to Ollie.

"Well, you'd know," Clark says.

I have absolutely no idea if he's trying to be funny or is snarking at me.

Ollie bursts out laughing.

"Sorry," Clark says. "This is me when I'm uncomfortable. I

make jokes that are totally funny in my head. Not so much out loud."

"I find them funny." Ollie snickers.

"No, you find my awkwardness funny."

"Isn't that the same thing?"

I find myself smiling at them.

When I first found out about Clark, it was hard for me to accept Ollie had found someone else when he promised he wasn't going to have another closeted relationship.

Now, I can see how genuinely happy Ollie is, and all I have in return is respect for the guy who's making that happen.

"We'll be there in a few minutes," Max says and shoves me toward Clark.

I'd throw him a quip about owing me later, but this situation is already awkward enough. Now's not the time for sex jokes.

Clark and I make our way toward the Strömberg house in uncomfortable silence. So silent, I'm sure I can hear the blades of grass being squashed under our feet.

Over-exaggeration, maybe, but that's how I'll retell this to Max later.

Since when is this walk so long?

"How are you and Max doing?" Clark asks.

"Great." I don't have to force a smile. "You and Ollie?"

"Umm, yeah, really good."

"Cool."

Clark nods. "Cool."

I have to remind myself running for the front door would be considered rude.

"It won't always be this weird, will it?" I ask.

Clark lets out a loud breath. "Fuck, I hope not."

I manage a laugh and stop him right as we reach the porch.

"I think the only way they aren't going to go crazy in there is if we do act like we're completely cool with our situation. Don't treat it like a big deal and they won't."

"In all truth, it's not a big deal to me. I don't know if you've really thought about my position in all this, but I'm happy Ollie's ex has found someone else."

"Even if it's Ollie's brother and that means we'll have to see each other?"

Clark shrugs. "Hey, as long as it's not Ollie. I may not be able to fight, but I'm friends with the Chicago Warriors football team if that's more threatening to you."

I'm going to have to tell Ollie that his boyfriend is adorable when he's trying to be all growly and threatening. "Max is the person I was supposed to end up with all along. You don't need to call your NFL buddies."

Clark smiles. "Good."

"Then there really is no problem, is there?"

"Nope."

"Glad we could settle that. I guess we better get in there."

"Guess so." Clark takes a deep breath.

We walk through the empty house toward the loud chatter in the backyard.

And, as predicted, as soon as we hit the back deck, the first thing out of Ollie and Max's brother Vic's mouth is, "They've swapped again. I'm convinced they're in a four-way relationship."

I give him the finger, because I'm allowed to. I've known these guys for years.

Surprising me though, Clark doesn't shy away. "Jealous, Vic? Maybe you'll be able to hold on to a girlfriend if you had three of them."

The Strömbergs crack up, and before Vic can say anything else, I cut him off.

"You're being nice. That's assuming he can even get three girls."

Vic narrows his eyes. "I don't like you two being friends."

Hey, at least we pull off acting cool with this. I have faith we will be fine in the future, but it'll be an adjustment.

Clark makes his way over to Max's dad to wish him a happy birthday. I'll do that later. I go to the other end of the table where the rest of Max's brothers are.

"Where's Max and Ollie?" Leo asks.

"Max wanted to talk to Ollie about something."

"What?" Nic asks.

"How am I supposed to know? I don't know every single thing that goes on in Max's brain."

"Are you sure?" Vic asks. "I've always thought you two shared a half a brain each."

"At least then we'd have one full brain more than you."

"What is this, pick on Vic day? I'm going to go get a beer." Vic storms off.

Of all the Strömberg brothers, he's the smartass, the thoughtless one, and he often speaks before he thinks. He can dish it out but can't take it. It's why we all target him.

Leo leans in closer to me. "Are you sure it's safe to leave Ollie and Max alone? I don't think that's happened since you two—"

I gesture toward the back doors where Ollie and Max appear. "Does it look like they're trying to kill each other?"

They're both smiling. Ollie locks eyes with me and smiles wider before making his way over to his boyfriend. He says something in Clark's ear, and then even he looks at me and smiles.

I purse my lips as Max approaches and sits in the seat next to me. He leans over and kisses the top of my head.

The whole backyard goes silent as if everyone at the table is holding their breath.

Max and I have been a couple in front of all of them before except for Ollie and Clark. This isn't new. But with the way everyone's eyes flit between Ollie and Clark and then me and Max, you'd think they're waiting for a fight to break out or something.

Ollie breaks the silence in the only way a hockey player with an insane metabolism can. "Is it cake time yet? I'm hungry."

Clark snorts. "Of course you are."

The family lets out a collective sigh of relief.

"Dinner first," their Ma says.

Here's the thing about the Strömbergs: everyone knows if they're quiet, something's wrong. Food is the only exception, so maybe that explains the silence as everyone shovels dinner in their mouths, but I get the sense it's something else.

When the low chatter is absent between dinner and cake, I know there's something up.

I lower my voice and whisper in Max's ear. "I think your family is broken."

"I know," he mutters. "I'm going to fix it." My boyfriend stands. "I have something I want to say."

Oh God, he's drawing more attention to the elephant in the room. That is not how you handle this group of people.

"I know you're all worried what will happen with family gatherings now Ash and I are together."

I hang my head. Can I go hide?

"You don't need to be. Because before I came here tonight, I asked Ollie a kinda important question." Max stares down at me. "I told him that when the time comes, I'm going to ask Ash to marry me."

Both our mothers squeal in excitement.

My mouth drops open.

Max takes my hand and pulls me up next to him.

My heart beats erratically, because as much as I want this, I don't think I'm ready.

And as if reading my mind, Max says, "I'm not going to ask today. In fact, it's going to be a while. The last eighteen months have been filled with confusion and heartbreak and doing the wrong thing, so I'm going to wait until we're both ready for it. But I had to ask for Ollie's blessing today, because I know it is going to happen. One day."

I swallow hard. My best friend is giving me everything I've ever wanted without actually doing anything. The thought makes me laugh.

He's promising me forever but not pressuring me or making me think we have to do it. We'll take this step in our own time.

Max will always be there for me, just as I am for him.

"I always thought our parents were lucky because they've all found someone who doesn't drive them crazy," Max continues.

"Oh, your father does that every day," Mrs. Strömberg says. "But I love him in spite of it."

Max sighs. "It wouldn't be a romantic gesture without input from my *mother*."

"Sorry," she says. "Go on."

"I thought what they had was unobtainable. I didn't think I'd ever find what we have. I've loved you since we were kids, but it hasn't been until these last six months that I've realized exactly what it means to love someone as much as I love you. I used to think love always came with a side of doubt, but I have none when it comes to us. Not anymore. Whether it takes a year or five years for it to happen, just know I'll be asking you to marry me one day."

I try to speak, but only a rasp comes out, so I clear my throat and try again. "Just so you know, when that day comes, my answer will be yes."

Max kisses me our hundredth, thousandth, millionth kiss—I don't know, I've lost count—but the promise sealed in it has my chest filling with the type of love I've been searching for my whole life.

When Max pulls back, everyone surrounds us for hugs and congratulations even though we're not actually engaged yet.

Ollie steps up to us and hugs us both at the same time.

"You're really okay with this?" I ask.

"I didn't even get the whole question out before Ollie told me to go for it," Max says.

"It's still weird," Ollie says, "but I'm genuinely okay with it because I've assumed this would happen as soon as I found out how serious Max's feelings were. You want to get married, and Max will give you anything you want. It's a no-brainer."

"And you have Clark," I say. "Who's pretty cool, by the way."

Ollie glances over his shoulder. "Yeah, he is."

Max nudges his brother. "When are you two gonna get married?"

Ollie grins. "We've spoken about it maybe, possibly, being a future thing, but dunno. We're in no rush."

Well, at least that hasn't changed. It wasn't until we broke up that I began to see Ollie's promises of marriage in the future as something to placate me and our mothers. I don't think he ever wanted it.

Ollie's eyes meet mine. "I'm happy you found someone who can give you everything you ever wanted."

"Same to you." And I'm being completely honest.

I've thought a lot over the last six months if I would've done anything differently and wondered what would've happened if Max had told me how he felt in college.

It's hard to believe things happen for a reason when today has been one of the most awkward in my life, but I also have to have faith that everything between me and Max happened the only way it'd work out.

Because of Ollie, and because of Taylor, I know the only reason to get married and pledge my life to someone is because of bone-deep love. Not because I'm owed it. Not because I want to prove something.

Marriage to me is something to honor and cherish.

And Max is the only man who has ever come close to that.

Max is mine, and I am his.

Forever and ever.

THANK YOU

Thank you for reading *It's Complicated.*

WINNING YOU

FAKE BOYFRIEND 4.5

PREMISE

Marty:

The only reason I'm at this charity raffle is to win the music festival tickets I've been chasing for months. Yeah, I'll have to go on a date with whoever the other winner is, but it's a price I'm willing to pay to meet my future husband—Jay from Radioactive.

Only, when I come face to face with my date, I'm not sure the tickets are worth it. The guy has a permanent scowl on his face and insists on calling me a kid.

I'll admit he's alluring for someone who's rude and grumpy, but no. I'm here for Jay. I will not fall for the tall, hot, older guy.

Luce:

The kid's sass almost makes me want to change my original plan of ditching the date as soon as we get to the festival.

I may have had ulterior motives trying to win these tickets, but it's obvious the same goes for Marty.

The easiest thing to do is split up.

Then how do I find myself buying him dinner and hanging out with him?

If I knew how much this guy would change my life in one night, I might not have been so surly to him when we met.

Now I don't want to let him go.

Winning You, while set in the same universe as the** *Fake Boyfriend* **series, is set in Australia and uses AU English. It is technically a prequel to** *Hat Trick, Fake Boyfriend book 5,* **but** *it can be read in any order.*******

1

MARTY

Desperate times call for desperate measures. Radioactive is playing at the Joystar Music Festival, and I'm skint. Serves me right for doing the whole PhD thing. I'm supposed to be smart and shit. Obviously not too smart considering I'm twenty-three and can't even afford a concert ticket. Hell, I could barely afford the cover charge to this event tonight.

After weeks of scouring eBay, Gumtree, and Melbourne buy-swap-sell groups on Facebook for tickets, I've got nothing. I can't afford an actual ticket, let alone a scalped one. Even if I found the money for a real ticket, the festival is completely sold out now.

That's why I'm at the Heart2Heart charity event, hoping to be set up on a blind date with someone else who wants to get free passes to Joystar—the last tickets available *anywhere.*

Of course, that's if I even win the date. A mate who works here slipped me some extra raffle tickets, which I promptly dumped into the festival giveaway, but it still might not be enough. A whole heap of prizes were donated by local businesses, and everyone else seems to be spreading their luck around on different date options—the more expensive and elaborate dates like hot air ballooning or deep-sea diving—but that doesn't stop me from glaring whenever anyone puts one in Joystar's box.

"Need another drink, Doc?" Gray asks from behind the bar.

"Yeah, thanks."

The nickname annoys me—always has—but this guy is practically family to me. He's buddies with my brother and completely straight, but he works here because he says he gets better tips than at a straight bar. It works well for me because I get free drinks.

The Doc nickname started when I got accepted into the accelerated science program in high school. What else are people going to come up with when I've been on track to get my PhD in molecular engineering since I was fifteen? Doesn't help I was named after the main character from *Back to the Future*.

The argument that Marty wasn't the physicist in the movie makes people call me Doc even more. Or nerd. Although, the only people who call me a nerd are my very best friends or family, because I may be shorter than average and on the skinny side, but I've been told by dates repeatedly that I'm way too pretty to be smart.

Thanks … I think?

I down the rest of the beer in my hand just in time for Gray to give me a new one.

"You nervous?" he asks.

"I'm nervous I'm not going to get the passes. I *need* to go to this show."

Gray leans on the bar. "Do you really think the lead singer's going to look at you and fall in love?"

"Yup."

"You realise if you do win, you need to take your *date*? Hope he's a Radioactive fan. What if he drags you to the other stages?" He gasps. "He could like EDM."

"Shouldn't you be working?" I grumble. If the date likes EDM, he's on his own.

Gray snickers. "The raffle's about to start, so good luck. Hope you and Radiohead are happy together."

I grit my teeth. He knows it's Radioactive, not Radiohead. He's trying to get a rise out of me like always. Instead, I flip him off and rejoice at the retreating sound of his laughter as he goes to serve someone else at the other end of the bar.

Radioactive aren't big in Australia yet—they're a relatively new band out of New York—and the only reason I know of them is because I saw a video on YouTube and fell into an obsession.

I listen to them when I study, when I work out, when I sleep … basically, they're all I listen to.

The obsession is deep with this nerd.

The raffles start getting called, and everyone else seems more in the spirit about the whole thing than I am. They all look excited with love hearts in their eyes when they meet their dates. I should feel guilty about being here for the wrong reasons, but … it's *Radioactive.*

My heart leaps into my throat when the festival date comes up. First name: not mine. I get a sinking feeling in the pit of my stomach that they're gonna Primrose Everdeen me. Someone with only one entry will win it.

The first guy takes to the stage, and I've already forgotten the name that was called, but he's the epitome of tall, dark, and handsome. I'd totally volunteer as tribute to climb that.

He's wearing a tight T-shirt, loose jeans, and muscles. No wait, he's not wearing muscles, his muscles are wearing him.

The only downside of the look is it's completely ruined by a backwards baseball cap.

Seriously? Where's the class?

A burp flies out of my mouth, and all I taste is beer.

Oh, right. Ain't no class here either.

I'm so busy checking him out that I don't hear my name being announced until Gray shoves me from behind the bar.

"You got it!"

I won? Holy fucking shit, I won.

I'm one step closer to Jay falling in love with me.

2

LUCE

The guy who's supposedly my date for the night bounds up to the stage in an excited ball of energy. Almost to the point he looks like that cartoon Tassie Devil going a hundred miles a minute. While cute, his floppy light-brown hair and black polo shirt make him peppier than a One Direction concert. Shit … he's probably younger than all the 1D boys.

Kill me now. He looks about fifteen years my junior. This … *kid* isn't going to want to go on a date with me.

Jesus H Christ, when did I get old?

Maybe since working nonstop after graduating high school? Paying your dues, working your way up …

I shake that thought free and grab our tickets and tram passes as we're sent on our merry way to the sound of cheers and applause. Some of the dates up for grabs don't take place until next week, but ours is one of the few that start right now.

"I'm Marty," he says when we step outside.

"Luce."

"Loose? Not really a great name if you're a bottom."

I come to an abrupt stop on the sidewalk, wondering if I heard him correctly. Who says shit like that? Then I look him over again, from head to toe, and realise teenagers say that kind of shit. "L-U-C-E."

"Oooh. My bad. Is that short for something?"

"For something," I mumble and keep walking.

"What is it?" His legs are about half the size of mine, so his strides are fast and bouncy, which makes him look like an excitable puppy.

"My personal assistant doesn't even know my full name, so you've got Buckley's, kid."

It's his turn to stop walking. "Kid? How old do you think I am?"

"If you weren't in a bar just now, I would've said ... seventeen? Are you even old enough to vote?"

"Man, I'm twenty-three, but I don't know whether to kiss you or tell you to fuck off."

"Bullshit you're twenty-three."

Marty pulls out his wallet and shows me his driver's licence. Well, shit. He's twenty-four in a month.

"Are you sure this isn't a fake ID?" I ask.

"Trust issues much?"

Another card in his wallet catches my eye. "University of Melbourne. That's the fancy school in Parkville, right?"

Marty snatches his wallet back off me. "Geez, didn't your mother ever teach you not to snoop?"

"Why are you still at uni if you're twenty-three? Shouldn't you have graduated last year?"

"Bitch, I graduated three years ago, got my master's at twenty-two, and now I'm in a PhD program. What have you done with your life, old man?"

Old man? I have to hold in a laugh, because he's even

cuter when he's angry. I'd like to dispute what he said, but I feel a hell of a lot older than I am. The greys in my hair don't help. Hence the baseball cap. I haven't had a chance to dye my hair recently, and until this afternoon, I had every intention of blowing this charity event off. But I need these festival tickets.

I grunt. "I'm not old. I'm thirty-two."

"Look, I have a proposition for you. Obviously, you think I'm too young, and I think you have too much arrogance going on. How about you give me my ticket, we'll part ways, and then maybe we can enjoy the show as singles?"

My eyes narrow, and I realise he was never here for the date. I'd be offended if I wasn't here for the exact same reason.

I split the prize and go to hand over his passes but don't let go. "You just wanted concert tickets."

Marty's mouth drops open as if forming an excuse, but nothing comes out. I can't help noticing his plump lips.

When I cock my brow at him, he scowls and snatches his ticket from my hand.

"That may be true, but I was at least open to going on this date until you opened your mouth."

"You're dismissing me because I said you look young? Fuck, I'm a monster. Are you even gay? Or are you some straight boy trying to score free tickets?"

"Did you seriously just accuse me of faking being gay for festival tickets?" When he storms off, I can't help following.

He had no intention of going on this date, yet when I call him on it, he's the one who's pissed? For some inexplicable reason, I find his attitude funny and a tiny bit adorable.

"Throwing a hissy fit doesn't really have the desired effect if you're both going the same way," I say and try not to smile.

"Hissy fit this." Marty throws up his middle finger.

That just entertains me more. "Are you *sure* that's not a fake ID?" I taunt. "What with your stellar maturity and all …"

I expect him to get more pissed off. Instead, his feet falter and I hear the most heartwarming laugh I've ever heard in my life.

"I don't think anyone has ever called me out on my shit before. Most guys would've let me run off."

Most guys are idiots.

"How is it possible you've never been called out when you have such a stunning personality? What kind of people do you hang around?"

Little dimples appear in Marty's cheeks. "Molecular engineers, mostly."

Damn, the kid *is* smart. "Ah, so you all got picked on at school and don't know how to smack talk each other?"

"Hey, I never got picked on at school. I was on the rugby team."

This guy? With his skinny frame and being so … vertically challenged? Not that I'm complaining about his tight little body, but rugby? "*Seriously*?"

"No, dude. Look at me! You know what's worse than being a nerd growing up? Being a gay nerd. High school was not fun. Adulthood hasn't been much better, but at least I have the balls now to tell people to fuck off if they're a wanker."

Meaning me. I think I've been so removed from social situations I have no idea how to behave like a normal human anymore. My entire life since leaving school has been about proving to my mother that I don't need to go to university to be successful. I was stubborn with a one-track mind about working and making a big name for myself. And what do I have to show for that? No social life and an empty, but fancy, apartment. Yay, middle management.

"I'm sorry."

Marty's eyebrows shoot up.

"For being a wanker," I clarify. "And for what it's worth, you certainly don't look like a nerd now. You're gorgeous."

He stares at me as if I've been smoking crack.

"I mean, you're still young, but gorgeous."

"And we're back on the young thing. Just when I thought we could turn this conversation around." He walks faster, but I keep up.

"Wanna know what my first thought was when you took to the stage? You know, apart from *get this guy some ADD medication, stat*."

He doesn't say anything, but his lips quirk as if trying not to smile.

"First thought was that you are way out of my league. Young, hot, and fun. Everything I'm not. I'm in my thirties, look like I'm in my forties, and I work eighty hours a week. It might've made me defensive from the beginning."

Marty slows to another stop and just stares at me. His eyes are soft, but his lips are pursed, and I don't know what he's thinking. Then his eyes roam over me, agonisingly slow, and I feel his gaze as if it's burning my skin. Vulnerability seeps in, and I run my hand over the back of my neck. The move makes his eyes catch on my arm and the muscles there. I may work a lot, but hitting the gym in my apartment block is the way I de-stress after a long day.

A tram heading for St. Kilda pulls up to the stop ahead of us.

"Is that …" I point.

"Shit, that's the one we need." Marty legs it to the platform, and I'm right behind him.

I'm met with his smug smile as he settles into the last available seat. It's one of the sideways facing rows, right next to the standing section.

With a sly grin, I ask, "Isn't it customary to give up your seat for the elderly?"

Marty lets out more of that amazing laughter but doesn't move.

"All right then. I'll just have to stand here." I step forward and reach for the bar above my head, knowing it puts my crotch right in Marty's face. Maybe this will get him to move.

I stare down at him and pretend I have no idea why his cheeks are suddenly pink, and he licks his lips as if his mouth is dry.

His really pretty mouth.

I forgot the worst part about cockteasing someone is it backfires. My dick generally wants in on the action too. Instead of being put off by the growing bulge in my jeans, Marty smirks.

Then the fucker looks down at his shoe. "Damn. My laces are undone."

They're so not undone.

He keeps his eyes trained on me as he bends forward, reaching for his shoe. That pink tongue darts out again, licking his lips, and his mouth is so close to my groin, I can practically feel his breath on my cock.

A growl rumbles loud in my throat.

Marty's shoulders bounce as he laughs. "Sorry, I need to tie my shoe." His shaggy hair lightly brushes against my thigh as he "ties his shoe."

"Fuck," I mutter and take a step back.

Marty grins up at me. He has to know what he's doing. Those lips, his head so close to my cock …

"You're the devil." Which is funny coming from me.

"I have no idea what you're talking about." He sits back in his seat again and has the gall to wipe his mouth suggestively, which makes my cock even harder.

"Smug kid."

He shakes his head. "We've already established I'm not a kid."

"According to your birthdate. I'm still trying to figure out if your shoe size is a more accurate comparison to your age."

Marty bites his lip as if he's trying not to smile, and either the older woman next to him is disgusted, or takes pity on my cock tenting in my jeans, but she gets up and moves towards the door of the tram.

I immediately throw myself into her vacated seat, and when I think it must've been a coincidence and her stop is next, she sends a glare our way as the doors open and she rushes off.

I tsk him. "Corrupting little old ladies. You should be ashamed of yourself."

"You're the one who put a cock in my face."

"Didn't hear you complaining."

"From what I could see, there wouldn't be much to complain about." The challenge in Marty's compliment isn't lost on me, and I'm reminded of how much fun it can be to flirt.

I check my watch. We've still got a while on the tram, and I'm going to make the most of it.

"So, who are you excited to see?" I ask. "At Joystar?"

"Radioactive." The name flies out of his mouth without so much as a thought put behind it.

I try to place the band, but there are more than seventy acts performing over the course of the weekend. It takes a few minutes, but then—

"Small American band? Mix between rock and grunge? Lead singer is gay …" I don't know why that detail seems important right now.

Marty pulls back in shock. "You've heard of them? None of my friends have heard of them! They don't get my obsession. And Jay is not only gay, he's my future husband."

That makes me laugh. "Wow, you *really* didn't want this date, did you? Apparently, you're already spoken for."

He sees my amused expression and rolls his eyes. "He just has to meet me."

He might have a point. Marty definitely has an alluring quality to him.

"So, are you gonna tell me your real name yet?" Marty asks.

"It's Lucas."

He narrows his eyes. "I call bullshit."

"You're calling bullshit on my name? The origin of Luce is Lucas."

"You said no one knows your real name. If it was something normal like Lucas, you wouldn't keep it a secret."

"Damn smart people," I mumble. "Maybe Lucas is my dad's name and I have daddy issues."

His eyes do the scrutinising thing again. "Nope. Not buying that either. Is it Lucille? Naww, Lucy!"

"I wish it were Lucille."

"Come on, it can't be that bad. Can't be any worse than being named after Marty McFly."

My entire face lights up. "No way."

"Way." His lips form a thin line and his forehead scrunches in concentration. "Hmm … is it Lucius? I know I wouldn't want to be named after a villain in *Harry Potter*."

I nod. "Yup. There you go. You guessed it. I, uh, hate that Lucius character."

Marty cocks his head this time. "And which character is he?"

"The one with no nose?" My voice cracks, and Marty's eyes widen.

"You don't even know *Voldemort's* name? What kind of grown-up are you?"

"Uh, one who doesn't watch kids' movies?"

He gasps. "You refer to them as movies and not books? I … and … you … I can't … I can't even."

I chuckle. "That's good, because our stop is here."

And playtime is over. Now that I'm here, I have something I need to do.

3

MARTY

As soon as we step off the tram and begin to make our way toward Catani Gardens where the festival is held, Luce flips his baseball cap around to the front.

Because in his mind it's cooler? I guess?

I don't have the heart to tell him he should lose it altogether, but then again, it seems whenever I give this guy attitude, he thrives on it and shoves impressive appendages in my face.

And for some inexplicable reason, I don't find that as creepy as I should. In fact, I find it so far from creepy, that old lady is lucky she didn't get an even more explicit show on the tram.

His dismissive attitude over my age still pisses me off, but it's almost refreshing in a way. A lot of older guys love having a young twink-looking guy on their arm—to the point where it's annoying, even. They want me to be the pretty thing to play with and don't expect me to have a voice. They generally lose interest once I open my mouth.

We arrive at the entry gates, and Luce follows closely

behind me. Almost too close. His hand goes to the small of my back as if this were a real date.

After showing our lanyards to security posted out front, Luce puts distance between us again.

"So …" he says. "I guess this is where we part."

Even though it was my idea to go our separate ways, I thought, maybe, that our little tram encounter might've changed that plan.

Obviously not.

"Oh. You're … so we're … okay …" *Tongue and mouth, get it together! A normal sentence would be good right about now.*

"I wouldn't want the lead singer to think you're taken." He winks.

Damn him.

It's not that I actually think Jay from Radioactive will give me a look-in, let alone fulfil my fantasy of jumping off the stage and dropping to one knee to ask me to marry him on sight. I mean, the hope is there, but I'm not delusional, and I thought Luce and I … I thought we might've been able to scrounge up a real date in between the bickering.

"Sure," I say with what I hope is a nonchalant shrug. "Wouldn't want him to think that. Well, you know where I'll be hanging out if you want to come find me later."

He nods. "I'll do that. I just wanna go check out the main stage first, but I'll meet you. I wouldn't mind seeing your man play."

When he teases me about Radioactive, it doesn't piss me off like when my friends do it. It's more like he's playing along with me and entertaining the insane notion that rock stars fall for their fans mid-concert all the time.

I watch as he walks away, and my gaze gets stuck on his

tight butt in those expensive designer jeans. Then I stare down at my cheap clothes and realise …

I'm young *and* broke. He's so not gonna come find me.

It seems stage three is where they send all music to die, and after only an hour and a half, I pray for a zombie apocalypse to break up the concert. Right now, I'm not sure if Radioactive is worth it.

They so are, my stupid brain reminds me.

Unlike stage two, which is all EDM, and stage one, which is where all the big headliners are performing, stage three is a mixed bag of *Please, can I cut off my ears?* and *How the hell did you get a better stage time than Radioactive?*

When a band called Rabid Skunk takes the stage, I know I need a break.

I sacrifice my great view near the front—there's no way I'll survive until Radioactive's call time—and make my way through the small crowd of people who are high, drunk, or both.

Stage three is right near the food vans, and the smell coming from the trucks reminds me I didn't have dinner tonight, so I peruse the row of fast and greasy food and settle on ordering a dagwood dog.

The noise in this part of the grounds is a hell of a lot quieter. Or I've gone deaf. One or the other.

As I round the corner to find a place to sit, I put the phallic-shaped fried food to my mouth and freeze at the sight of Luce leaning against one of the food trucks and peering around the other side as if hiding from someone.

Then he turns and sees me, his mouth opens in surprise,

and his eyes focus on the stupid sausage shoved halfway down my throat. His face hardens, but not in an angry way. His gaze burns with heat I can feel from here.

I bite off a piece and chew, talking while my mouth is full. "I was hungry."

"Hungry for what?" he growls.

I chuckle. "Guess these things do kinda look suggestive."

"*Kinda*?" His voice has a weird shrieky thing going on. "It should be illegal for you to eat one of those in public."

"Everyone or just me?"

"Definitely just you."

I step forward. "That mean you like what you see?"

Luce sighs heavily and looks around the corner of the van again.

"Who are you hiding from?" I ask.

He flinches. "I, uh … umm. I'm not hiding."

"Liar."

"Okay, I'm hiding. Come 'ere."

I approach, and he lowers his voice.

"Can you go out there and see if there's still security guys hanging around?"

"What did you do? Maybe I don't want to protect a fugitive."

"No, it's nothing like that. I just … umm …" He hesitates, as if debating whether to tell me the truth or a lie. "I used to date one of them, and he got all stalker-like, and I'd prefer not to see him right now. Or all of his security buddies."

Well, shit. I know what that's like, thanks to a crazy stalker date I met on Grindr once. Called the cops on him and everything.

"Say no more." I tilt my head around the corner and see

two burly shadows coming this way. "Uh, don't know what to tell you, man, but you might wanna run."

The figures of the security guards also leave me disheartened. Clearly, if one of them is his ex, Luce is into buff and bulky guys. I only go to the gym the bare minimum of twice a week, when my brother practically drags me.

"How close are they?" Luce asks.

I peek again. "Umm, like you have three seconds to get out of—"

Luce grabs my arm, and I drop my food on the ground as he spins me. In a swift move, he throws his cap underneath the wheels of the van and then pins me up against the side of the food truck and presses his insanely delicious body against mine.

That's not a problem though. The problem is his wet, hot mouth covering mine in a searing kiss that feels more than a ploy to shield his face from his ex-date-guy-whatever.

It comes out of nowhere and takes me a few seconds to get my bearings. My tongue licks the seam of his lips on its own, I swear, and even though the small gasp that comes from Luce is from shock, my tongue totally thinks that's an invitation for more. Yep, my tongue. Totally separate thing from my brain. Not my brain at all.

Actually, I think my brain has completely melted by this point.

He smells like expensive aftershave and mint.

Footsteps crunch on the grass and then head away from us, but Luce doesn't stop kissing me. In fact, he presses against me more and grinds that impressive cock against mine. Back on the tram, I could already tell he'd be huge and he was only at half-mast. Right now, it feels like he has a steel bar between his legs, and mine's in a similar state.

His tongue expertly massages mine, but when I groan, it's as if he snaps back to reality.

Luce pulls away but stays close enough that we share shaky breaths.

"That tasted better than my dinner," I say and pull back a fraction more—giving us just enough space to see my discarded food on the ground at our feet. "Which is lucky, because it's ruined now."

"I'll buy you a new one," Luce says.

Good, because I spent my last ten bucks on that thing. I don't say that aloud though.

"Do you think they're gone?" he asks.

"I want to say no so you'll kiss me again."

The grin that takes over his face is nothing less than breathtaking. This man should always look that happy. It suits him more than the judgemental guy I met earlier. "The sassy kid knows how to flirt."

I grit my teeth. "Call me a kid one more time …"

Luce screws up his face. "I guess it's not the most attractive thing to call you. Especially when I want your lips again so damn bad."

I give him what he wants and press my lips to his for a quick, chaste kiss. "Mmm," I hum when I pull back, "the old dude is a sweet-talker. Hey, is that grey hair I can see?" Reflexively, I reach up and run my hand through his hair, which definitely has grey streaks mixed with dark. It makes him look distinguished.

"I am not old." He swats my hand away. "I started going grey in my twenties. Genetics suck."

"Of course, you did … *old man*."

"*Kid*."

We both wince.

"Permission to stop with this weird-ass creepy role-playing thing now?" I ask.

He laughs again and pulls completely away. "Agreed. So, dinner?"

My stomach beats me to replying by rumbling loudly.

4
_____

LUCE

Maybe I've lost my mind, because this isn't me. I've always chosen work over anything else. The end of my last relationship five years ago proves that. He left because I never made him a priority.

Yet here I am, following a cute guy and buying him dinner when there's other shit to be done. On my list of priorities, it should be: stay away from security—none of whom I've ever dated. I lied about that. Second should be finding a way backstage so I can fix the clusterfuck my second-in-charge has created since I was kicked out of here this afternoon.

This festival was supposed to be Australia's Coachella, but with how it's going, we'll be lucky to get another year out of it.

Amanda had promised me she knew what she was doing. The bigwigs of the label forced me to take the weekend off even though I'm the one who organised this whole damn event.

No way was I staying away, and now that I'm here, I should want nothing more than to storm backstage and take over—fix the mess Amanda made. Acts are going overtime, the changes between bands is way too fucking long, and from what I can see from the sidelines, none of the bands or their management are happy. This is my baby—the thing I've worked on for eighteen months straight. When I was told I couldn't work this weekend due to contract law and doing so much overtime that my salaried hourly pay rate had fallen below that of a sweatshop worker, the first thing I'd thought to do was go to the Heart2Heart charity event to win the tickets I'd donated under Joystar Records' name to get back in here. Morally grey area, maybe, but I'll be sure to make an extra donation to Heart2Heart to make up for it.

Mum calls me a workaholic, but that has negative connotations. I don't think there's anything wrong with being invested in your work. That's what separates you from the rest of the pack trying to get ahead.

The festival is falling to pieces in front of me, but all I can think about is buying Marty some food and hopefully getting to experience his mouth again.

One kiss has me knocked for six. Up is down, left is right, and the world spins the other way now. No one has ever kissed me like that before.

Is it possible for one kiss to cause a lobotomy effect?

At least I don't have to worry about the food side of the business. It's running smoothly, if a little busy, but that means more revenue. And I don't think anyone knows how long the wait or how shitty the food is when they're all wasted.

Near the front of the line, I turn to Marty. "Are you sure you want another dagwood dog? I can't guarantee it won't end up on the ground again. Especially if you wrap your mouth around it the way you did before."

The innocent smile he sends my way isn't fooling me.

"You'll just have to keep buying me one until you can restrain yourself."

The alcohol van catches my eye, and I grab out my wallet. "You want a drink too?"

He stares at my wallet and then at me, and he bites that lip I'm quickly becoming obsessed with. "Dinner and drinks?" he asks. "You trying to win back brownie points for being a dick earlier, or you trying to get me to put out?"

"Would that even work?" I ask.

He hesitates just a fraction before leaning in and whispering, "After that kiss? I don't even need the dinner."

Oh, holy mother of hell. Where did this guy come from?

I have to restrain myself from throwing him against the side of another food truck.

"Get what you want, but can you grab me a Jack 'n Coke?" I hand him a crisp hundred-dollar bill.

"I can get anything I want?" he asks. "The most expensive drink they have?"

"That'll be the cheapest beer on the market with how much they mark up in these places, but sure."

He laughs. "Okay, I'll be back soon."

When he turns and walks away, I realise his ass is just as tempting as his mouth.

We take our food and drinks to the stage three field where my ears are assaulted by a horrible band with a screeching lead singer.

"What the fuck?" I mutter.

"I know, right? How did these bands get stage time over Radioactive? It's been shitty act after even shittier acts. I guarantee whoever organised this thing is deaf or has never heard these bands play."

I would be offended—hell, I *want* to be offended—but he's

right on the money. I'm not deaf, but I haven't heard every band I booked. I looked at sales, social media followers, and tour schedules before booking them, and then I chose their stage time accordingly. I guess this is a good lesson in knowing quantity of fans doesn't always equal quality of music.

"Maybe we can find a patch of grass toward the back where we can't hear them so ..." I try to think of the perfect word because *loudly* doesn't seem to cover it.

"So our ears won't be murdered?"

Perfect. "Exactly."

Marty and I sit on a small hill, a fair way away from the lights, the people, and the sound coming from stage three. I have to look the other way while he eats his food, because I know if I don't, I'll run the risk of pouncing on him.

The cool night air blows past us, but it's refreshing. From back here, the festival doesn't appear in shambles. It's a perfect night weather-wise, the loud cheers filter through the dark, and I can smell a mix of beer, grass, and the smoke coming from the allocated bonfires.

God, the arguments I got into with the bosses over those damn bonfires. Safety hazard, insurance premiums, permits, wah, wah, wah. They provide ambiance, dammit, and I wanted them.

Can't really think of a reason why now, seeing as I'd never planned on enjoying them like this.

"Dinner, drinks, and what some people would call music," Marty says. "Looks like we ended up going on the date we won after all."

The date neither of us wanted. Yeah, I'm so not telling him that after I was an ass about him coming for the wrong reasons. I'm just as guilty.

"So, tell me," I say, changing the subject, "what's so good

about Radioactive?"

"What's *not* good about them?" Marty's face lights up, and he starts rambling about how the band changed his life. "Jay's lyrics are so relatable. It makes all the bullshit seem okay, because it's not just you going through it, you know?"

"You sound really attached."

Marty shrugs. "Haven't you ever been that invested in a band or a piece of music? Or something that makes you feel like you aren't alone, even though you are?"

His passion doesn't fill me with warmth like it probably should. It fills me with a sense of longing which makes my chest ache. I hate it. The intense fandom he has for this group of people he's never met makes me remember why I wanted to get into the music business.

"Yeah. I know exactly what you mean." Even if I haven't felt that connected to music in a really long time. Working in the industry has ruined it for me. It's *work* now. Not an escape like it once was.

I want to feel Marty's level of excitement about music again. Not only because it makes my life seem empty to be without it, but the way Marty sells it, it looks really good on him. I've never seen someone glow from talking about music —the thing I claim is my life.

"My first cassette—"

Marty coughs the words "old" and "man."

"Ignoring that. The first cassette I ever bought was Pearl Jam."

"Eddie Vedder is sexy."

"I was ten."

Marty shrugs. "I was in nappies."

"Fuck." I laugh. "Anyway, they were kind of my gateway drug into that nineties, grungy-pop genre. Nirvana, Green

Day, Sister Hazel, Counting Crows, U2 …" They're the reason I do what I do, but the enjoyment is gone.

"Yet, you know who Radioactive are but have never heard them."

"How do you know I've never heard them?"

"Because when I talk about them, you have nothing to say. You look at me like my friends do when I talk about them—like you want to pat me on the head and tell me I'm precious. Like it's cute to be this obsessed over something, but you don't actually care."

My lips quirk. "What if I'm just mesmerised by you and can't find any words to say?"

Marty pulls back, with an almost shocked expression clouding his face. "Wow, you're really trying to get lucky tonight, aren't you?"

"One hundred percent serious. I love how animated you are about this stuff. It … well, shit, I'm only going to sound older now, but it reminds me of when I was a teenager."

"I'm not a fucking teenager," he says.

"I know. That's not what I meant. I meant I haven't felt that way about *anything* since I was a teenager. When I left school, my life became about proving myself to the world, and when you're too busy trying to build a life, you don't get much time to actually live one. I'm envious you were able to hold on to your passion."

Marty stares blankly at me for a few seconds, as if trying to figure out why in the hell this random guy on a random first date would bare his soul, but when he blinks out of his wonder, he reaches into his pocket and pulls out his phone, and then he grabs his earphones out of his other pocket. "I want you to listen to something."

"Okaaaay." As I put the buds in my ears and Marty loads up a song, the opening rifts pull me into another mind. Another life.

And it's sad and happy and bittersweet all at the same time. To have no support and to be alone, and then finding that one person who fits into your life perfectly and makes everything better.

A lump gets caught in my throat at the raw emotion, and I can see why Marty is in love with this band. When the song ends, I reach over and tap his phone so it repeats.

Marty doesn't say anything, because he understands.

After the second time, I take the earbuds out and hand them back, but I have no idea how to put in words how touched and affected I am by the song.

I go for the best defence mechanism and misdirection technique known to man: humour. "Sounds like your man's already taken."

"He's single."

"You said they write their own songs, right? That song is way too personal to be made up."

"I've tried stalking online and have read everything I can on the song, but no one knows who it's truly about, and the band hasn't said anything publicly."

"Ooh, *intrigue*."

"I suspect Jay suffers a broken heart—that it didn't work out with the guy from the song—but it'll be okay, because I'll be there to mend it."

I know I'm supposed to laugh again, but I can't bring myself to do it. "And what do you think your man will say if he finds out you've been kissing a much better-looking guy tonight?"

Marty shrugs. "Have to kiss some toads before I meet my prince."

There's that damn mouthy attitude that I somehow find charming.

"I'm pretty sure if you kiss toads, you hallucinate. They have that poison-y thing on their back. I think you mean frogs."

He nudges me, and the spark of humour in his eyes does things to me. "You'd so fit in with my friends, Mr. Useless Trivia."

"I'd … uh, say the same about you if I had any friends." And isn't that fucking sad?

"You? The guy who refuses to tell anyone his real name and within minutes of meeting me said something offensive has no friends? *Shocking*."

I finally find my laugh. "Hard to believe, I know."

A silence falls between us, and I have to avert my gaze from his scrutinising stare. The truth is when work and sleep take up ninety-five percent of your time, friends drift away. It's a fact of growing up … or so I thought.

Marty makes me question everything about my life, which is intense for a guy I met only a few hours ago.

His gentle hand slips into mine. "I'm not completely delusional, you know. I know Jay won't see me from the stage and know we belong together. I just thought I'd clarify in case you think I'm batshit crazy or something. It's a fantasy. I came for their music."

"And you got stuck with me tagging along."

He leans in so slowly his breath becomes warmer against my skin. In whispered words that send a shiver right through me, he says, "*Stuck*? I prefer to think of it as I found you instead. Someone who appreciates Radioactive? Hottest.

Thing. Ever."

A tortured groan flies from my throat as my dick thickens, and I take the opportunity to close the short distance between us. My mouth meets his, and just like the kiss we shared earlier, I might've been the one to initiate it, but Marty takes over. Being with a guy who knows what he's doing and takes control is a definite turn-on. I'm in control at work all day every day. I want to come home to someone who'll take the decisions out of my hands and take me the way he wants.

I cup Marty's face and pull him closer, my tongue seeking his in a sloppy and wet kiss that's all parts consuming. Between my heightened emotional state because of the song, and the way he's appreciative of my reaction, we get lost in each other, our mouths exploring until it gets to a point where it's not enough. My hand wanders and slips under his shirt, and I'm surprised to find hard muscles along his abs.

I pull back, breathing deep. "Do all molecular engineer grad students have tight abs?"

"I kinda feel like molecular engineer and the words *tight abs* shouldn't be in the same sentence." Marty chuckles. "Did I mention my brother is a personal trainer?"

"Guess we know where all the brains went in the family," I joke.

His eyes widen. "Thank you! I say that all the time, but apparently it's mean to point out the truth."

I shake my head. "You really are something else."

I don't give him a chance to respond, and instead, I lie back on the grass and pull him on top of me. Our mouths come back together for more of his talented tongue.

My cock is hard, pressing against the fly of my jeans, and just the pressure of Marty on top of me has the ability to get me to the edge. If he were to start moving, it'd all be over and the rest of the concert would be pretty damn uncomfortable.

Which is why I run my palms down his back and slip my hands into the waistband of his jeans to cup his firm ass. It's supposed to keep him in place, but all it does is make my hips pump upward. And when he moans into my mouth, I swear I almost come.

It's been way too long.

I almost don't care if I'll have to clean myself up with my underwear and then dump it and go commando, because at this point, it feels way too good to stop.

At the sound of cheers and a wolf-whistle, followed by a deep voice saying, "Oh fuck, it's two guys," I break away, and my head slams back on the grass as we're brought back to reality. I wasn't really thinking—getting so hot and heavy in public, even if we are in a quieter area.

I gently move Marty off me and to the side opposite the three guys who interrupted us in case there's trouble, but they move on with one of them giving an apologetic stare at his drunken friend's comment.

I let out a breath of relief. "My place is a five-minute walk away."

Marty's brow furrows as he stares toward the stage and back again.

"Right," I say. "How could I forget about your prior engagement with your future husband."

He bites that lip again, and fuck, he doesn't even know what that does to me. Or he does, and he's doing it on purpose. "They're still not due to go on for an hour and a half. You said you live five minutes away?"

I've never gotten up faster in my entire life.

5
———

MARTY

The walk is five minutes if you have legs as long as Luce. It takes almost ten with me trying to keep up with the giant pulling me the whole way. By the time we arrive at his apartment block, which had obviously been a single mansion at one point that's been turned into individual dwellings, I'm panting as if I've already gotten off.

Should've brought my asthma puffer.

Yeah, because that's so sexy …

No sexier than the wheezing I'm doing right now.

This totally wasn't the plan for tonight, but I can't bring myself to be upset about that. I already thought Luce was hot *before* he got choked up listening to Radioactive. I saw the moment it clicked for him—the moment where I just *knew* he understood like I did. There was no keeping me off him after that.

As soon as the door to his apartment is closed, Luce is on me again. His mouth and strong hands—he exudes sex and confidence, and I'm putty under his touch.

His lips trail down my neck, and I can't breathe, but I don't know if it's because of him or still my asthma. When his hands cup my ass, and he grinds his hard cock into me, I know without a doubt my breathing problem has nothing to do with needing Ventolin.

As if he's magically sprouted limbs, I feel Luce's hands all over me, while the close embrace of his arms surrounds me with warmth.

His mouth sucks and teases my skin, finding its way back to my lips.

Luce's chest rumbles, deep and sexy-like. "Bedroom." It almost comes out like a choked garble.

"Would be handy to know where that is," I point out.

He pulls back. "Right."

Without warning, he picks me up and tosses me over his shoulder.

Instead of protesting about my legs being in working order, I go a different route. "I demand this is how I travel from now on. My feet shall never touch the ground again."

Luce swats my butt. "There's that sass again."

"I'm beginning to think you like my sass."

"You're wrong. I *love* your sass."

He throws me down on the bed and then stands at the foot of it, slowly removing his T-shirt and then unbuttoning his jeans.

This is the part that's always awkward. The whole … which goes where, what's off limits, what you like, and if there's anything worth sharing—like *Surprise, third testicle.*

"How do we … uh, I mean … are you, you know—"

Luce smirks. "All I've been thinking about all fucking night is that pretty mouth of yours. I want your lips wrapped around my cock. If you're okay with that, then I'll let you do whatever the hell you want to me afterwards. Fuck me, rim me, demand I suck you off … hell, mug me for all I care—"

I laugh.

"I just want this." His hand cups my face while his thumb brushes over my lips.

I give it a small nip before kissing it.

His breath hitches.

Scooting my way to the edge of the bed, I pull Luce's jeans down his legs and look up at him.

"I'd be lying if I said I hadn't been thinking about doing this ever since you shoved your impressive cock in my face." My voice takes on a raspy sound I've never heard come from my lips before, but with the way Luce's eyes fill with heat, I guess it turns him on.

I skim my fingertips over his hard length with light touches.

A large hand fists my hair. "No fucking teasing."

His gruff, demanding voice makes me shiver in anticipation. I like it when a guy gets bossy, so long as he knows I'll tell him to go fuck himself if I don't want it. This though? Luce fucking my mouth until I choke on his dick? I can't wait.

I circle his tip with my tongue before engulfing the whole thing to the root.

He gasps. "Holy fuck."

Don't mind surprising guys with my deep-throating skills either. It usually takes them off guard. I like taking a guy to the back of my throat until my eyes water and they can't restrain themselves.

Seeing a guy lose control and knowing I'm the one making him go bananas is the hottest thing there is.

Luce's hips thrust forward, making his cock go a little too

far, so I grip his ass cheeks and dig my thumbs into his hips so I have more control.

He mutters my name so loud I almost lose my rhythm, because there's affection in his voice that doesn't belong in a hook-up. This should be fast and hard, and instead I find myself slowing and staring up at him while I continue to move my mouth over his velvety tight skin.

He senses the change from rough to gentle, and the hand gripping my hair loosens and travels to the side of my face. That damn caressing thumb softly trails over my cheek in a loving manner, and the admiration and awe in his gaze makes my cock harder than when he was trying to shove his dick down my throat as far as it could go.

"This is better than I anticipated," he whispers. "I don't think I'm going to last long."

I nod and my cheeks hollow as I suck harder, because I'm unwilling to pull off him even for a second to beg him to come in my mouth. Luce throws his head back, and we moan in unison when the first spurts of his release hit my tongue.

Salty musk fills my mouth, and my own dick responds by leaking precum into my boxers.

"So good," Luce murmurs, his legs trembling until his cock falls from my lips. He climbs on top of me, pushing me onto my back, and his lips skim my cheek until his mouth is next to my ear. "Now, how do you want me?"

Unintelligible mumbles fall from my mouth. When he laughs, I shake my head to clear it. I manage to get out, "How about on your hands and knees?"

"Mmm …" Luce's hands skim over my polo. "Right after I get you naked, first."

"That'd help," I quip.

He pinches my side with a laugh, and I love that it's

playful between us. Some guys are so serious in bed, it feels clinical and all about getting off. I like to have fun with sex, because that's what it's supposed to be.

I also love that he's up for anything, and I want nothing more than to get inside his ass.

Luce undresses me, and I can't bring myself to help him. It's way too hot watching him do it for me. Muscular arms yank at my clothes, and before I know it, I'm spread out in front of him, completely bare.

He takes my nipple into his mouth and hums around it. "I know you said you want my ass, and I promise you're welcome to it, but I want to play first."

"Who am I to deny playtime?"

With a grin, Luce moves down my body, kissing and tonguing my abs and belly button, then down the thin trail of hair leading from my navel to my groin. He avoids touching my cock though, with his hands or mouth, and I want to cry. Instead, a whine comes out.

He nuzzles me as his tongue darts out and licks my balls. "You smell delicious."

I want to joke about showering helping with that, but when he moves to take the head of my dick into his mouth, I know he's not talking about the freshness of my skin. He licks at the precum pooling in my slit and moans as if being served a gourmet meal. The vibrations from his mouth go straight to my balls, and I know if he doesn't stop, there'll be no chance to fill his ass, because I'll be too busy coming down his throat.

"Wait, wait, wait." I grip his hair and pull him off me. "You're way too good at that."

"No such thing."

"There is when I want this to last."

"Fine." He climbs off me and goes to his bedside table to

pull out lube and a condom. "But I think you're forgetting I'm nine years older than you. I need more recovery time, and I wanna feel good while you're inside me."

I send him the cockiest smile my face owns. "I'll get you there, baby."

He looks sceptical, but I'm determined to get him off again. He climbs onto his hands and knees, and I tease his hole and balls with my mouth and coax him back to hardness. I take my time adding lube and pressing my fingers into him, because I want this to be good for him too. The break from having any attention on my cock is what I needed to calm down enough so I won't be so quick on the trigger, but that doesn't mean I'm not achingly hard.

By the time Luce is writhing against my fingers, his breathing ragged and his hands fisting the comforter, he's begging for me to fuck him. I rubber up and add more lube to my cock, but as I push against his hole, a hand reaches out for mine.

"Just … it's been a while … okay?" He sounds unsure now it's my dick and not my fingers.

"I won't hurt you," I promise him.

He nods and releases me, and as I slowly enter him, I feel him push against the intrusion and hold his breath.

I lean forward and kiss between his shoulder blades. "Breathe," I whisper.

"I'm okay," he croaks. His head drops, and I feel the tension ease below me.

Starting small, I rotate my hips in short thrusts. His breathing picks up, and his body accepts me willingly.

The tightness surrounding my cock is almost too much.

"Fuck me," he begs.

"Can't. Too tight."

"I'm okay now." His voice is breathy, and it does nothing to calm my racing heart and throbbing dick.

I grit my teeth. "I'm not."

He laughs, and I feel it all the way up my dick as his body shakes.

"Not funny," I say, but now I'm laughing too.

Luce pushes back against me, and I groan. I reach around to stroke his cock and find him hard as granite. I slide in and out of him in time with my hand pumping his dick.

"God, you feel good," he mutters.

"Ditto. Best. Date. Ever." The saddest thing is I'm not even lying.

A few more thrusts and neither of us can talk anymore. It's all moans, grunts, and loud breaths as we chase our release. I try to hold out for him, but I know it's imminent.

He pants in between trying to talk. "I'm gonna go … any … minute."

"Thank God. Take me with you," I plead. "Send me over with you—"

Luce comes on a shout, covering my hand with cum while his ass milks my dick. It tightens around my cock, and I thrust in and out a few more times until I have absolutely nothing left.

He collapses onto the bed, forcing me to pull out of him. The sight of his used, slicked-up hole makes another ripple of pleasure shoot through me, and when he rolls over and stares up at where I'm still resting on my knees and leaning on the heels of my feet, his flushed face and happy smile make me come even more.

Tenderly, Luce reaches for the condom and removes it, tying it up and throwing it on the floor beside the bed. Then he reaches for tissues on the bedside table and cleans his cum off his chest and my hand.

"Come 'ere." He throws the used tissue on the floor and beckons me to lie on top of him, where I fit perfectly on his chest, my head below his chin.

"The old guy's a snuggler, huh?" I can't help myself.

A meaty hand pinches my ass, and I'm working out that's his go-to move when I'm giving him attitude.

"Back in my day, it was customary to snuggle after sex."

I snort. "Back in your day, you also had to walk fifteen miles to school barefoot, right?"

"In the snow," he mumbles. "Can't forget the snow."

Silently, we catch our breaths and calm our racing hearts. A content feeling I've never experienced after sex makes me want to not get up. Ever.

"It's Lucifer," he eventually says.

I pull my head back and stare up at him. "What?"

"My real name is Lucifer."

That content feeling? Kinda gone. Fear of having come home with another crazy person tries to take over it. Maybe I'm a psycho magnet.

It's hard to tell if Luce is serious or not, but his grimace doesn't imply he's joking. He's waiting for me to respond, but I have no idea what to say to that. If I ask if he's joking and he's not, that's gonna suck.

I swallow hard and try to make a joke. "Was this some sort of sacrificial virgin ritual? Because I have bad news for you. My virginity has been non-existent for a while now."

He laughs. "Damn. There goes my master plan for world domination. Like Hell isn't hard enough to control."

I purse my lips. "How … I mean, how is it even legal to have the name Lucifer?"

Luce's hand runs through my hair and cups the side of my head. "My mum had planned on calling me Lucas, but when I put her through forty-eight hours of labour, she decided Lucifer was a better fit. She still uses the excuse that she was high on pain relief when she filled in the birth certificate forms. Pretty sure I'm the reason you're allowed to change your kid's name for free within the first twelve months of birth now."

I try to hold in my amusement, and he must sense it.

"It's okay to laugh. It's a horrible name."

"Why do you go by Luce now and not Luke or something close but more … normal-ish?"

"Punishment," he says with a smirk. "Mum hates it, but I always ask her how she thinks I felt growing up with the name Lucifer."

"Why didn't your dad stop her?"

He shrugs and pierces me with stormy grey eyes that make his greying hair shine in the dark. "Never knew him. It's always been just me and Mum."

"I'm sorry, Satan."

Again, with the pinching.

"Stop pinching me." I laugh. "If you keep doing it, I'll start spouting random sarcasm if someone pinches me. You know, like Pavlov's dog."

He cocks his head. "Do you have a lot of people pinching you?"

"Maybe I do … maybe I don't …"

Luce runs his arm down my bare, sweaty back. "We should get up and go before we miss your man."

"Few more minutes."

And even though we have every intention of doing just that, I don't realise when sleep pulls me under, because I'm too warm, sated, and happy lying in Luce's arms.

6
LUCE

I wake to an incessant buzzing with light streaming through my windows and a warm body against me. It takes a while to get my bearings, but when I do, I know I've fucked up.

"Shit!" I hiss.

Marty mumbles and rolls away from me.

"Shit, shit, shit, shit, shit," I whisper to myself.

He missed his band—the whole reason he put himself through the awkwardness of a horrible blind date. He's gonna hate me when he wakes up, and that's the last thing I want.

I don't know if it's Marty or the fact I only realised last night how truly lonely I've been lately, but I do know I want to see him again. That's not gonna happen when he'll blame me for screwing up his chance to see Radioactive live.

My stomach churns knowing he'll wake up soon and realise what happened.

Pushing myself out of bed, I find my phone in my discarded pants. I have a gazillion missed calls from Amanda.

With a sigh, I pull out a pair of fresh sweats and head for my kitchen. Coffee is needed before dealing with work.

Once I'm settled at the dining table with a cup of adulting elixir, I hit the Dial button on Amanda's number.

"Where have you been?" she screeches. "I've been trying to call all morning."

"All morning? It's seven a.m. on my forced days off that you only have yourself to thank for." Okay, so coffee isn't helping me act human just yet.

"We need you to do damage control, because—"

"Because you fucked up and a whole heap of shit went wrong. I know. I was there last night, watching."

"And you didn't do anything?" she screeches again. "Why not?"

The smile that spreads across my face is involuntary. "You wanted to handle it yourself, and you got your wish."

"You do realise this looks bad on both of us?"

I shrug, even though I know she can't see me. "I met someone who made me realise there's more to life than work."

The line goes completely silent.

"Are you still there?" I ask.

"Who are you and what have you done with the real Luce?"

"Funny."

"We need your help."

The urge to say yes and take back my baby is almost over-powering, but then I think of Marty lying naked in my bed and the conversations we had last night about music and the way I miss having that connection to it.

"Nope. Mandatory days off."

"Luce," she whines.

"Maybe you should've thought of this before you went to our bosses and got them to take me off the festival."

She's been gunning for my job ever since I was given it. This was her perfect chance.

"I'll tell you what," I say. "I'll help you do damage control with all the bands when I get back to work in two days *if* you give me the number we have on file for Radioactive's tour manager."

There's a small pause. "Radioactive?" She has no idea who they are.

"They're an American band who played stage three last night around three a.m."

She sends through the details, and I get to work on making something else right before I fix work problems.

Look who's learning shit about prioritising.

———

My heart thumps loudly against my rib cage as I stand at the foot of my bed, watching Marty sleep. Then I think about how creepy it would be to wake up to that, so I place my peace offering cup of coffee on the bedside table and climb into bed with him.

"Marty?" I whisper and pull him close.

He keeps sleeping. Guess he's a heavy sleeper.

"*Marty*," I say a little louder.

He throws his arm around me and then a leg, clinging to me like my very own koala. "I don't wanna get up," he mumbles. But then, as if he realises the same thing I did when I first woke, his eyes widen. He sits up and looks around the bright room, and his shoulders slump.

"I'm so sorry," I say and sit up next to him.

I'm expecting him to reject my embrace as I wrap my arms around him, but he welcomes my touch. Thank God.

"We fell asleep," he says.

"Wow, you really are smart, huh?"

He doesn't respond, and I realise now's not a time for jokes.

"I'm so, so, so, so sorry," I say again. "You can yell at me, or—"

"Wait." He turns in my arms. "You think I'm mad at you? I'm mad at myself. Not for coming back here or doing … what we did. I don't regret that at all. Just, I wish I hadn't fallen asleep."

Relief washes over me, and I lean in and kiss Marty's temple. "I have a plan to make it up to you."

"How?"

"So, uh, first of all, I need to confess something."

"Uh-oh."

"Coffee first?" I hand him the mug from the bedside table.

"Thank you." After Marty takes a few sips, I continue.

"You know how I gave you shit for not going to the Heart2-Heart benefit for the right reasons?"

He eyes me suspiciously. "Yeaaaah."

I raise my hand. "Guilty."

"What do you mean?"

"I work for Joystar Records. I organised the entire festival, and at the last minute—"

"*You're* the reason Radioactive had a shit stage time?"

I laugh that the first thing he thinks of is the band, not that I'm a liar. "Guilty again. In my defence, you were right about me not hearing any of those bands play before. I worked on stats—sales, online presence, and followers. If I'd heard them …" Last night would've been organised way differently.

Marty's brow furrows. "I don't understand. Why did you need to win tickets if you were running the whole thing?"

"My second-in-command stabbed me in the back and took over on launch day. That's the real reason I had to stay away from security. I didn't want Amanda to know I was checking up on her."

"You … and …" The adorable little scrunch in his brow doesn't waver. "But …"

"Spending the night with you made me realise how obsessed I can be about work. I ended up forgetting all about it when I listened to you talk about Radioactive and how much you love them. Which is why I feel like a total shit for making you miss out on seeing them perform."

Marty cracks a small, but fake, smile to placate me. "It's okay. They'll be back another time." His tone betrays his words, because we both know a small international band like Radioactive won't be coming back unless they make it huge.

I lean in. "You gave me something last night. You reminded me why I got into this business to begin with. I want to discover new bands and help guys like Jay from Radioactive make it big. The way their music speaks to you … I want to give that to people. It was my original plan until I got stuck climbing the corporate ladder. I haven't felt your type of passion for my job in years. *Years.* I've been wasting my life."

"You're welcome? I think?"

I cup his gorgeous face. "I've found a way to say thank you properly."

His eyes light with heat and mischief. "Is it you bending over for me? Because I'm pretty sure you nailed that last night."

I chuckle. "Because of my co-worker running my event into the ground, I have to do some sucking up to some bands. Guess who we get to go visit in their hotel room in about one hour?"

Marty's face drops and his expression turns cold-sober. I thought he would be excited, but he looks like he could puke. "Are … are you shitting me right now?"

I shake my head.

"You're … you're gonna take me to meet Radioactive? *The* Radioactive?"

"*The* Radioactive. Only, I have one condition."

"Anything," he blurts.

"When Jay falls at your feet in love with you the second you step into that hotel room, I'm kinda hoping you might tell him you're dating someone?" My voice cracks like a preteen, and I have to clear my throat.

I might be mistaken, but I swear Marty's cheeks pinken.

"Well, I did spend a fun night with a pretty awesome guy. I'd love to see him again."

"Then you better get dressed, baby. Because I'm about to make your biggest dream come true." When I pull away and get out of bed, he stares up at me with glassy eyes.

"You're really not shitting me about this?"

"Deep-seated trust issues?" I ask with a small smile.

"No, I don't think you understand. This … this really is making my biggest dream come true. If you're not shitting me, there's a good chance I'll propose to you on the spot."

I laugh. "How about a second date first?"

"Deal." Marty's grin lights me up in a way no one else ever has.

For the first time in so long, I have something to look forward to. My mind races with plans and ideas of where I can take my career now. I don't want to be bogged down in events management when I should be doing something where I can make a difference.

Maybe band management.

Marty's made me rediscover that side of myself, and I'll be forever grateful to the guy who showed me my love for music isn't dead.

"I'm glad I won you," I say.

Marty's lips twitch. "Well, I am an awesome prize," he says dryly.

But little does he know, he's probably the best prize I've ever won.

7

MARTY

Oh my God, oh my God, oh my God, I am not standing in front of Radioactive's hotel room. I can't be. Someone pinch me.

"Hey, Luce? You're a dickhead."

Instead of doing what I want him to though, his brow creases like he can't tell if I mean it or not. "Umm …"

"I'm trying to get you to pinch me, because this has to be a dream. Did you drug me last night, and now you're doing God knows what to my passed-out body while I hallucinate all this?"

His stormy eyes shimmer in amusement. "You don't sound too upset if I actually did that."

"Dream Jay, real Jay, I don't care. Although if this is a hallucination, I'm gonna be pissed when I come to."

"Can I knock yet, or you need a minute?" Luce smirks.

I let out a big breath and mutter to myself. "Okay, Marty, this is it. I won't ask anything of you again. Just, for once in your life, be fucking cool." I turn to Luce. "I'm ready."

"Nice pep talk."

I ignore the mocking tone and smile. "Thanks."

Luce's arm comes around me. "One thing first."

His mouth descends on mine in a kiss hotter than any of the ones we shared last night. Either that, or my memory is already failing me and dimming the explosiveness that was yesterday. I definitely remember Luce's mouth being mind-blowingly awesome, but this awesome? I'm not so sure.

He tries to pull back, but I don't let him, following with my mouth and kissing him harder.

But Luce forces our lips apart and then smiles down at me. "I'd say that should hold you until the Jay mania dies down."

I still can't believe I'm going to meet *the* Jay, and that Luce is making it happen.

"You know, when he falls at my feet and worships the ground I walk on, I could totally ask if he'd be up for joining us." I'm only kidding … well, half-kidding, and I have to hold in my amusement at Luce's frown. "Dude, I'm joking. I promise I won't hit on Jay. Fanboy, sure, but I meant what I said last night, I'm not delusional."

Luce huffs and pulls me against him tight. "You don't get it, do you?" His voice tickles my ear, and I suppress a shudder. "You joke that it'd be impossible for someone like Jay to fall fast and hard, but you have this charismatic energy that's impossible not to be drawn to. I know because I witnessed it last night, and now I'm wondering if it's a really stupid mistake to let you in there."

"*Let me*? I don't know whether to be pissed or turned on right now."

Luce laughs. "Figure it out and let me know. I like you just as much when you're argumentative. It will make for an inter-esting day."

The door opens and a guy in his forties with a grumpy face

stands there staring at Luce and me wrapped around each other.

Luce clears his throat and steps away from me. "Wayne?"

"Thought I heard voices out here," the guy grumbles. "Coming in or what?"

Pleasant guy.

We follow him into the suite with a small sitting area and a king bed in the one room.

There's a lump in the middle of the bed—a shirtless lump with shaggy dark hair over his face.

Holy shit, Jay is, like, right there. Asleep. Lying on his stomach and … okay, that kinda looks like drool coming out his mouth, but who cares. He's *Jay.*

The dimples right above his ass crack peek out the top of a blanket, and oh, how I wish the blanket was an inch or two lower.

"I'm Luce Riley." Luce holds out his hand towards the old guy.

Wayne ignores it and moves to the bed to smack Jay's ass. "Hey, fuckboy, get up."

Did he just call him "fuckboy"?

Luce looks just as confused. This is supposed to be Jay's tour manager, right?

"It's fuckin' early," Jay moans and rolls onto his back. "Because ya know, we went on stage late, the roadies set up our equipment wrong, so our instruments were fucked, we got booed off stage, ain't got much sleep, and now your sleazy-ass voice is in my ear. Leave me alone."

I have to hold in squeeing like a groupie. I don't even care his words are hostile, his Southern accent is too much.

Luce clears his throat.

"Suits from the label are here," Wayne says.

I scoff at the suit comment because I'm in my clothes from last night, and Luce, while in suit pants and pressed shirt, doesn't exactly look like a stuffy suit type.

Until I study him closer and realise, actually, yeah he does. He looks like the guy I met last night with the uptight vibe. I wonder if I'm only seeing him in the post-sex, laid-back way because I've seen Luce drop his guard. He should drop it more often, because he's so damn gorgeous. And hot. And distinguished.

I'm too busy staring at him that I miss Jay get out of bed and slip on pants. My eyes catch on the small patch of fuzz above his cock as he pulls them over his hips.

Motherfucker.

Would it be considered rude to ask him to rewind and do that again so I don't miss the good stuff this time?

The rock god stalks towards us, tight muscles on his thin frame and a delicious V peeking above low-hanging sweatpants.

Yep. This can't be real.

When I drag my eyes up to his face, I take it back, because fantasy Jay would never scowl like that.

He throws himself on the small couch and looks up at his manager. "Go get Benji. If he's not in his room, try Freya's because they think they're being sneaky about their hook-ups, but they totally suck at hiding it."

"Why don't you get off your lazy ass and go get them?" Wayne asks.

"You're our tour 'manager,' so go fuckin' manage."

Wayne grumbles something about a spoiled brat as he leaves the room.

Jay glares after him. The Jay I've built up in my head is nothing like the real Jay, and that's something I don't want to accept. I can't accept it. This guy has gotten me through so much shit.

So instead of acknowledging the hostility, I play up the dumb guy people seem to assume I am before I talk. I gasp. "The bassist and drummer are doing each other? Oh my God, that's so adorable. Though, I was kinda hoping Benji played for our team, but this could be even cuter." I even bounce on the balls of my feet for good measure.

Jay narrows his eyes. "Are you sure you're from the label?"

Luce smiles but tries to contain it by rubbing a palm over his jaw—clearly seeing through my charade. "I'm from the label. He's …" He glances at me. "My assistant. Marty."

I don't know if he omitted the fact I'm his date for my stupid fanboy dreams or if he did it for professional reasons, but if it's the former, it only makes me want him more.

Jay nods. "Makes sense. No one important at the label seems to have any love for us." He looks at Luce. "I bet you didn't even know Benji or Freya's name."

"That's true," Luce admits, and I admire him for telling the truth.

That doesn't stop me from coming to his defence. "He did know you're from New York, that you're gay, and he knows how many followers you have on Twitter."

"Fifteen point nine thousand," Luce supplies helpfully.

"Wait …" I say. How is that possible? "That seems really low. Like, my friend has a skateboard-riding pug who has over thirty thousand followers, and that's only like … three-quarters of the talent Jay has."

Jay bursts out laughing. "This guy for real?"

I frown because I can't determine his tone. The laugh seems genuine but his words harsh. "Yes, I assure you I exist." I gesture to my body.

Jay rolls his eyes. "Not what I meant. But good to know I'm slightly more talented than a dog." Finally, I get a bit of a playful vibe, but I'm still not sure.

"Dude, have you ever skateboarded? That pug has skills."

He breaks into a grin. "Talk to me when he plays a guitar."

"Oh, I'm so all over that." I take out my phone and start texting my friend to get a photo of his dog with a guitar.

"Are you here to drop the band, then?" Jay asks Luce. "Send us out of the country and then tell us to find our own way home or what?"

Luce takes the seat opposite Jay, while I remain standing to the side.

"The opposite," Luce says. "First, I'm here to apologise for the fuck-up that was last night. That was on me—"

"No, it wasn't," I argue. "It's on that co-worker who tried pushing you out."

Luce holds up his hand to stop me. "Thanks for defending me, but I organised the event. It's on me even if I wasn't allowed to be there to fix it."

Jay cocks his brow and glances between me and Luce. "So first the apology. And then?"

"Secondly, I want to talk to you about your management team, because Marty's right. You should have more followers on Twitter. And Instagram and Facebook and YouTube. You should have more exposure. You guys are so fucking talented, but you've been overlooked by the label. They've done a lot of things wrong, but probably the worst is assigning you *that* for a manager." He gestures to the door where Wayne left. "He shouldn't be treating you like a rent boy."

Wait … did I miss something?

Something flashes in Jay's eyes, but he schools it. "That's

what happens on tour. People get lonely." He shrugs. "It's not a big deal."

Whoa, he's fucking the surly, older guy? How did Luce pick up on that?

Maybe while you were ogling Jay's half-naked body.

Oh, right. Point.

Luce shifts uncomfortably. "Kinda is a big deal. Especially if you're not really into it?"

"He's not forcing me to do anything."

"You're not exactly pleasant with each other. Doesn't seem like a healthy relationship, especially between manager and lead singer. I literally spent thirty seconds with you guys and picked up on that."

"Anyone would. Wayne is a dick," Jay says, his tone dripping with *duh*.

I can't help myself. "So, you're voluntarily sleeping with him even though he's a dick?"

"You know, he could be fired for even going there," Luce says.

Jay sighs. "I don't want him fired, but as a manager he is super sucky. He says our music isn't good enough to hit number one and it's our fault the first album didn't do well. But that's not anything different to what the label is telling us too."

"Yet, you still slept with him," I say, still not understanding it. Why sleep with someone you hate and who treats you like shit?

"Momentary lapse of self-esteem. Benji and Freya are drama central, and I hate taking sides. When they get along, I hate being the third wheel. Wayne's there when Benji and Freya aren't. It's just sex." He shudders but scratches his shoulder as if trying to blame the disgust with an itch.

"Sounds more like regret than sex. Sex is supposed to be fun."

Jay glares at me. "Thanks for the insight. Are you even old enough to be having sex?"

Luce practically chokes trying not to laugh.

"Shut up, you," I grumble at him and then turn to Jay. "Oh, I'm old enough. And also flexible enough. Just ask him." I nod in Luce's direction.

Luce immediately stops laughing now.

There's nothing funny about Jay's pissed-off scowl. "My manager can't fuck me, but you can fuck your assistant?"

"He lied," I say. "I'm not his assistant. I'm just a fan."

I hate that I'm disappointed. Jay doesn't seem like the guy singing his songs at all.

"Let me get this straight. You come to my hotel room to apologise for messin' up last night by lyin' and telling me the label doesn't care about me." Jay stands. "Well, this has been fun, but I think it's time for y'all to leave."

Okay, admittedly I melt a little at *y'all.* So bloody adorable.

Luce stands too. "Jay, I've seen the ugly side of this business. I've been in it for fifteen years and worked in a lot of different departments. You might've only caught my attention last night, but thanks to this guy"—he gestures to me—"you're now on my radar and I want to fight for you. If you'll let me."

Jay's hesitant, his eyes flicking between me and Luce. "Benji and Freya too?"

"Yes!" I blurt. "Sorry, Luce. I know I can't tell you how to do your job, but they can't be left behind now I know they have something going on. I need to follow this like a soap opera. You're never getting rid of me now. You're my connection to Radioactive."

Luce smiles at that. "Then I guess I better do everything in my power to show the label they need to treat the next big thing better."

"Ugh. Happy people," Jay complains. "You two look at each other like my brother does with his husband."

Luce cocks his head. "How so?"

"Sooo in love," Jay says. "It's disgusting."

My heart sinks. "You don't believe in love? What about the song?"

"Song?"

"'*He's Mine*'!" I exclaim. "It's about the love of your life."

"Common misconception. That song is about my brother."

I screw up my face. "Eww."

Jay rolls his eyes. "My brother and his *husband*."

I deflate even more. "Oh. That's less incest-y, so yay."

"'Hat Trick Heartbreak' pretty much explains my love life if you wanna look it up."

I gasp. "No way." That song is upbeat but so fucking sad.

"Unfortunately. But I am impressed you know of it. The only evidence of it is a shaky video from a show we did in Ohio."

I start singing. Badly. "*Chasing a dream I want to be real. A heart I'm gonna steal. You fit the mould. The perfect hat trick. But you slipped, and then you flaked. Now you're nothin' but my hat trick heartbreak.*"

I've stunned Jay speechless by my lack of talent, I know this.

Still, his lips twitch. "That was … uh … I think that's the first time a fan has ever sung me my own words, so thanks for that. I guess."

Luce chuckles quietly.

"Hey, I'm a genius. Smart people can't sing."

"And now you call me dumb." Jay sighs wistfully. "If only you were single."

Luce winks at me. "Told you that you could win him over, hon."

I want to groan. I suck at humaning. This is not how my meeting with Jay was supposed to go.

"Talk to your bandmates," Luce says to Jay. "If you want me to fight for you, I'd want to sign on as your manager."

"And I should trust that you'll do a great job even though it was your event that tanked last night? I should trust you to keep it professional when you burst into my hotel room with a fan who"—Jay glances at me—"doesn't seem like a fan at all?"

Yay me. I've reached a new level of Marty-ism.

"You don't need to trust me at all," Luce says. "All you need is to ask yourself if I can do more for you than Wayne can."

Jay stands and offers his hand for Luce to shake. "Easy answer. We're in. Benji and Freya hate Wayne more than I do."

Luce shakes his hand but holds it before he lets go. "Still, talk to them without making a decision first. You want them involved, so they get a say."

Jay's smile is blinding. "I will do that. And I have to say, even if you woke me up, have a mouthy boyfriend, and screwed up last night, I have a good feeling about you."

Luce hands him a business card. "I'll get the ball rolling. Call me as soon as you've spoken to the band without Wayne."

Jay holds up the card. "Will do."

8

LUCE

As soon as we hit the corridor of the hotel and the door clicks shut behind us, I throw myself against a wall. Any wall.

"I can't believe I just did that."

Marty approaches, his hands going to my waist. At first, I think it's to help hold me up, but then his warm lips are on mine, his tongue seeks entrance, and he moans into my mouth.

I wrap my arms around him and hold him to me, but he pulls back.

"You handled that really well."

It's impossible to stop the smile from taking over my face. "Thank you. I still can't believe it. I might've just fucked everything up, but I'm excited."

"I'm guessing this isn't as easy as walking up to your bosses and saying you're taking over managing the band."

"Considering I'm not even in band management, yeah, no, it's not that easy." My hands trail down to his ass. "But I don't want to think of the logistics now. I want to celebrate."

"Mmm, and how did you want to do that?"

"I have a few ideas ... most of which would be illegal in public, but first I want to take you on our second date."

Marty fans himself. "Two dates in twelve hours. I am a lucky boy."

"That is, unless you want to go back in there and offend your idol some more. Do you have some sort of condition where you blurt out everything on your mind?"

He gives an adorable little shrug. "It comes from years of not speaking my mind. I realised one day that life's too short to put up with bullshit, but maybe now I'm too much on the other end of the spectrum. I can't believe I talked to Jay like that." His head falls on my shoulder. "I'm an idiot."

"Even with your mouthy attitude, I could tell he liked you. Maybe too much for my liking."

Marty raises his gaze, and he smiles. "Can I confess something to you?"

"Intriguing ..."

"I—"

The elevator dings, and Wayne and the two I assume are Benji and Freya step off.

Marty and I quickly jump apart but probably a little too late.

Wayne appears indifferent, and the other two narrow their eyes at us.

"These are the suits?" Benji asks.

Meanwhile, beside me, Marty's trying not to jump up and down in excitement. A little "Eeee" comes out of him, and fuck, I love how passionate he is. It really isn't about boning the lead singer, who I have to admit has some charm underneath his bitterness, but about their music.

Marty seems to be fanboying just as hard over Benji and Freya as he was with Jay.

"Luce Riley," I say and hold out my hand to Benji.

He shakes it but still seems wary.

"I've already spoken to Jay about what happened last night. He can fill you in."

"Are we getting dumped from the label?" Freya asks.

It makes me want to pin Wayne up against a wall and tell him to stop being such a shithead. He probably likes putting these guys down to make him feel more superior and important. Managers shouldn't be like that. Bands need all the support they can get. Managers aren't just there to tell the band where they have to be and when. They also have to sell the band. Book gigs and events. If a manager thinks a bigger and better act will come along, I guarantee it will because this is a fickle industry. You could be on top one day and gone the next. Just like that.

Radioactive needs someone to believe in them, and after just one night, after hearing just one song, I'm more invested in Jay's band than their current manager.

"You're not being dropped," I assure her.

A warm hand intertwines with mine. "It was lovely meeting you all, but we have to get going. A lot of bands we have to grovel to today after last night's fuck-up."

"Wait, that's why you're here?" Benji asks.

"Talk to Jay," I say and get on the elevator they vacated.

I almost let out a "Hope to see you all soon" before the doors close, but I don't want anything to tip off Wayne of the band's plans. Especially while in a foreign country.

The small niggle in the back of my brain tells me that if they do take me on as their manager, I'm going to have to pack up and move countries, and the part of me that's still hung up on last night protests at leaving.

Which is ridiculous. I haven't even known Marty a full day. He shouldn't even factor into this kind of decision.

But he is the reason I'm here at all, trying to chase a dream a decade old.

"Brunch?" he asks with an adorable smile.

"A quick one. I need to get you back to my place as fast as possible."

"I like the sound of that."

We don't make it to brunch. Hell, we barely survive driving to the restaurant, which is why I'm pulled off to the side of the road, while Marty sucks hard on my dick.

As soon as we got in the car and I started driving, Marty reached for my suit pants and unzipped them, muttering something about payment for introducing him to Jay.

Who was I to deny that?

"Fuck, I love your mouth," I say.

I can't get over how hot Marty looks with my dick sliding in between his big, pouty lips.

"Take your cock out. I want to see you get yourself off."

Marty doesn't stop working me over while he unbuttons his jeans. Only when he has to get his pants down does he release me so he can pull himself free.

If anyone was to walk by, there's no way they wouldn't know what we're doing.

My head's thrown back on the headrest, and now Marty's bare ass is facing the window while he leans over me and sucks me down to the base.

His hand on his own cock strokes lazily, but his mouth is working overtime.

"You must really appreciate meeting Radioactive."

"Mmhmm," he hums, sending vibrations through me.

"I'm close," I warn.

Apart from the radio, which I couldn't tell you what song was playing if my life depended on it, Marty's slurps and my heavy breathing are the only other sounds to fill the car.

Marty's breathing joins mine in being stilted and erratic, and when I glance over to where he's stroking himself, I can't hold my orgasm back.

His cock is leaking like crazy, the wet head sliding in and out of his hand with ease, and I let my release go, the visual too much for my poor little brain to handle.

After he swallows my release, he pulls away and slinks into his seat while he jerks himself.

His back arches, his thighs tense, and I can tell he's close, so I quickly lean over him, sucking him into my mouth just as the heady flavour of cum hits my tastebuds.

I keep licking him clean until he puts his hand in my hair and forces me away.

Our chests heave, and I swallow his taste down. My eyes are closed, my head resting back on my seat.

A chuckle comes from beside me. "Great brunch."

"Awesome brunch. But I'm still taking you for croissants."

"Mmm, cum and French food. Most perfect date ever."

We tuck ourselves away, and Marty uses the sun visor mirror to fix the mess I did of his hair.

I take his hand and bring it to my lips before dropping it to my thigh and steering the car back onto the road.

An 11OZ song comes on, and Marty grunts. "Ugh." He reaches for the radio, but I stop him.

"Wait …" There's something in the catchy beat that gives me an idea. "Didn't Eleven Ounces just announce their worldwide tour, but supporting acts haven't been determined yet? I swear I read that. Or heard it somewhere."

"Okay, if you tell me you're a boyband fan, you're about to lose all your musical cred and all of my respect. I mean, you were skirting the line with Green Day, but Eleven? Hell no. They're worse than One Direction."

I laugh. "I'm not big on boybands, no, but … hear me out, okay? Radioactive's sound is emo-ish, a little pop rock, with a dash of grunge, yeah?"

"Yeah, I guess."

"Jay has a serious identity problem, but they have a sound that will speak to emotional teenagers—"

"I'm not a fucking teenager. Fun fact, and this may shock you, I'm two years older than Jay."

I love how defensive he gets over his young looks even if he is frustrated by it. "I wasn't actually talking about you. Just in general. And granted I've only heard one of Radioactive's songs, but the impact of that one song would kill with the teen demographic. What's that 'Heartbreak' song you were singing? Terribly, I might add, but the lyrics were good."

Marty reaches into his pocket and pulls out his phone. "The only recording of it is a pretty shitty one from one of their shows, but it's got an angry edge to it. It's basically about not being good enough and telling the person walking away that he's making a big mistake."

I glance over to see him open the YouTube app and pull up the video.

He's right about the quality being shitty. I have to glance back at the road, but I can still listen.

The hunch in my gut gets stronger with every note Jay belts into the microphone. It's peppier than "He's Mine" but has grittier lyrics. It's perfect. Because if there's one thing teenage girls love more than love, it's the drama that follows a breakup.

"I need to get Radioactive hooked up with Eleven some-how. Like what 1D did for Five Seconds of Summer."

"That'd put them in boyband territory. I don't see Jay going for that."

"A worldwide stadium tour? Yeah, he'd turn that down," I say sarcastically. "Plus, there's a girl. Therefore, no boyband."

"Okay, but isn't the appeal to that demographic wanting to hook up with the lead singer? Jay's out; there's no shoving him back in a closet."

"All the girls will want to be his best friend."

"If you say so." Marty shifts in his seat.

"Plus, Benji's hot, so …" I cock my head at him. "What's wrong?"

"It's nothing. I'm being stupid."

"Since when don't you speak your mind no matter what?"

"You've known me a day …"

"And I knew within ten minutes of meeting you that you don't hold back, so don't do it now."

He side-eyes me. "Okay, but you asked for it. You're about to realise how batshit crazy I am."

"Not gonna lie. I'm pretty sure you can't shock me."

Marty punches my arm but not hard. Well, too hard.

"Ouch. Driving here."

"So here's the thing. I want Radioactive to be huge. I want everyone to love them like I do … but … I also want them to be mine. I don't want them to be ruined by mainstream shit with bad lyrics and boyband dance moves."

I burst out laughing. "You just want to claim them. I can see it now. In a few years when they're big and famous, you're going to be telling people, 'I loved them before they were cool.'"

"Exactly!"

I smile. "I don't think that's batshit crazy. It's adorable."

Marty folds his arms and sulks. "I'm not adorable, fuck dammit."

"No. Of course not. The way you spoke to Jay wasn't adorable as fuck either."

He throws his head back. "Ugh. Don't remind me. Though … I have to kinda admit I wasn't exactly swept off my feet by him."

"Calling him out for sleeping with his manager and then implying he's dumb probably didn't help." I snicker.

Marty sighs. "I guess this is why they say you shouldn't meet people you admire."

I purse my lips. "I hate to say it because I know it's not what you want to hear, but I think no matter how that meeting went, you were probably going to be disappointed in some way. And he was a bit grumpy, yeah, but he's allowed to be. The label has been screwing that band over since the beginning. They deserve better. And I'm sure once I make them super famous, Jay will be super nice to you. Because I will make him."

Marty's lips twitch. "You'd do that for me?"

"Yup." I pull into the parking lot of a trendy café. "But before I do all that, I need food."

9
———
MARTY

I love how animated Luce is getting over Radioactive. I love that he wants to help them make it big, and that he's in an actual position to do something about it. If I could make people listen, I'd tell the entire world about their music.

But I'd be lying if I said I wasn't facing as big of an identity crisis as Luce claims Radioactive is going through.

Yesterday, I was delusional about meeting Jay, and while I knew my delusions were far-fetched, I guess I never thought I'd walk away from him less interested than I was before.

The funny thing about that is, I don't know if it has anything to do with *him*. Yeah, he's messier than I imagined, but I held him at an impossibly high regard. I thought he'd be too good for cheap tricks with managers and a typical rock star life.

Maybe I wanted him to wake up spouting philosophical shit. I was expecting kind of a pretentious douche. Not a guy who seemed lost.

But again, I don't think that's what's gnawing at me.

I think the whole exchange isn't sitting right because while

I was there, I was keenly aware of everything Luce did. Of his every move. Admiring the way he commanded attention and controlled the room.

If someone had told me yesterday that I'd choose to be having brunch—eager for it, even—rather than talking to Jay from Radioactive, I would've told that person to fuck off and get off drugs.

Yet, as we sit here in the crowded café, and I watch Luce scarf down eggs Benedict and pastries, there's a bittersweet feeling that I might've just met the man of my dreams and he's about to chase a different dream. One of representing a band halfway around the world.

Luce smiles at me. "What're ya thinking about?"

I smile, but I know it's weak. "That you're gonna kick ass at managing Radioactive."

"Then why are you looking at me like I've set fire to a litter of puppies?"

"Because that probably means that our first and second dates might be our only ones?"

Luce's hand pauses halfway to his mouth with a forkful of food.

"I mean … I'm not, like, obsessed with you or anything after one night. But I am having fun."

Luce puts his fork back down and reaches across the table for my hand. "Me too. However, the good news is, if this is going to happen, it might take a while. Hell, it might not even happen at all. I have to get the label to sign off on it, and then work visas and all that paperwork crap. It'll be a slow process."

I squeeze his hand. "It'll happen. The label will see how passionate you are about them, and your idea to make them mainstream to get exposure will work."

Luce's brow furrows. "What are you saying? That you want this to be our last date?"

"No. Just because I'm sure it'll happen, doesn't mean it will. Like, I'm sure one day I'll succeed in using a molecular structure to create a composite plastic harder than steel, but until that day, I'm not going to disown all my friends before I'm a famous scientist. Like, that's just stupid."

He laughs. "Right. You're going to wait until after you're famous to ditch everyone."

"Duh. I'll have the money to buy new friends then."

"Do scientists really make that much? Even famous ones?"

"Don't spoil my fantasy!"

Luce throws his hands up. "Okay. Sorry. One day you're going to be so famous you won't even remember my name."

I shake my head. "Sorry, Lucifer, there's no way I'm forgetting your name."

Luce grits his teeth. "I shouldn't have told you."

"Ah. Then you shouldn't have had sex with me. It's like the gateway to people's secrets. A man is never more honest than after he blows his load."

There's a woman next to us who chokes on her coffee. Serves her right for eavesdropping. I mean, really—she's the one being rude here. Not me talking about coming.

Luce smirks at her. "Well, I propose that if our time is limited, we spend as much time together as possible."

"Deal."

"Better eat up, because unless you have plans later today, I think we're going to have plenty of time to …" He looks at the woman beside us and then back to me. "Be honest with each other."

I wipe my mouth with a napkin and stand. "I'm done eating."

———

Luce's definition of plenty of time? A full thirty-six hours where we don't leave the bed except to eat, go to the bathroom, and hydrate.

When we're not having sex, we're chilling in each other's arms or watching TV on the big screen he has in his bedroom. He said at one point he wanted to check in with the festival that's still going on, but then apparently I got up to take a piss and distracted him with my retreating ass.

In his defence, I do have a good ass.

It's been the best weekend of my entire life, which is quite sad but not really if I think about it. I've spent most of my life since my early teens with my head in a book. I've dated, I've met guys off hook-up apps. I've *never* experienced the kind of connection I have with Luce.

Not even through music. Not even with Radioactive. Though, meeting them this weekend helps lift the last few days to best-weekend-ever status.

Come Monday morning, we're woken by Luce's phone going off.

I need to get home to shower and go to the lab at uni to get some work done, and Luce needs to get to the label. We knew this morning we'd have to say goodbye, and as much as Luce keeps telling me he wants to see me again, I can't help thinking this is all fleeting.

Perhaps it's because I know what he's planning to do, and I have all the faith in the world he'll achieve it.

"Luce Riley." He throws his legs over the side of the bed and stands, pulling his boxers up his legs as he tucks his phone in between his head and shoulder. "I'm so glad you called." He looks over his shoulder at me and mouths, "It's Jay."

Yeah, don't think I'll ever get used to that. Not that I think I'll have the chance to though anyway. Because this is it. This phone call is the thing that's going to make this weekend come crashing down.

"I actually have some ideas," Luce says. "Some of them you may not like according to Marty—" He chuckles. "Yeah, the mouthy boyfriend who loves your band."

My stomach flips. I've never had a proper boyfriend before, and I don't think after spending two days with someone I can call him that. I mean, I've dated guys for months and never called them my boyfriend before. But the description falling from Luce's mouth makes me want it.

"I'm going to try to get something set up at the Joystar offices here in the city today when I head in for work. When do you go back to the States?" Luce bites his bottom lip. "Two more days? That doesn't give us a lot of time. Do you have any plans? I'm wondering if we could meet up to discuss my ideas before pitching it to the big guys. You coming with me to headquarters will help gain some urgency too." He nods. "Great. I'll see you in …" He looks around the room, his eyes landing on his watch beside the bed. "An hour good? I'll send you the location so you can Uber or cab it. Oh, and bring Benji and Freya but not Wayne."

He ends the call and stares at his phone in shock.

"He actually called," I say.

"He did."

"It's a lot sooner than I thought—"

"Me too, but this … this has been my dream forever. It got lost somewhere along the way." He climbs onto his bed and crawls towards me. "And you brought it all back for me. You made this happen. I … I don't think there are enough words to ever thank you."

I smile mischievously. "Then maybe you should thank me by *not* talking."

Luce groans. "As much as I would love to thank you all day again, I need to get a move on if I'm meeting the band."

Just like that, the fleeting sensation is back.

"Can you come back tonight, or can I call you?" Luce asks.

I nod. "Call me when you're done. I'll come over. I'll also bring over some clothes and a toothbrush so I don't have to keep using your stuff."

He leans down and brushes his lips against mine. "I'll see you tonight."

"Tonight."

From the couch in our living room, my mum gives me a look as soon as I walk through the door of our small townhouse in Pascoe Vale. "Have a fun weekend, did we? Thanks for the two-word text letting me know you weren't dead."

"You're getting better at hiding your mocking tone."

She smiles. "Darn. I wasn't trying to be subtle at all."

I approach her and kiss her cheek. "I'm going to go shower and then get to the lab."

"Can I expect you home for dinner at least?"

I freeze. My immediate response is to say no, but that niggly feeling that he's not going to call still gnaws at me. "Don't bet on it, but that doesn't mean I definitely won't be."

"So will I cook something for you or not?"

"Not. If I do come home, I'll fend for myself."

She scoffs. "Well, then, good luck."

"I haven't given myself food poisoning since I was a teenager, and I thought chicken came in medium and well-done like steak." Will never make that mistake ever, ever again.

Mum laughs at me.

I start to head for my bathroom, but she stops me again.

"Was he worth it?"

I grin at her over my shoulder. "He's amazing."

"Who is he?" Her eyes shine in a knowing way.

"Gray told you, didn't he?" My brother's friend from the bar. God, he's worse than my brother with this stuff. "I swear he and Adam are like two little gossiping queens." The funny thing being they're the straight ones.

"Gray said he's older."

"Luce is not that much older. He's an exec for Joystar Records, and he got me a meet and greet with Radioactive because he knows how much I love Jay. He's a good guy."

"Wow."

"Wow, what? That I'm dating someone older or that he's a good guy?"

Mum blinks. "That you met that band you won't shut up about, but you're telling me about *the guy* instead. Jay not fall head over heels for you?"

"Okay, there was no attempt to hide *that* form of mockery. And no, he didn't. He was … kinda a mess. Not like, high or drunk kind of messy you'd expect of a rock star, but … I dunno. I felt *sorry* for him."

"Aww, hon, I'm sorry."

I find a smile because I'm not as distraught about it as I thought I would be. "It's all good. I met someone who understands and even calls me on my bullshit."

Now I just have to wait for him to call me, period.

"I like him already," Mum says.

Yeah, that's my problem too.

And I wish I could say I'm being cool about it and have the attitude that if I hear from him again, great, if not, oh well. But I don't.

After I shower, I check my phone. Which is stupid, because he's probably still with the band and talking to the label.

I get to uni late, I can't concentrate all day, and I keep incessantly looking at my stupid screen, willing a message or his name to pop up as it rings. Well, technically, Tom Ellis's name —the guy who plays Lucifer on TV. I couldn't resist.

Instead of going home at five, I figure I need to do something productive seeing as I failed all day. He still hasn't called, so going to the library to check out a dissertation I wanted to read seems like the responsible thing to do.

The second my feet step across the threshold, my phone chimes. I can't get it out fast enough.

TOM ELLIS: *WE'RE GOING OUT TO CELEBRATE. MEET US AT MECCA BAR?*

The amount of excitement in the pit of my stomach hits all new levels of pathetic. I do wonder who he means by "us"—if he means him and the band or if he talks like my uneducated brother and says "us" for "me" in sentences. Because, you know, that's good English.

ME: *WHAT TIME?*

TOM ELLIS: *WE'RE HEADING THERE NOW. RACE YOU?*

Play it cool, you doofus.

ME: *I'LL MEET YOU GUYS THERE. I'VE JUST GOT SOME WORK TO FINISH UP FIRST.*

TOM ELLIS: *GOOD LUCK WITH ALL THE MOLECULES AND ATOMS AND SHIT.*

ME: *YES, THE 'AND SHIT' PART IS THE TECHNICAL TERM FOR WHAT I DO.*

TOM ELLIS: *I WOULD USE THE PROPER TERMINOLOGY, BUT IT'D BE SO TECHNICAL THAT EVEN YOU'D HAVE TROUBLE UNDERSTANDING ME. DUH. CAN'T WAIT TO SEE YOU. WILL IT BE LAME IF I SAY I MISSED YOU TODAY?*

No. Not lame at all.

ME: *YUP. BUT I'LL LET IT SLIDE BECAUSE YOU'RE SO HOT.*

TOM ELLIS: *HOW GRACIOUS OF YOU.*

ME: *I'M A GRACIOUS KIND OF GUY. I'LL SEE YOU SOON.*

On the way to my car, I have to tell my legs to slow down.

When I hit a yellow light, I tell myself to stop and do the safe thing.

And when I get to Smith Street, I tell myself to find free street parking farther away from the bar than the parking garage that costs more than I can afford. Which isn't hard.

I enter the bar, and it's easy to spot who I'm looking for. He stands tall above the crowd. The shouting and woo-hooing around him helps. I also have my answer for what he meant by *us. We're* celebrating. Jay, Benji, and Freya are here too.

They all down shots at the bar, and there are smiles all round.

Luce's face lights up even more when he sees me coming, and I can't stop my own reaction.

"Babe! You're here." He pulls me in, but with Mecca not being a gay bar, the kiss he gives me is brief. "I don't think you officially met Benji and Freya the other day, but I know you know who they are. Guys, this is Marty. He's the entire reason I'm here with you at all."

Freya—the Freya from fucking Radioactive—hugs me. Benji high-fives me.

Jay gives me a nod and a smile. "Apparently, I need to

apologise for being an emo dick the other morning, but in my defence, it was before caffeine. I can't be held responsible for anything that happens before that."

"It's true," Freya says. "We know not to try to rationalise with him."

I smile. "It's all good. I've been told my bluntness could be considered rude."

Luce pulls me close. "Now who would ever tell you that? Your bluntness is adorable."

"Wow, he must really like you," Jay says. "How are you two gonna be with Luce coming back to the States with us?"

Just like that, my heart sinks to my stomach. I turn to him and fake a smile. "You're … you did it."

"Almost. They want to take it to the guys in L.A. and we'll see what happens after that. I might be home in a week."

"Oh," Jay says. "Okay, now I am an asshole. Sorry, I didn't realise you hadn't told him yet."

Luce shrugs it off. "There's nothing really to tell yet."

I nudge him. "Yes, there is. This is an amazing opportunity, and I know you're gonna rock it."

"If it was up to us, it'd be a done deal," Benji says. "Wayne has to go."

"I'll admit I'm a little surprised you guys are okay with Luce's crazy idea."

Jay shrugs. "It's not that crazy. We're pretty eclectic, so that just means we'll pump out a few pop-rock songs next and tap into Eleven's market."

Luce leans in. "I'm going to make 'Hat Trick Heartbreak' their first single on their next album."

"It's a great song."

Which only reiterates Luce is gonna be offered the job and he'll take it.

"More drinks?" Jay asks. "My treat." He holds up some money. "Australian money is pride coloured. It's weird."

I laugh. Guess that's one way of looking at it.

While he and the band order more drinks, Luce pulls me close, wrapping his arms around me from behind. "Can we pretend I'm not leaving in a few days and don't know when I'll be back?"

No! "Let's just celebrate tonight."

"You still coming home with me?"

"Of course. I'm nowhere near done with you yet." Even if this can't go any further.

"Good. Because neither am I."

Jay passes drinks all round, and after we toast to the band and drink them down, Benji wraps his arm around Freya. "Wanna play wingwoman and dance with me?"

She nods, but I frown and turn to Jay.

"Wingwoman? Aren't they—"

Jay sighs. "They're in major denial. Too much drama for me to keep up with."

They're on the dance floor for only a few minutes before they're each dancing with other people. I can't help wondering if they do it to torture themselves or each other or what. I've never understood that type of craving for angst and heartbreak.

Then I look at Luce and wonder if I'm not doing my own version of the same thing. I want to spend as much time with him as possible before he leaves, knowing that once he gets on that plane, the chance of him coming home is slim to none.

And if I can feel this strongly after only a few days, what will another few days do?

"They're going to be doing this to each other all night and

eventually go home together," Jay says. "It's actually getting quite boring to watch. Are there any gay bars around here?"

I grin. "There is, but if we go, I need you to do me a favour."

Both Luce and Jay cock their heads at me.

"Trust me. It'll be fun."

I lean on the bar and yell over the music. "Hey, Gray."

My brother's friend grins and makes his way over to us. "What can I get you, Doc?"

"Three beers, and I want you to meet someone. This is Jay." I pull Jay forward. "From Radioactive."

Gray's smile drops, and he glances between me and Jay. "No fucking way."

I nod. "Way. Told you he'd jump offstage and fall at my feet."

Jay puts his arm around me. "Marty here is just too irresistible."

A growl comes from my other side, but Luce reins it in. That is until Jay cups my face and pulls my lips to his.

It takes a second to register what's happening, but then it clicks.

Jay's mouth is on mine.

Jay.

From Radioactive.

His tongue teases my lips, but I don't open for him.

Because I'm in shock, because it wasn't part of the plan, or because it feels … weird, I'm not sure.

How long have I fantasised about Jay kissing me? How long have I wanted this?

Now it's actually happening, all I want is for it to stop.

And thankfully, it does.

He pulls back and nods to Gray. "Totally irresistible."

Apparently, that's too much for Luce to handle, and he steps in between us. "Okay, fun time's over." He turns to Jay. "That's the only one you get."

He throws up his hands in surrender and laughs. "You got it, boss."

Luce's arms hold me possessively. "Mine."

My brow furrows as I look up at him. "Did you just claim me?"

"Yup."

"I'm so confused," Gray says.

I wave him off. "That really is Jay. But this is Luce."

Gray nods. "Ah, the guy who won Marty."

"Yup. That'd be me. Luckiest winner in the world." And when Luce kisses me, it's so much different than when Jay did it.

It's warm and gentle yet filled with passion too.

"I'll get your drinks," Gray says and turns to the fridges to get us a Corona each.

I stand on my tiptoes so I come closer to Luce's ear. "How long do you think we have to stay until we can go home and celebrate on our own?"

Luce's eyes flick over my head, and he grins. "Not long at all." He lifts his chin, and I follow his line of sight to where Jay's already talking to a hot guy and flirting.

Good. Because if we don't have much time together, I want to make every moment count.

10

LUCE

Sweaty, breathing heavy, and losing my goddamn mind, I push in and out of Marty's perfect body. "I could wax poetic about this ass."

I have him facedown on my bed, his pants around his knees, his shirt riding up enough only to expose his lower back, and his ass in the air.

Marty mumbles something into the mattress, but I can't make out what it is.

I pause, my cock still deep inside him. "What was that?"

He turns his head. "I said I'd dare you to write poetry about my ass, but I don't want you to stop."

"Maybe later I can write you a limerick."

"How about now you keep fucking me?"

I pull out slowly and slam back in.

He grunts.

"Like this?" I ask and do it again.

As soon as he said he wanted me to fuck him tonight, it was a mad rush of tangled arms and legs until I could get him inside my place and on my bed.

"Faster."

I do as he says.

"Harder," he begs.

Gripping his hair, I close my fist through the short strands and tug.

"Oh, fuck." Marty trembles beneath me. His ass pulses around my cock. "I'm … I'm …" He lets go, and I feel it in the way his body tenses and shudders.

"Nothing hotter than a guy coming hands-free."

Marty takes in deep gulps of air, and I give him a second to recover.

"You all good?" I ask.

He nods. "Keep going. I want to feel you come inside me."

I want to promise him that one day there'll be nothing separating us, but for now, he'll need to settle for the feeling of my cock throbbing inside his ass until I empty into the condom.

It only takes a few thrusts until I collapse on top of him.

When we're both able to breathe normally again, I pull out of him slowly and roll onto my back. "I promise the next round will be slower."

Marty doesn't reply, and when I turn my head, I meet his warm gaze. He looks at me with a pensive expression.

"What's wrong?"

"Nothing. I just … I can't get over how perfect you are for me."

I hear the things he doesn't say in that sentence. "I'll be back at some point."

"I know, but … Can we keep a pin in that?"

My arms pull him closer to me so his head is on my chest. "We can put a pin in it as long as we can."

So, we do that. At some point, we get up and clean ourselves off and then fall back into bed.

I'm woken at fuck knows what time to Marty kissing my neck and looking to go again.

The next time I wake up, the sun is peeking through low-hanging clouds as dawn breaks, and it's my turn to wake him up for sex.

He calls in sick to his lab.

We enjoy each other's bodies. We talk music. We talk families. We talk shit and mock each other, and then make out until we're horny and struggling to breathe.

We only have one more night together before I'm flying to the States with the band. Part of me wants the label to shut me down so I can come home and stay in my current job, but the thought of losing my passion for music again while doing that makes me hope that everything works out with Radioactive.

I don't know what the future holds, but a bitter thirty-two-year-old shouldn't be factoring in this guy I don't even know. That's insane.

But so is meeting someone and turning your entire life upside down because they inspire you that much just by existing. Marty makes me believe in shit I'd long gotten over—like the notion that things happen for a reason and people come into your life for a purpose.

If this does work out, and I chase the dream job I originally went into this industry for, I will owe everything to Marty.

I don't want that to be all he is though. I want him to be more.

"We could do long distance," I say while he lies in my arms.

"Putting that type of pressure on a three-day-old fling is relationship suicide."

I know he's right, but it doesn't feel that way with him.

"You could come with me."

Marty snorts. "Yes, with all my disposable income, that's a brilliant plan."

I don't suggest I pay for him. I already know him well enough to know he's too headstrong for that kind of thing.

"I kinda feel like I'm about to live your dream without you," I say.

"I have no dream of managing a band. I don't have enough patience to deal with divas or people. That's why I work in a lab. With other lab rats. Where we barely have to speak, let alone be social."

"I'm sure you'd be okay having to be social with Radioactive every day."

"Hmm, true. But there's that little annoying thing of money. In the sense that I need it, and you don't get paid for being a groupie."

"Well, no, because that would make you a hooker."

Marty laughs.

"I wish there was a way we could make this work," I whisper.

"Me too. But you'll be back at some point, and then you can look me up. Until then, there's Facebook and Skype if you want to talk. I'll be available. You know all I have in my life is research and working on this stupid dissertation that's stupid."

"How long do you have left until you get your PhD?"

"As long as it takes to create a stable molecular structure that can—"

"Okay, you already lost me. So … like, I'm guessing it's not possible to do that in the next week or two?"

Marty laughs. "Doubtful. Even then I have to finish my dissertation which can take years. I'm not even close."

"So maybe a month, then."

Marty slaps my chest.

I sigh. I don't want this to end.

———

"I don't want to say goodbye," I say, but seeing as I'm also mauling Marty's face while saying it, I don't think he hears me.

He pulls back. "It's just a few days. You'll need to come back for visa interviews, I'm assuming, so I'll see you again. This isn't the end."

"When did you become so rational? I thought that was my job."

"Since I'm trying to hold my shit together."

We kiss again, standing in the entryway to my apartment, my luggage by the door and the whisper of goodbye on our lips.

Why does leaving him feel wrong?

Everything has happened so fast, it's hard to believe the last week has been real at all.

But I'm really about to go meet Radioactive at the airport. I'm really about to hop a fourteen-hour flight to L.A., and I'm really about to leave this guy I really fucking care about already.

Anyone on the outside would think I was crazy—factoring in my ever-growing infatuation for Marty, but until they've ever met Marty Van Gent, they can't know the type of charismatic and blunt charm the guy has.

"Go," he says. "Or you'll miss your flight. Not that I'd complain about that, but this is your dream."

With that last reminder, I kiss him again and leave, staring after him long after my Uber turns the corner and I can't actually see him anymore.

This is my dream job. It's what I've always wanted and has been my goal forever. I just got sidetracked the last few years.

This is my chance.

I check in at the airport, go through security, and find the band waiting at the gate. "What are you guys already doing here? If you're gonna be a rock band, I really need to talk to you about punctuality and how it's not cool."

Jay laughs. "Yeah, except when your label doesn't give a fuck about you and you miss your flight? You're paying for a new one. Not them."

"Point taken. I'm going to make sure they start giving a fuck about you." I scan the airport. "Seen Wayne anywhere?"

"He went back a few days ago after we fired him to beg to rep another band," Benji says.

"Oh. So he's not only not your manager anymore, but—"

"The label isn't impressed with him," Freya says.

Jay leans back in his seat. "I might've told them some of the shit he did."

"Like …" I hold back from saying *fucking him.*

Jay nods. "When we spoke to the US guys, I found out he's fucking *married*. To a woman. I might've gotten a little mad."

Benji snorts. "I'd say. You threatened to walk completely which we don't really have the luxury to do in our position."

"Jesus," I breathe. "You guys are having my work cut out for me, huh? Is this like some sort of initiation?"

"It was a calculated risk," Jay says. "They were salivating over your idea, and Eleven needs an opening act. For the first time since signing with the label, we feel like we have an actual shot." He pierces me with his deep brown eyes. "Because of you."

"Fuck, no pressure." I laugh.

Jay grins. "None at all."

But I feel it like a weight bearing down on my chest. This is no longer just a possibility. Wayne is completely gone. They don't have another manager lined up, and they liked my ideas. I have this job in the bag.

My first response is to want to call Marty and tell him, but then I realise that'd be like boasting to him how ecstatic I am about not coming home to him.

I can't call him.

It's probably best I don't at all.

11

———

MARTY

A week after Luce leaves, I get a message.
Seven days it took him to pluck up the courage to
tell me he wasn't coming back. His visa was being handled
through the consulate in Sydney, and the label was only flying
him home long enough for his interview, and then he had to
get back on a plane and re-enter the US on a temporary visa
until his sponsorship with the label came through. He rambled
something about needing to leave the country to re-enter or
something, but I didn't really follow it.

All in all, it was a "Hey, sorry I haven't had the decency to
pick up a fucking phone and tell you I'm not coming home,
like, ever, so, uh, you know, it was fun while it lasted. Have a
nice life" text. Only, it was more sugar-coated and full of shit
about coming to see me when the band is touring Aus.

Whatever.

It's better he cut ties now.

Only, the sucky thing about it all is my love for Radioactive
has now been tainted by Luce's connection.

He got his dream and crushed mine in the process.

But it's not Luce's fault. Not at all. It's me who can't listen to a Radioactive song and not think of Luce.

It's me who keeps playing that weekend I spent with him on a loop over and over and over again.

It's me who wishes I'd never told him about the band.

All that *it's better to have loved and lost than not love at all* crap surely isn't accurate. If it was, I wouldn't be hurting now.

Word in the Twittersphere is Radioactive have officially landed the supporting-act gig with Eleven.

The tour starts in two months, and they have that long to record and release their second official album.

Hopefully two months is long enough to forget about Luce so I can actually enjoy the new songs.

Spoiler: it isn't.

My phone rings next to me, and I don't even look at who's calling. No one calls me but my mum, brother, or telemarketers.

No one else has called me, because apparently, they don't have phones in America. I'm guessing.

"I'll keep in touch," he said. "We can still be friends," he said. *I'll like your posts on Facebook but not reply to your messages until days later ...* Okay, he didn't say that one, but he did it.

When he would eventually message me back, it'd be "Hey, sorry, been super busy. Hope life is treating you well."

Yeah, well, I'm still bitter. How about that for treating me well?

"Hello?"

"Hey, Marty."

I bolt up in bed. I know that voice. I've wanted to hear that voice for two months now. Since right after he left.

"I know I haven't been in touch, and that might make me a dick."

"A huge dick."

Luce laughs. "Fuck, I've missed your snark. I have a good reason for being absent. I promise."

"I'm listening …"

"I could give you a million excuses about working so hard on this album and working to gain followers for the band's social media, and jumping into a job I've never done before, but … babe, I did it. *We* did it. The band fucking did it."

"Did what?"

"We're number one. With the song *you* showed me."

"'Hat Trick Heartbreak'? No way."

"Way. And listen … I've been pulling some strings …"

"Strings?"

Luce hesitates, and I can practically hear his insecurity when he asks, "How do you feel about taking a gap year?"

"A …" My mouth drops open. "A gap year …"

"You said it yourself that you've been working towards your PhD since you were fifteen. You went from high school to doing an accelerated degree and master's, and you're only twenty-three."

"Twenty-four now, thank you very much. You missed my birthday."

"I'm sorry. I hope this will make it up to you. I'm offering you a once-in-a-lifetime opportunity, and I want you to take it."

"Take what? What are you offering?"

"I need an assistant for the tour. I already have one who's staying in L.A. to make sure everything I need booked is good to go and everything sticks to plan, but I convinced the label I need someone with me on tour too. Someone to grab coffee for me and the band. Fetching all the shit for me I forgot. Someone who doesn't leave my side ..."

"A-and you want me to do it?"

"I want you to experience your favourite band the way you deserve to. I want you backstage with me. But most of all, I want to explore what we started months ago. I want more. I ... I've missed you."

"Then where was my phone call, asshole?"

"I've wanted to call. I ..."

"You what?"

"I've been telling myself I need to make Radioactive a success for *you*. I thought leaving the possibility of us meant I had to make this work. And now I have, I want to make it work *with you*. The label will be paying your wage, and you won't have to worry about money, and we could spend the next year getting to know each other properly."

"What if I get over there and we hate each other?"

"Then I fire you. Or you can quit. I just ... I want this to happen for us."

"Gee, no pressure."

Luce sighs. "It's not a perfect plan. But really, what's the worst-case scenario here? It doesn't work out, you go home again and go back to your dissertation. Best-case scenario? You get to travel the fucking world with Radioactive and maybe, hopefully, fall in love. Uh, I should clarify with me. Not Jay."

I laugh.

It sounds too awesome to be true. I mean, who the fuck does this? How would I explain to my mum, "Oh, that guy I met a few months back? He got me a job as an assistant for a fucking rock tour …" Hmm, well, pop tour. It's with *Eleven*. Wait—

I groan. "I'll have to put up with listening to Eleven every night? I don't know if I can do that."

"Even knowing Jay's giving them one of his songs?"

I perk up. "He has? Oh my God, I bet it's amazing."

"So, will you come? Tour kicks off in a few weeks. We'd need to do a rush on a visa application for you like they did for mine."

"I …" I can't do this, right? It's insane. I have a dissertation to write. I have research to complete.

"I understand if you can't give me an answer right now, but please think about it. And fast."

"I'm totally going to sound my age here, but I need to talk to my mum."

Luce laughs. "Hey, we're never too old to turn to our mothers. Who do you think convinced me to accept my dream job when I was hesitating thanks to a sexy molecular engineer I met?"

"Oh, so I can blame your mother for missing you?"

"Ah-ha, so you do miss me."

"Yeah … I do."

"Come on. Even if you don't do it for me, do it for yourself. Everyone deserves a gap year."

"I … I'll call you back."

"I'll be waiting. We're going out for celebratory drinks, but I'll have my phone on me. Oh, this is my US number, by the way, so call this one, not my Aus number. I'll talk to you soon."

"Hey, Luce?" I blurt before he can end the call.

"Yeah?"

"Congratulations on hitting number one."

"They literally wouldn't be there if it weren't for you."

The call goes dead, and reality sinks in.

They want me to go on fucking tour with them.

Radioactive.

Holy shit.

How can this be my life? Seriously. What the fuck?

It took Mum a whole five minutes of screaming excitedly before she did the actual parent thing to talk it out with me logistically. She encouraged me to take it. It's a once-in-a-life-time opportunity, and it's not like I can never go back to working towards my PhD.

And that's how I've ended up here, in a first-class seat, on my way to the States to follow Radioactive around the fucking world.

Deep breaths, Marty.

I don't know what's making me more nervous—the tour or seeing Luce again.

He was ecstatic when I said I was coming, but it's been a few months since I've seen him, and what happens if I see him again and he's nothing like the Luce I remember?

What if that spark isn't there?

And, I mean, technically, he's my boss. Then again, it's not like I'm doing this for the *job*. The job is a mere vessel for me to do this at all.

Landing at LAX, I'm tired, have plane on me, and all I want to do is sleep. Turns out first class isn't so easy to sleep in either. Or maybe I'm just too wired to sleep.

This is it.

Luce should be out there waiting for me.

I take a deep breath. And then another. It doesn't help get oxygen to my lungs.

I better learn fast to breathe like a normal human being or customs are gonna think I'm smuggling drugs in my ass, and I don't want anyone's fingers up there unless they're Luce's.

I follow the signs and the people being herded like cattle to the immigrations and customs desk.

The guy behind the counter when I reach him wears a solemn expression, and I wonder if it's a prerequisite to have a permanent "I just tasted something sour" look on your face to be an immigration agent.

"You look nervous," he says.

"I … eh … umm …"

He cocks his eyebrow at me.

"I'm meeting someone," I blurt. "My boyfriend."

Oh God, don't tell him you're gay, idiot. Though, you know this is Los Angeles, not some redneck, bible-preaching town.

"Let me guess. Met him online?"

Apparently, I'm amusing to him now.

"Uh, yeah," I lie. Because I don't care enough to explain the situation right now.

He looks over my visa information, stamps my passport, and gives me a smile. "Welcome to the United States."

"Thank you," I mumble and can't get away fast enough. I have to tell myself to slow down. Strip searches are still a possibility.

Waiting by the baggage claim is even more nerve-racking, because I know the minute my bags arrive, the only thing separating me and Luce is two glass doors.

When that moment comes, I find myself standing by the exit and holding my breath.

Then someone goes and ruins my self-preparation by walking past me.

The doors slide open.

And then he's there, waiting for me at the end of the welcome section, and he looks … utterly amazing. He's still hot as fuck and makes my mouth dry.

Then Luce smiles. Probably at my feet stalled by the exit.

His shoulders shake from light laughter as I make my legs finally move and carry me toward him.

"How is it possible you look even younger right now?" is the first thing he says.

"Fuck off."

Luce laughs hard and wraps me in a giant hug. "I have missed that mouth of yours."

I pull back and tilt my head, but our arms stay around each other. With the way his cocky face stares down at me, I'm guessing Luce hasn't picked up on the double meaning of his words. Or maybe he meant to say it that way and that's why he looks so smug.

Before I can get out an equally obnoxious retort, Luce leans in and kisses me.

It's soft and warm, and I've been thinking about these lips for *months*.

I've been trying to remember what they taste like, what they feel like, and how they turned my world upside down, but no memory, no fantasy can live up to this.

Luce pulls back long before I'm ready. "Mm, you taste like peppermint, which is surprising after a long flight."

"They gave us a free travel toothbrush and toothpaste on the plane. I thought I'd put it to good use in case you were as hot as I remembered."

"Am I?" He turns his head from side to side.

"Were you always this grey?" I reach up and run a hand through his hair.

"You know I was."

"I know, but it's fun to tease."

Luce takes my suitcase handle from me. "Let's get you home."

"About that. Where will I be staying while I'm here?"

His gorgeous lips twitch. "Well, we're about to hit the road for the first leg of Radioactive's tour, so you'll have your own hotel room, but that's not for another two days."

"And until then?"

Luce clears his throat. "I was hoping you'd stay with me."

I try to act nonchalant, but I know my entire face lights up.

Shocking. Nerdy lab rat can't act remotely cool to save his life.

I don't even have to answer.

"Then it's settled," he says and takes my hand.

"Yeah. Settled."

12

LUCE

Marty is just as charismatic, just as unapologetically snarky, and just as good-looking as I remember.

Granted, it's only been a few months, but it feels a hell of a lot longer than that.

As we make our way to my car, I can't stop staring at him.

I can't believe he came. I can't believe he actually did it.

It was a long shot asking him to take a year off from school and his PhD just to see if this could work between us, but I haven't been able to stop thinking about this guy since the moment I met him.

I'm here because of him.

Radioactive have a platinum single because of him.

And yeah, any other uni student or post-grad would jump at this chance because who wouldn't want to tour the world with their favourite band? But with Marty, his work is too important. He's been working at it since he was fifteen.

Yet, he's still here.

With me.

Giving us a real shot.

I ride that high until we get about halfway to my small West Hollywood apartment.

I went from a middle-management label-exec position to band manager, which is basically two pay grades below what I was before. I can't afford much, and L.A. is ridiculously expensive, but in the few months since I've been managing the band, I've already made them ten times as profitable as they were last year. If we keep on this trajectory, I'll be buying my own mansion soon.

"So, have you … like, well—"

I grin. "You can ask me anything, Marty."

"Oh. Okay. Umm, have you seen anyone since …" He waves a finger between me and him.

Okay, he can ask anything but that.

I shake my head. "Nah." But fuck, even I hear the guilt in my tone when it's really all quite innocent.

I've had a million offers since arriving in L.A. When the band plays shows and people realise you can get them backstage? Yeah, people throw themselves at you. There was even one girl who, when I told her I was gay, turned to her boyfriend and got him to come offer to blow me.

I wasn't tempted by any of them.

But there was this one guy …

I sigh. "Okay, full disclosure. No, I haven't been with anyone else since I left Australia, but there was this guy who works at the Joystar label here. He's one of the assistants who float from person to person. Kinda like a permanent temp? He goes where he's needed."

I glance at Marty and see disappointment in his eyes.

"Let me finish, okay? Nothing happened between us, but it almost did."

"Did you kiss him?"

I purse my lips.

"Luce, it's okay. We weren't together after you left. You ghosted me. I fucked heaps of guys these last few months."

My hands grip the steering wheel tight, and I speak through gritted teeth. "Really?"

"No, not really, you dickhead. I've been working and trying to get my mind off *you*."

"That's what I'm trying to say. This assistant. Rory. He reminded me of you. He's got the same colour hair, same cute features. When he smiled, I thought of your sarcastic smirk. I thought we were done, and I couldn't go back. I thought long distance wouldn't work and that it'd only hurt us if we kept in touch. But the thing is, when this guy tried to kiss me? It wasn't you. My head knew it wasn't you, and my heart definitely knew it wasn't you. That's what made me ask the label to create your position and offer it to you."

I let out a deep breath. Rory's lips were on me for not even a full second before I pulled away and said I wasn't interested because I was hung up on someone back home. And even though Marty and I weren't even together, that half, maybe three-quarters of a second has made me feel guiltier than anything else I've done in my entire life—even torturing my own mother as payback for calling me Lucifer.

"You didn't kiss him?" Marty asks, his tone hopeful.

I shake my head. "He tried to kiss me, and I stopped it. And I'm telling you about it, because I want you to know why I asked you to come to L.A. and take a job that you're way overqualified for. I want to start us off the right way."

Marty looks relieved, but then he throws his head back on his headrest. "This is crazy, Luce. How did I get here?"

"Plane. Duh."

"Who takes a year off their real life to follow some guy and a band around the world?"

"You do. Again, duh. You'd think with that big brain of yours, you'd know these answers."

Marty's voice drops. "What if it doesn't work out?"

"You can leave your contract with Joystar at any time, and if you're not happy here, I don't want to force you to stay. It's only twelve months. The tour is eight. We have plenty of time to work out what we want, how we work as a couple and at our jobs, and if this is something we both want. If it doesn't work out, it doesn't work out. This isn't even your chosen profession, so you're not risking a career. All either of us are risking are broken hearts."

"I don't want a broken heart."

"Neither do I," I admit.

Our first conversation in person in months has gone dark pretty fast, but then Marty breaks the mood by smiling again.

"So we give it twelve months."

I nod. "Twelve months."

13

MARTY

I never imagined a brainless job could be so exhausting. I also couldn't imagine being so good at it. Or loving it.

Because it's kind of a bullshit job, I've semi-become a personal assistant for not only Luce but the entire band. I never thought I'd be someone's bitch-boy or that I'd enjoy it so much.

Getting to watch Radioactive onstage every night would be payment enough.

That, and getting to spend my days next to Luce and my nights wrapped up in him.

My doubts about Luce when I took this job were unfounded, and these last six months on tour have only strengthened what we had back in Melbourne.

It amplifies every day, and I'm so fucking in love with him.

Can I tell him that though?

Nope.

Too fucking scared.

Because it could change everything.

I enter Radioactive's dressing room to find Benji, Freya, and Luce. No Jay.

Luce scrolls on his phone, not paying attention to the scowls Benji and Freya are sending each other. Must be a fighting day. They tend to alternate between being loved-up and arguing. Jay says they're perfect for each other. I'm honestly surprised they've lasted this long without killing each other or walking out on the band.

But we don't get involved. It's their thing.

I have a feeling I know where Jay is, and if I'm right, every teenage girl in the world will hate him. "Where's Jay?"

"He went to get a Pepsi."

I point to the chilled bucket full of Coke. "You didn't think that was weird considering his rider asks for Coke?" I should know. It's my responsibility to make sure the venue gets every item on the list right.

Luce lifts his gaze from his phone, and even though he's a clueless idiot, he's a gorgeous, clueless idiot, and he's mine. "Maybe he felt like something different?"

"I'll go find him."

I step into the corridor and try to think where he could be. I have a feeling I know who he's with, but where …

Jay appears in front of me, sans Pepsi. "What's up?"

I eye him from head to toe. "Find your Pepsi okay? You know, you can ask for that on your rider so you don't have to do it yourself."

Jay and I have become good friends over the last few months, but I've seen a switch in him in the last two. He's acting cagey and disappearing before shows. When I've gone to check on him in his hotel room, he hasn't let me in.

He smiles a trademark Jay smile. "I'm not going to be one of those celebrities who can't fend for himself."

I purse my lips. Maybe I'm wrong about him.

Maybe.

Jay tries to get by me, but I step in front of him.

"Just be careful. With Pepsi. If you're not careful, it can make a big mess."

Jay narrows his eyes. "What would you know about … Pepsi?"

"Nothing. And I think it'll be better that way. I don't want to have to lie to Luce."

"About Pepsi?"

I nod. "About Pepsi."

We stand quietly, just eyeing each other.

"Marty?"

"What?"

"You're the weirdest person I know, and that's saying a lot, because my brothers have this whole crazy gay brigade they hang around who are nuts."

I grin. "Thanks. Total compliment."

Luce opens the dressing room door. "Good, you found him. You need to be onstage."

"I'm ready," Jay says.

Benji steps past us. "So are we."

The band has been kicking ass. Gold album. Platinum single. If they keep going the way they are, next year they'll get their own headlining tour.

They're at the level of fame where a lot of people still won't know who you mean if you say the band name, but hum a few bars of "Hat Trick Heartbreak" and the entire population would chime in. Or tell you to shut up because it got played to death on the radio and stayed high in the charts for months.

Luce takes my hand and leads us to where we usually watch the band from the sidelines.

You'd think I'd be sick of listening to the same songs every night, watching the same routine, and while artists will never say they have favourite cities or audiences, the truth is, each city is different.

The atmosphere is charged with a different energy with the varying crowds.

No show is the same.

And I'm still mesmerised every time Jay sings.

Luce wraps his arms around me from behind, catching me off guard.

Everyone in the crew knows we're together, but we still make sure to be professional in public.

The band is onstage singing "He's Mine," but the meaning of that doesn't register until Luce lowers his head so his lips are by my ear.

"It's the song that brought us together."

It's the song that changed my entire life. I don't know what will happen in another six months, but if the label and Luce ask me to stay, I'm staying. End of story. No doubts, no regrets, and I have absolutely no desire to go home and get my PhD anytime soon.

Maybe one day.

"I love you," Luce says.

I freeze in his arms, only turning my head to look up at him. Either I've heard something I've wished for him to say or he actually just said he loves me.

"I've fallen for you."

Again, his mouth moves. I hear the words. But—

"I'm so in love with you," I blurt.

Luce kisses me while Radioactive plays our song, and it could very well be the most perfect moment ever.

14

LUCE

I hold my breath and prepare myself to walk into a hissy fit of epic proportions. I just got word from the label that instead of Radioactive headlining their own stadium tour like they deserve, that they'll be doing a second tour with Eleven. As their opening act.

Jay, Benji, and Freya have worked so hard at this album, worked so hard on the last tour with Eleven, and it still hasn't been good enough for the label.

They spouted something about Jay not being ready and needing the exposure being linked to Eleven that has already done amazing things for the band. That might be all well and true, but Radioactive is so much better than an opening act. They deserve to be headliners even if it's in concert halls instead of arenas.

They're on the brink of greatness, and I'm worried touring with the boyband again will seal their fate. Always the bridesmaid, never the headliner ... or something like that.

I stand outside the band's Hollywood Hills mansion that

they bought as a group the minute their first big royalty cheque came in, and I just hope they take this news well.

Oh, who am I kidding. Jay's going to flip his lid.

Not only that, I was hoping if they got their own head-lining tour that I'd have a valid argument for Marty to stay on and stay with me. He's great at his job, no doubt. He seems to sense what the band or I need at any given time, and he's two steps ahead, but I'm not sure he gets anything out of it. It's not a rewarding job.

We said we'd give it a year. It's now been eleven months. They've been the most meaningful eleven months of my life. Waking up next to undoubtedly the most amazing man I've ever met every morning has made this whole experience ten million times better.

I also got word today that the label has offered to extend his one-year contract, but it's up to Marty.

He took his gap year. It's done. He has a PhD to get back to.

If he does go back, I want to find a way to make us work, because I've never been with anyone like him.

Someone who challenges me.

Someone who's fun to be around.

Someone who makes my life complete.

Ugh. I need to deal with the tour problem first. Then my love life.

I push the front door open and head straight downstairs to their main living and entertaining area.

There's a deck out back that overlooks the hills, and that's where they're all lounging with beers in their hands as they watch the late-afternoon sun cast an orange hue across the valley.

Marty sits up on his deck chair at my entrance, and the way

he smiles at me creates longing in my chest. I left him in our bed this morning, and I'm already aching for him.

I can't imagine what it'll be like if he decides to go back home to Australia.

He shifts forward so I can squeeze in behind him and he can lie back between my legs with his head on my chest.

Jay, Benji, and Freya all stare at me, waiting.

"So, what are we doing?" Jay asks. "New album, a tour … what?"

Marty must feel me tense because he sits up and turns to face me. "What is it? What's wrong?"

Jay bites his lip.

I slump. "A tour." Smiles begin to take over their faces, so I have to stop that fast. "With Eleven."

Benji frowns. "Dude, that was last year. Did you look at the calendar wrong?"

"You're gonna be their supporting act again. The first tour was great exposure, and—"

Benji stands. "What the fuck? No. We … no. This was our moment. If they're not going to give us a tour, they should at least give us another album."

"That'll happen after this tour," I say.

Marty's gaze darts between me and Jay. "Jay?"

Jay shrugs. "Same shit, different day with the label. No point being angry about it."

He walks into the house deflated, which is so not how I thought this was going to go. I expected a lot of whining and fighting. Not accepted defeat.

I turn to the others. "One good thing is we've got our own jet this time. No more cramped tour bus."

Benji becomes less mad but still not happy. He follows Jay, and Freya sighs in resignation.

A second later, she's gone too.

I take Marty's beer that's on the table next to us and take a sip. That's when I notice the concern in his gaze. "What's wrong?"

"Did … did they say anything about me?"

I take another sip and try to smother my smile, because I don't want to influence his decision. I want him to stay, but not out of guilt. "They offered to extend your contract, but I told them I want a new model."

He shoves me. "You did not. You better not have."

I cock my head. "Oh? Why's that? I thought you were gonna go home in a month and go back to your lab."

"No fucking way. Even if I wasn't totally in love with you, I'd still have to stay to see how this tour goes."

There's definitely no stopping the smile this time. "Totally in love with me, huh?"

Marty rolls his eyes. "Duh. It's not like we haven't said it to each other before."

"Just because we're in love, doesn't mean we can't make it work if you wanted to go back to Australia."

Marty shakes his head. "I want to be wherever you are. Doing whatever you do. You're stuck with me and my sass."

"Your sass or your *ass*?"

"Both."

"Promise?"

"Would I ever lie to you?"

My lips purse. "What about the time you and Jay went out to a bar before their set, turned up late, and while I stood there getting yelled at by label execs on the phone, you tried to tell me there was an impromptu running of the bulls and it was too dangerous on the streets so you were stuck in the bar?"

"We were in Spain. It could've been true."

I laugh and shake my head. Such a Marty answer. I lean in and kiss him. "So, you're staying?"

"I'm staying until this ride gets boring, and it hasn't happened yet. I can get my PhD when I'm fifty for all I care right now."

"You have no idea how happy that makes me."

His hand reaches for my cock confined by my suit pants. "I might have some idea." Shifting so he's crawling on top of me, he kisses me and rubs his hand over my hardening dick until I'm gasping for more.

"No fucking on the deck chairs!" Jay yells from somewhere in the house.

"That's creepy," I say. "Maybe we should go home?"

Marty nods and climbs off my lap, yelling, "We're out" to the others.

As soon as we're in the car, I turn to him. "Hey, what did you mean by even if you weren't in love with me, you'd have to stay for this next tour?"

He side-eyes me, and I get the sudden feeling he's holding something back.

"What is it?" I'm only slightly panicking.

"You didn't think Jay's reaction to having to go on tour with the boyband again was less than … indifferent?"

"It was a little understated compared to what I was expecting."

"Please, we all know we ain't there for Eleven's songs."

"I've totally heard you singing that song of theirs … what was it? 'I Like You'?"

"So? Their songs are fucking catchy. Like crabs. You don't want to catch it, but sometimes you do."

I laugh. "You've had crabs?"

"Not recently."

Now I'm howling with laughter. "I love you so much."

"I know, right? I'm a fucking delight. But for real. Jay. I totally think he's fucking one of the Eleven boys. I need to see how this turns out."

Aww, shit. "Please tell me it's just a hunch and you think you could be wrong."

"Umm, well, it is just a hunch, but I don't think I'm wrong. Why?"

"It's in the Eleven guys' contract that they can't disclose their sexuality to the public. If he is with one of them, I can see it now. It's only going to end in heartache."

"Damn. Why the hell is that in their contract?"

"Remember how we talked about their target demographic? Teenage girls are more likely to buy albums if they can fantasise about being with the guys."

Marty looks confused for a moment. "I didn't realise teenage girls were homophobic twatwaffles."

"They're not. They'll just hate that they can't get a piece of them."

"Still twatwaffle behaviour."

I laugh again. "Marty?"

"Yeah?"

"Never change. Please."

"Never plan to."

"Good."

THANK YOU!

Thank you for reading *Fake Boyfriend Breakaways: A short story collection.*

Obviously, when I started writing the *Fake Boyfriend* series, I had every intention of using the fake boyfriend trope for the entire series. But during the writing process, many side characters were not okay with that. Or that it'd only be three books. My plans changed drastically, which isn't surprising. I suck at planning.

Thank you to my readers who hounded me to write Max and Ash's book—a couple I never intended to write. I'm so glad I got the chance to put their story in words as opposed to just knowing what happened in my head.

If you want to keep up to date with Eden Finley news, new releases, and more, join my reader group here: https://www.facebook.com/groups/absolutelyeden/

Alternatively, you can join my newsletter here: http://eepurl.com/gln68n

I want to thank my beta readers, editors Sandra Dee from One Love Editing and Kelly Hartigan from Xterraweb, and my cover designer Kellie from Book Cover by Design. I also want to thank every single member of my team who helped me get this out into the world.

EDEN FINLEY BOOKS

FAKE BOYFRIEND SERIES
Fake Out
Trick Play
Deke
Blindsided
Hat Trick

STEELE BROTHERS
Unwritten Law
Unspoken Vow

ROYAL OBLIGATION
Unprincely (MMF)

ONE NIGHT SERIES
One Night with Hemsworth (MF)
One Night with Calvin (MF)
One Night with Fate (MF)

One Night with Rhodes (MM)
One Night with Him (MF)

Printed in Great Britain
by Amazon

38865117R00179